DEVIANTS

ALL-ENCOMPASSING ANSWERS TO WHY NORMAL PEOPLE HAVE ABNORMAL SEX.*

Book One: The Lifestyle

By Charles Martin and Will Weinke

* No answers actually contained herein
A work of fiction

Edited By Amber Losson
Cover By Halo Sama of Shonuff Studios
Deviants Copyright © 2011 by Charles Martin. All rights reserved. To be printed in the United States of America. No part of this book may be used or reproduced in any manner whatsoever without written permission from the author except in the case of brief quotations embodied in critical articles and reviews. For information, visit www.literatipressok.com.

FUN FACT: Swing Clubs (a.k.a. Lifestyle Clubs, Sex Clubs)
Swing Clubs are the modern day watering hole for Middle America's middle class, where the pillars of the community congregate. Secrecy is the water they all drink from and the spring is governed by the law of mutually assured destruction.

DISCLAIMER:
Intercourse is a splintered thing. One simple, instinctual act that has been complicated, sophisticated, and commercialized by mankind so that the modern image of intercourse covers a vast array of tastes, fetishes, and differing images of sexual ideals. Do not believe the claims of gurus, psychologists, or medical professionals. Any individual or organization that boasts definitive knowledge of human sexuality is merely trying to sell you something.[1]

What this particular book can tell you are the things that sex are most certainly not:

1. **Love**. Love and sex are often entangled, as are chocolate and peanut butter and coffee and cigarettes. Sure, one can enhance the other, but a responsible adult shouldn't be ashamed that they occasionally want their chocolate with caramel or their coffee

---

[1] Like this book, for instance.

poured directly on their bathing suit area.
    2. **Fate.** Sometimes sex is just an impulse that, in hindsight, was perhaps not the wisest use of one's time and/or money.
    3. **Marketing.** If corporations could truly tell humanity what we are attracted to, then 90 percent of the population would be in serious trouble.
    4. **An Inherent Bonding Experience.** Mutual respect and emotional attachment are not necessary ingredients to a successful sexual tryst. In fact, sometimes it's more enjoyable that way.

    It would be cynical to say that love has no role within a sexual relationship or that sex isn't an important tether within a devoted marriage. The sticky point comes as women overestimate the bonding power of sex, just as men undervalue it.
    If love and sex were as conjoined as popular culture likes to imply, then long-devoted lovers would not need to close their eyes to orgasm. Vast studies of sexual partners[2] have confirmed that orgasm is more easily reached when the individual is allowed to fantasize about:
    1. Other people
    2. Other places
    3. Multiple partners
    4. Family friends
    5. Unethical and/or criminal acts

    Why? Because loving partners are compelled to have sex to renew a physical bond with each other,

---

[2] Ten and counting!

but the payoff is very far from a hormone and firework laden consummation of love. If anything, the female orgasm is just a confirmation that she has become comfortable enough with her partner to pretend he's not even there.[3]

That said, love can improve a couple's sexual dynamic. For instance, it takes love:

1. To stick one's legs under the sheet to find the "wet spot" is on their side of the bed AND not to insist on switching places even though you really do need a good night sleep.

2. To not admit to how dismal or uncomfortable a particular romp was because the other person has had a rough week.

3. To pretend that all the weird sights, smells and sounds of sex never happened.

4. To spend much longer performing oral sex than originally intended, thus missing the first fifteen minutes of one's favorite TV show.

5. To not mind that 60 percent of a couple's sex life has fallen into a routine.

6. Even during the most vile and depraved dirty talk, to not mention the mortal enemy of one's partner regardless of how badly you would really like to see him/her naked.

7. To cuddle.

So, now that the connection between love and sex has been given the appropriate asterisk, we can

---

[3] Want proof? Say "I love you" and see how she responds. I'll wait….Ha! I told you!

proceed to the meat of the book.[4]

What follows is a detailed account of the comings and goings of individuals in the midst of sexual and/or emotional awakenings as well as analyzing the virtues and vices of various forms of "deviant sex." As such, there are subjects herein that might be considered lewd, but simply cannot be avoided.

It is not the desire of the authors to allow this work to devolve into a vulgar tell-all[5], but when we arrive at an impasse where propriety and the needs of the narrative beg for a certain word, a series of Xs will be used in its stead. In so doing, we shall maintain the decency of the prose, but the desired affect will be achieved—to a degree.

For an example:

"Young Man was endowed with a XXXXX that was exceptional in both length and girth and looked vaguely like a pensive baby elephant. The unfortunate byproducts of a well-developed XXXX were frustration with condoms and the abundance of foreplay needed before XXXX XXX or XXXXXXXX could be attempted comfortably."

The following accounts are fictional[6] but elaborate the many ways the normal ritual of sex deviates into something else entirely. Rather than treading through the abundant wealth of human perversions, Book One will focus on the "Lifestyle." This generic word refers to any extra-marital sex that is consensual by both committed partners. "Lifestyle"

---

[4] Pun intended!
[5] But just wait until the screenplay!
[6] See if you can guess which ones are true!

sex can consist of, but does not necessarily include, all of the following perversions:
1. Group Sex (The More the Merrier)
2. MMF (Male, Male, Female)
3. FFM (Female, Female, Male)
4. BDSM (Bondage and Discipline, Sadism and Masochism)
5. Soft Swap (oral only)
6. Full Swap (anything goes)
7. Exhibitionism (Show Offs)
8. Voyeurism (Pervs)
9. Photo/Video Swapping
10. Swing Clubs (Venues catering to the Lifestyle)
11. Open (Dating outside the marriage/relationship[7].)

We explore all this to show that, for such a small part of the human experience involving such a relatively insignificant amount of the body[8], sex is by far the most complex and obsessive instinct.

---

[7] Not the same as polygamy. Swingers maintain a male/female emotional bond like a traditional monogamous relationship, even if they are free to seek out new sexual partners.
[8] It's not the size, etc, etc, etc...

FUN FACT: What Causes Swinging? Many think that trauma early in life is the leading cause of abnormal sexual behavior. That can be a predominate factor in other deviant behavior and a contributor amidst some swingers, but the majority of those that chose the Lifestyle did so in response to repression during the formative years of their sexual identity. When one or both members of a relationship realize they missed out on sowing their oats, they can be compelled to make up for lost time. This can cause many divorces, but with the right couple, it leads them to the Lifestyle. This is why swing clubs flourish in the Bible Belt[9].

The Ballad of Jerry and Carey/Cynthia/Veronica
Part I

Introducing Jerry. This quiet, virile farm boy was nagged by a curious mind early in life. He had perpetually sun-bleached hair and a tan etching the outline of a t-shirt on his otherwise pale chest. Jerry often disappeared for hours while he wandered the countryside in search of mystery.

Jerry could spend an afternoon studying the tireless work ethic of ants, stalking a dear across hundreds of acres of woodland or strike up a friendship with stray dogs that had yet to be eaten by coyotes.

Of his youthful fascinations, girls are what

---

[9] Or so I've heard.

piqued his curiosity the most, particularly a 13-year-old, raven-haired beauty that family friends sent to his farm one summer. She was bold, brash, argued with his mother and was two years older than Jerry. She came from a distant city named Tulsa, which made her exotic to a boy that had never been out of his county, let alone to a bustling metropolis.

Her training bras were the first women's undergarments that Jerry had ever seen. He stared at them in wonder as they hung over the edge of the laundry hamper like a speck of cheese in a mousetrap.

His first sighting of one of those pink satin sirens came while brushing his teeth before bedtime. He tried to ignore the limp, frilly thing. He spit the foamy toothpaste in the sink and decided he would look just once, for research's sake. He wondered if it felt as soft as it looked, so he reached out and fingered the satiny strap.

"Jerry!" his mother belted. He jammed the bra under the other clothes and bolted from the bathroom.

Like all sons, he believed his mother possessed mystic abilities enabling her to track his missteps within the house and all across the property. He was relieved to find she was only calling for help with the dirty dishes. She could see the guilt splayed out on his face, but Jerry knew he'd gotten away with something significant.

It was invigorating, and he couldn't hide his smile the rest of the day.

Still, to be safe, he decided to not even look the raven-haired girl in the eyes for a week. Surely the girl possessed that same second sight, and since it was her bra, she must be able to see the sin that had escaped his mother's radar.

The beauty that had so befuddled our hero was named Roxie. She tied off the front of her shirt to show her navel. She brushed her hair and applied makeup before arriving at the breakfast table. She had a drawer in the bathroom that Jerry was warned to not "go digging through." He interpreted this to mean not to reach a hand in the drawer, but he could peer inside if the drawer had been left open a smidge.

On a hurried day before church, Roxie had left the drawer wide open, revealing a pale blue box and white wrapped objects that looked like they held cigars.

He was both curious and disappointed, but managed to stifle the urge to further examine.

Roxie constantly rifled through beauty magazines, disappearing into the bathroom to soak in the tub for an hour, leaving the magazines piled on the floor like used Kleenexes.

To impress her, Jerry began reading whatever magazines he could find in the house, which ended up being a meager stack of dusty *Car & Driver* issues. The technology was hopelessly outdated, but he read them cover to cover and asked his father to buy him more the next time he went to the pharmacy.

"Do you want some of those hot rod magazines with the pretty girls in bikinis?" his father smirked, nudging the boy with his elbow.

"Harold," Jerry's mother sighed.

"No," Jerry finally muttered while Roxie grinned. "Gawd."

"Jerry, language!" his mother snapped, then

whacked the back of his neck with a wooden spoon.
    It didn't hurt, just stung a little. The embarrassment at being harassed by his mom in front of the raven-haired girl stung much worse.
    Whenever the family went into town, older boys flocked to Roxie, which infuriated Jerry. What could he say? His mother insisted the girl was like his cousin, though that wasn't how Jerry saw it.
    No shared-blood relatives meant no retard babies. Simple, irrefutable math.
    Toward the end of the summer, the moment finally arrived that would change the way the poor farm boy would look at women forever.
    A simple mistake, really. Jerry failed to knock on the bathroom door, instead walking in on the girl while she changed into a swimsuit before taking a dip at the pond.
    His mother was tending to her garden. His father was rumbling through the fields on his rusted-out tractor.
    It was just Jerry and the raven-haired girl, naked as the day she was born.
    She didn't yell, she didn't cover herself; she merely looked at him, mildly annoyed and entirely unthreatened.
    "Occupied," she stated.
    Frozen for a brief moment, he finally took a step backward, eyes still locked on the girl. He tripped over a bookcase and fell on his butt. She sighed and closed the door.
    After retreating to his room, all he could really remember was the pubic hair and the small nipples. The two images created massive craters in his mind

and all the other smaller, trivial thoughts like Bible study and chores were consumed by those mystifying details.

It felt like his body and brain had just been jumpstarted. Things got really weird, really quickly.

"Your gettin' just like your pa," his mom growled the following day after Jerry forgot to check the oil in the tractor and nearly burned up the motor.

Indeed, Jerry was beginning to feel a bit more like a man and had learned his first lesson of sexual maturity. He was incapable of keeping a pretty girl from making him feel like a little boy.

Jerry was so enthralled and ashamed that he avoided, at all costs, talking to Roxie again. He would still go out of his way to cross paths with her, but without making it look too obvious.

Instead of spending hours staring at beehives like last summer, he plotted his day. He arranged his chores so as to increase the likelihood of passing by her, but pretending to be too preoccupied to even give her a glance.

The days leading up to her departure, Jerry found excuses to sit next to her. Perhaps plodding across the field, exhausted by a day's worth of work and just looking to cool his heels. If she was already sitting on the swinging bench by the house, what could he do? He sat next to her, no big deal. He was just tired.

Maybe it was a lazy weekend and there was nothing to do but lounge on the couch for hours. She would read about revivals in hippie fashions and he would read a Reader's Digest he'd found at his aunt's house. Of course it meant nothing. Like his mom said, they were nearly family.

Jerry really hoped that the raven-haired girl didn't believe that crap and had done the math in her head too.

Him + Her – Blood Relation = No Problem!

He was careful never to tip his hand, though. He never looked over at her when she was near, but breathed in the sweet, fruity scent of her chapstick and bristled after the slightest touch of her arm against his.

He couldn't tell if she meant to brush against him; she retreated so quickly that it could be accidental. Or perhaps she was torturing him. Or communicating.

When the family friends left, the memory of the girl's beauty continued to haunt the farm.

Jerry's developing knowledge of sex was:

1. It was important

2. His parents could be heard having it from time to time, and they seemed to enjoy it.

3. Puberty meant becoming obsessed with sex. Once adolescence went into full swing, he would think of little else.

4. It was supposed to feel good, but experiments on his bed and with his pillow made him sore and the skin raw. It would be another year before a tip from a friend would lead him to search the bathroom for his mother's hand lotion.

The church sporadically mentioned sex, but only in dismissive terms. This was among the growing reasons why Jerry had lost respect for religion as a whole.

His parents often hugged. They rarely spoke of sex but when they did, it was usually positive and using euphemisms they thought he didn't understand. Jerry thus formulated an equation:
Happy Marriage = Sex
Sex = hugging + late night + X

Jerry had no answer for X, but was relatively certain it somehow involved his penis, which was entirely different than what he saw on the raven-haired girl.
When he could find an answer for X, he would then understand how to forge a happy marriage, ideally with the raven-haired girl.
Again, Him + Her – Blood Relation = No Problem.
Jerry's first true education on sex came when a junior high friend acquired a ten year old porn video. The unlabeled VCR tape had been copied and recopied so many times that 30 percent of the movie was white static, like it was shot during a snowstorm. The audio could be heard, but only sparse images could be discerned. Still, the moaning shadows that weaved and thrust amidst the static blizzard held the group at attention as they waited for the fuzz to pass.
The movie's first screening was with a select group of football players from the starting squad. The owner of the tape was the equipment manager who'd correctly guessed that the tape would elevate his social standing on the team.
The parents were away, and the young men sat, silent and studious. Laughter was sporadic; smiles were rare. Instead, all the boys watched and blushed, absorbing every sound and image on the fuzzy tape. It

was, after all, their study guide for a test that consumed 90 percent of their waking thoughts.

Once the blizzard cleared and real flesh and blood appeared, Jerry felt vividly weird. He wasn't exactly nauseated, but the images went down like foreign food that was spicy in a way his tongue didn't recognize, then settled in his belly awkwardly, so he felt satisfied and hollow at the same time.

After being entranced for over an hour, the absence of any immediate utility to the new information led the group to shut off the tape and try to discuss other things, like the AFC's inferiority to the NFC and whether Michael Jordan would be able to lead the Bulls to a championship.

Jerry, now a star of the small school's football team, was fully within the feverish grasp of puberty and the mysterious mechanics of sex were now answered.

That was only a small piece of the puzzle though. The how was nothing without the when, where, why and, most importantly, who.

Jerry struggled to become outgoing, which was made easier by his lofty position within the social structure of his school, where football players were the closest thing the town had to celebrities.

His first girlfriend was an awkward and somewhat over-weight band nerd he'd met on summer vacation. He didn't find her particularly attractive, but wanted to practice kissing someone. She lived close enough to his farm for him to visit in-between chores, so the relationship was more inevitable than magical. It didn't even really resemble what Jerry would later recognize as romance.

The girl's tongue was softer than he'd imagined, almost like dough, and she snorted when she laughed. He was compelled to visit her when he was lonely. She made him feel tall and dashing, yet he broke off the secret relationship for good before his first year of high school.

Though the bulk of Jerry's inquisitive mind was aimed directly at girls, there was still enough room left in his head to allow him to excel in academics. His barrel chest developed from years of laboring at the farm helped him excel in football, and college was discussed for the first time in the history of his family tree.

Jerry often wondered what the raven-haired girl would look like all grown. Part of him felt guilty, as if he was betraying his mother's trust. The other part of him, the majority shareholder in his fantasy life, vehemently resented the assertion that the girl was anything more than a family friend, thus fair game.

Even so, he grew accustomed to that curiously sweet taste of shame and fascination, and his sexual drive began veering toward the taboo.

And yet, the 5'11" football standout was still a virgin entering his freshman year at a college in southeastern Oklahoma. During an optimistic trip to a convenience store to buy condoms ahead of a date with a "sure thing," Jerry met a fellow freshman named Carey.

―

Introducing Carey. The brunette with dramatic cheekbones and an hourglass figure who was oft reminded by her mother that she was as skinny as a

broomstick when she was born.
    Carey grew up in a sleepy neighborhood tucked away in a rural community in Little Dixie, Oklahoma. It was too big to be a town and too small to be a city. It was, in her estimation, just the right size to be of no use to anyone, especially her.
    That bony frame she'd been born with lingered into late elementary school. She wore glasses and rarely talked to anyone but her menagerie of Barbie dolls handed down from her much older sister.
    Three events in childhood would affect her sexual identity dramatically:
    1. The sporadic presence of her father in the family structure.
    2. The removal of her older sister from the house for reasons unknown to Carey.
    3. The brief stay of her father's friend in the house.

    On issue one: Her father.
    The short, charismatic man liked a good drink, a shapely woman and was, to borrow a phrase, a rolling stone. Her father had been many things in his life: a soldier, a hobo, a construction worker, a college student, a train conductor and even published a novel about his time flying drugs over the border.
    He was also, at times, a husband and a father. During those short periods, when he decided to give family life another stab, Carey was delighted by the man's every word, every story and every gesture of love, no matter how small.
    Her father was a figure of such confidence, passion and zeal that he is worthy of his own chapter.

But he was also a man that could only be devoted to himself, so there is no place for him in this book outside of the damage his neglect did to poor, bony, little Carey.

On issue two: Carey's older sister, Pamela.

Her sister was in high school by the time Carey reached preschool. Pamela could be just as vibrant as her father. Pamela always had a plan and Carey would toddle behind her sister absolutely certain that whatever it was Pamela was about to do, it would be the most fun thing ever!

As vivacious as Pamela was when she was happy, when she was sad she disappeared from the world. Carey could hear her cry at night, and sometimes Pamela would come into her room, hug Carey tightly and they would fall asleep together.

Sometimes Carey awoke to hear Pamela mumbling about "The Bear." She would ask Pamela in the morning, but her sister would shrug and say, "you're just hearin' things."

On issue three: Her father's friend.

The man looked like a mountain to the young Carey: vast, dangerous, invincible and with eyes like a wild predator, always measuring, always hungry.

He rarely combed or cleaned his scraggily beard and there was an ever-present stale smell of sweat in whatever room he occupied. The man once grumbled to her that the pale blue tattoos on his arms were started in prison and finished in Mexico.

It was not the first time the man had stayed with the family. The one other time was long before Carey was born. Carey kept her distance from the man at first, but was encouraged to play with her "uncle" and sit on his lap.

When Pamela arrived home from school and saw the man sitting in their living room, she began the fight that would push Pamela from Carey's childhood life.

Carey was shoved into her room while Pamela and their mother whispered, then cussed, then screamed. Carey's father had no interest in the argument, so went out drinking with his friend.

That night, Carey was awoken by Pamela.

"We can't stay here or the Bear will get us," Pamela whispered.

"The Bear? Like the one from your dreams?"

"It is exactly the one from my dreams. But I'm taking you on a great adventure to a magical land where the Bear can't ever get us."

Scared and excited, Carey packed her clothes and together they left for a distant place called Oklahoma City.

Their mother reported the family car stolen, and the police caught up with Pamela and Carey on I-40 just east of Midwest City.

Carey was to be sent home, but Pamela had to stay for further questioning. As Carey was led to a squad car, Pamela called:

"Stay away from him, don't let The Bear get you, Carey! I will come get you, I promise!"

But she never did.

Carey's return home soon divulged a terrifying realization. The Bear that haunted Pamela's dreams was not a creature from the woods, but the massive man that greeted Carey at the door.

The first night he crept into Carey's bed

transformed her from a buoyant young girl into a quiet, damaged child whose only friends were dolls.

Two weeks later, the man would be in jail on drug charges, but to Carey, that stale body odor lingered for years, forever in the next room, waiting for her to fall asleep.

Carey was a smart girl, excelled in school, but was shy. As Jerry blossomed into an outgoing football player, Carey withdrew.

When puberty blessed her with breasts and curvy hips, Carey determined she was tired of feeling ashamed. So the clothes tightened, the skirts shortened and she held her chin up like a queen's—a queen that couldn't bend over too far without showing the class her panties.

Carey grew five inches to her final height of 5'8" and began playing soccer and basketball. It was just one step for her to reclaim her body and finally smother the scent of her father's friend.

Here is a brief summation of what passed between that moment of self-possession in high school and then meeting Jerry at a convenience store in college.

1. She dated an awkward 7th grader who obsessed over comic books, smelled like fruit roll-ups and worshiped her. They kissed twelve times and he timidly touched her butt once.

2. She decided she would date older. At a pizza place near the high school, she ran into a pimply-faced baseball player from another town spending the weekend with his cousin. She lied to the boy, saying she was also in high school. He asked her to go to a dance with him, but instead drove her out to the

country and demanded a handjob.

She never told her mother, knowing that if the woman hadn't protected her daughters from a Bear, she wouldn't protect Carey from a teenager.

3. She fell in love with a charismatic music snob named Donnie whose IQ was rumored to be at genius level. He underachieved, but the small school system passed him through each class anyway. When he spoke, it was like watching fireworks. His ideas were dazzling, he asked her challenging questions and was gentle with her, even when he took her virginity. He cheated on her four times, but they still dated for over a year.

4. She dated a rich kid who was a sophomore in high school while she was a freshman. Their first date was two weeks before she broke it off with the former boyfriend, thus beginning a long streak of never going a day without a relationship. She looked good in the rich kid's convertible and liked the lingerie he bought her, but he was unsure of himself sexually. A few times, his body seized up after only a few seconds, he'd growl "hold on, hold on," but ultimately be unable to hold off the premature ejaculation. He would then skulk to another room and not talk to her for hours.

5. On the side, Carey started an off-again, on-again relationship with a senior who drove a motorcycle and was planning on traveling the East Coast from Miami to New York City before college. He never offered to take her with him, though she prayed to God that he would.

6. Carey found Mr. Right her senior year. He was sexually adequate, sensitive to her mood swings and almost lured her into admitting the scars left by her

father's friend. He was also smart and had a bright future, which she saw as her escape. They broke up soon after graduation when he went to Yale and she went to a state school.

Upon her arrival to college, Carey had shed her accent and was determined to emerge from the school a professional woman, as strong as her older sister and as beautiful as a Barbie doll.

She also changed her name to "Cynthia."

Before long, every one of her friends, including Jerry, would only know her by the new name. She hoped that this new identity would wash away the stains left on poor, bony, little Carey.

But in her nightmares, she still walked in the shadow of the Bear.

FUN FACT: Activity
Swingers that are the most sexually active are those within a committed relationship with another couple or as part of an insular clique where trust and familiarity has already been established. Most couples within the Lifestyle for a prolonged period of time will eventually settle within a clique as part of the natural order of human interaction. There are exceptions.

Superswingers
Part I

Barry and Mary were both high school teachers and their emersion in that adolescent culture seemed to follow them beyond the halls and out into their civilian lives.

For instance, Mary read young adult horror romance novels and wore t-shirts from the mall with sassy, hip or cleverly worded sayings printed on the front.

Barry shopped mostly at thrift stores and continued to wear leather jackets, just as he had as a "stoner" in high school.

Teaching in high school gave them an adult's-eye view of how to be socially at ease and attractive. It offered both a second chance at building their identity from the ground up and they made the most of it.

Mary was blessed with large natural breasts, but thinned after having her last child so her waist to chest ratio was at its best proportions of her life. She shed all but a final, thin layer of baby fat, giving her a soft, girlish figure rather than the emaciated model/stripper bodies or the woefully flabby figures common among their Lifestyle peers.

Her new looks and new figure came with a defiantly buoyant and unflappable courage. Once she saw a target at a Lifestyle event, she wouldn't hesitate and charged in fully believing that the individual or couple would be wooed by her clever charms. She could be overbearing at times, especially when drunk, but was more often endearingly accessible.

Barry developed roguish good looks as he grew older and buried, for the most part, the geekish underpinnings that had haunted him throughout his young life. Mary's pet name for him was "Han (Solo)" which he loved, but also insisted that she never call him that in public.

Buying a Harley Davidson was a seminal moment in his life. It was a declarative statement.

"I ride this, therefore I am this!"

Once, when tearing through the open country, an older, wiser and tougher biker chick pulled up next to him. Her youth was beginning to wither underneath leathery, sun-exposed skin, but her smile sparked with vitality.

She told him to pull over at a nearby gas station. They talked briefly. They drove deeper into the countryside and f****ed behind a tree. They never exchanged names and her goodbye was a wink before her bike growled off into the horizon.

When Barry returned home and told Mary what had happened, she agreed that his life had found a new direction. Their relationship had been open almost from the beginning, but only now did they feel like they had, as a couple, blossomed to the point that they were ready to embrace all life's opportunities.

    A year and a half later, after giving birth to their third and last child, Mary bought a motorcycle. They drove together on the weekends, though never really took to the biker culture. It was partly due to Barry's reluctance to meet up with the woman again, fearing she would not live up to his vivid memory of her.

    Mary also preferred not to meet up with the famed biker chick, assessing the woman as possible competition because of how firmly she had became fixed in Barry's fantasy life.

    Like all budding swingers, they started in nightclubs and strip clubs, hoping to lure someone back home with the promise of pot and a hot tub. They eventually found their way to swinger clubs, at first nervous about being found out by the school district, but quickly settling in.

    The following interview was conducted at a Lifestyle club called The Rumormill. That particular night was a Meet and Greet for a prominent Lifestyle website which was considered one of the biggest metro-based events of the year. The website officials considered the Midwest and Southern part of the country its bread and butter.

    Barry – "The horny heartland."
    Marry – "And my goodness there are a lot of us. Starting out, all you can think about would be how horrible it would be if you ran into someone you knew."

Barry – "And you do."
Mary – "Yeah, but you learn to just run with it."
Barry - "There was that one time you ran into the parent at that house party. Tell them about that."
Mary (giggled) - "Oh, God, yeah. She was the mom of—Rafael?"
Barry - "Raul"
Mary - "That's right, Raul. Kind of your standard homely swinger mom."
Barry - "But nice tits."
Mary - "Fake, but yeah, pretty nice like inflatable throw pillows. At any rate, she said I should be ashamed of myself, I'm a teacher after all, blah, blah, blah. So, I said, 'Number one, you are here too. Number two, at least I'm not one of those cradle-robbing sluts that's trying to sleep with her students.'"
Barry - "And that worked."
Mary (exchanged a high-five with Barry) - "Yup, and she was a screamer. Really fun until she started insisting you give it to her up the butt. That was weird."
Barry - "If that's what you're into, that's cool, but I'm not really an anal kind of guy. Especially not with someone I just met."
Mary - "I don't remember the numbers on it, but the chances of picking up a blood-borne disease, like HIV, is dramatically higher through anal versus vaginal."
Barry - "Yes, but mostly on the receiving end, and I don't do that."
Mary - "I know, I was just explaining why I don't go backdoor with people we meet in the Lifestyle."
Barry - "Unless it's a dildo or strap-on or

something, cause you do that."
    Mary - "Well, yeah, but that goes without saying."
    Barry - "Does it?"
    Mary - "Yeah." (Then to interviewer) "Don't you think?"

    Barry and Mary met while in high school and continued dating throughout college, so the entirety of their relationship could be seen through the prism of academia. That might explain their sometimes utopian views of love and sex.

    Barry - "Orgasms are powerful things."
    Mary- "Just to warn you, this could go on for a long time."
    Barry - "No, I'll keep it short."
    Mary - "Sure you will."
    Barry - "I will. I believe, and I don't want to sound too mystical here, it's just what I believe. Every time you have an orgasm, you are reborn." (Mary rolled eyes, chuckled, but then kissed Barry on the cheek. He laughed acknowledging the joke at his expense, but continued undeterred.) "It's such an intense experience that you are reborn and can make yourself into anything you want to be. The human tendency is to settle back into what you once were because that's what you know, but if you want to make a serious life change or a serious life decision, you should orgasm first."
    Mary - "Keep it short, baby."
    Barry - "I will. So, after every spectacular orgasm I have, I try to reassess where I am in life, what I am doing and why. Your mind can focus better because

you are so depleted. There are no distractions anymore; you have been cleansed. That purity of soul will only last a very short time though, so you have to take advantage of it."
    Mary - "This used to be his excuse for not cuddling."
    Barry - "I cuddle."
    Mary - "You do now because I make you."
    Barry (mumbled while lifting his beer mug) - "I cuddle."

    Mary loved to dance. She bounced, writhed, and flirted on the dance floor, flush with attitude. In short, she danced like the girl she wished she'd been when she was younger.
    Barry would do his husbandly duty and dance with her unless he could convince another man to go instead. Mary was unlike most other Lifestyle women in that she rarely danced with other women. Mary considered herself an "old school" swinger, back before lesbian chic was all the rage.
    When Barry wasn't dancing, he was either chatting up new couples or sitting with Reginald and Fay Werster.
    Reginald and Fay appeared to be in their late seventies or early eighties and were one of the first couples Barry and Mary met when they entered the Lifestyle. Reginald and Fay sat at the same table at the same two clubs every time there was an event. They came early, left early and were just there to talk and watch.
    Barry and Mary loved the couples' stories of swinging throughout the later half of the twentieth

century, when the scene underwent dramatic changes. Reginald said the cycles of the Lifestyle were as regular as the tide. New talent always rushed in when social politics grew conservative. When terms like "Family Values" and "Moral Contract" were being thrown around on the state and national levels, it would be a good year for swinger clubs.

    Barry - "Tell them about Washington."
    Reginald (started to speak, but then smiled bashfully) – "No, no, they are here to talk to you two, not us old folks."
    Barry - "Well, they are being shy, but they have tapes from back when they were in D.C. that would make your hair curl. Incredible stuff from back in the '70s."
    Fay - "It was the sexual revolution and people still didn't think anything about letting someone with a high 8 camera come into an event. We were just so naïve back then."
    Reginald - "It was our camera and they trusted us."
    Fay - "And everyone loves to watch themselves doing it, even politicians."
    Reginald - "Especially politicians. Don't know why, its not like they are any good at it."
    Fay - "Some are, but most of them are just so self-centered. They want to have fun, but aren't too worried about anyone else."

    People like Barry and Mary are sometimes called Super-Swingers, couples who spend a good deal of time and money on the Lifestyle. It is the equivalent to calling someone a slut in normal life. Couples that are exceedingly liberated and engrossed in the culture are considered to be high risk for venereal diseases. In reality, many "Super-Swingers" are among the most vigilant with protection, but with every roll of the dice comes a new opportunity to crap out – so to speak.

Barry and Mary have tried BDSM, nudist colonies, soft swap, full swap, girl on girl, just about everything the Lifestyle affords, but have found that they are most comfortable with full, straight swap in a swinger club environment.

> Mary - "But we aren't too picky as long as it feels right at the time."
> Barry - "I find it interesting that even in the Lifestyle, you still run into the same judgmental people."
> Mary - "You'll **** someone all night long and then they'll tell you they need to wake up early so they can go to church. It's bizarre."
> Barry - "Well, I think it's good that people can still be Christians and be in the Lifestyle."
> Mary - "But it's weird and a wee bit hypocritical."
> Barry - "It can be, but not always."
> Mary - "It's weird."
> Barry - "It's like bisexuality. Neither Mary nor I are bisexual, but we aren't particularly repelled by someone who is. You see this double standard when a man is bisexual versus a woman. With women, it's a selling point and with men, it's the kiss of death. Especially in Oklahoma."
> Mary - "What was it that one girl said about bi-guys?"

Barry - "They'll get AIDS in the pool."

Mary (giggled and clapped her hands.)

Barry - "It is funny, but you see my point."

Mary - "Yeah, you say that, but you remember that time with that guy who grew up as a Mennonite?"

(Barry grimaced.)

Mary - "See, we were all having fun. The guy was a little unsure of himself and the girl couldn't suck the taste off a Tootsie Pop, but whatever."

Barry - "I think she was afraid of my penis and didn't really want to be there in the first place."

Mary - "Right, so it's like pizza, sex is still good even when it's bad. But all of a sudden Barry jumps. Apparently the dude tried to stick his finger in Barry's no-go hole."

Barry - "First I thought it was her, then I thought it was you."

Mary - "Why would it be me?"

Barry - "You were drunk."

Mary - "That's true."

Barry - "So, I just nudge the hand away. Then I catch the way he is looking at me as he tries again."

Mary - "Needless to say, that was the end of the night. Never saw them again."

Barry - "I saw them once, they were with that cute interracial couple."

Mary - "The one with the quiet guy?"

Barry - "Yeah."

Mary - "He is cute, I tried really hard with him, but he just didn't like me."

Barry - "Now we know why."

Vets vs. Newbies

Barry – "Hmm…I'm tempted to say experience over novelty. What do you think, honey?"

Mary – "It's apples and oranges in my opinion. I can't really say one is better than the other since, presuming they are both new to us, they both have a novelty appeal. I guess it's all about what you're in the mood for that night."

Barry – "A big difference between swinging newbies and straight out virgins is even newbies to the Lifestyle are still experienced in sex, just not necessarily sex with multiple partners in one night."

Mary – "That's very true. I have no use for a virgin."

Barry – "Exactly. For us, it would be like being NBA quality basketball players and deciding we'd rather play on a team with high school scrubs. What's the point? How fun can it really be?"

Mary – (giggles) "Nice. So would that make you the Lebron James of swingers?"

Barry – "God, no. I'm more of an Oscar Robertson type. I'm consistent. You know I'm going to get my rebounds, my assists and my points every night. I'm there to make everyone else around me a better player. Sure, every once in a while I might throw down a spectacular performance, but really I'm just a pillar you can build any great night around."

Mary – "Hmm. Okay."

Barry – "Am I wrong?"

Mary – "Not at all baby, I'll just start calling you Big O."

Barry – "Damn right you will."

Mary – "So, who am I then?"

Barry – "Kobe Bryant, definitely."

Mary – "**** you! I'm not Kobe Bryant! Why would you call me that? Why can't I be someone I like, maybe Kevin Durant?"

Barry – "You mean the guy who doesn't want attention, never talks trash but just plays out of the love of the game? That Kevin Durant?"

Mary – "Oh, yeah. Okay, then I want to be Lebron James."

Barry – "No, doesn't fit. James is overhyped. He has all the physical tools to be great, but doesn't have the heart to live up to his capabilities. He's a great player, but he's not a legendary player."

Mary – "So, I have to be Kobe ****ing Bryant then?"

Barry – "Yup, but hear me out. Bryant might have an attitude, he might be a diva that rubs people the wrong way, but there's no denying he's a great player. People can talk **** about him all day long, but there's no denying that he's the greatest closer in the history of the game."

Mary – "Hmm...I am a pretty good closer."

Barry – "You're a great closer."

Mary – "And I am a little on the rape-y side."

Barry – "Allegedly."

Mary – "Right. So, what the hell were we talking about?"

Barry – "Swinging is the NBA of sex. Newbies to swinging might not be as skilled as vets, but like NBA rookies, they've still got some skills or else they wouldn't be here. And grown adults who **** virgins are doing it because they have no game and are scared of a real challenge."

Mary – "Right. Can't handle the big show, ****ies."

FUN FACT: Fresh Meat
New couples fall into three categories: Those that were born to swing, those that like to rubberneck and those that have one member who is only there at the insistence of the spouse. The latter couple normally only stays in the Lifestyle briefly, but sometimes the reluctant member will see swinging as a calculated risk to keep their spouse loyal, in swingers' terms[10].

The Fishbowl
Part I

Setting the date for her suicide was the single most liberating moment of Michelle's life. Two Weeks. Fourteen Days. Three hundred thirty-six hours. Twenty thousand, one hundred sixty minutes. One million, two hundred and nine thousand, six hundred seconds.

Like most important decisions in her life, it came in a flash in the middle of the night. She was wrapped up in her comforter, staring up at the darkened ceiling, and listening to her mind spin.

The thought had haunted her for years, decades even, but only at that moment did she truly believe she could gather the strength to follow through.

Brad would be fine without her, might even thrive under that widower's glow. There were also no

---

[10] The enemy you know…

children to pine her departure, so the decision was simple. She would finally move ahead on her final, most decisive declaration of independence.

The time: 12:00 a.m.

Providence, she thought.

The big announcement came seven hours, twenty minutes, and thirty-eight seconds later.

"You see, Brad," Michelle stated in sharply trained diction. "This is my decision. My life is a possession, so it is mine to dispose of."

The declaration was directed at the long glamour mirror in the master bathroom. Brad would not hear this speech. Even if he did know, Michelle doubted he would care enough to earnestly try to keep her alive.

Perhaps he would surprise her, but after thirty-five years of marriage, she was tired of waiting on him. Besides, this was hers. Brad had the house, he had the friends, he had the fame, but he could not have this.

Michelle breathed in and then finished applying mascara to her tragically short eyelashes. They were her most loathsome detail. False lashes helped, but were only temporary. It was the one place on her body that she felt was beyond the reach of science.

The sweet irony was her recent discovery of a new prescription medication that would grow her lashes, but would take longer than two weeks to really be of any use.

They were just a small aspect of a body that was truly a work of wonder, a testament of her ability to stop the clock via a strict diet, rigid workout schedule and copious use of cosmetic medicine.

Breast augmentation increased her chest size

just enough to be larger than naturally proportionate, but not enough to embarrass her country club friends. She underwent liposuction every five years to capture that ten pounds that packed on no matter how stern her diet. She tightened her skin and received chemical peals to shed years, but not so much that it was laughable.

She did not smile often, so that helped minimize smile lines.

"Do you think I should color my pubes?" Brad called from the bedroom.

"I don't know that it matters, no one wants your old man balls in their mouth, no matter what color they are," Michelle quipped.

She blinked into the mirror, opened her eyes wide. She fussed with her short auburn hair, cut into a subtle bob and then stood and opened the door. Brad stood naked in front of a full-length mirror on the inside of the door to their walk-in closet. He was cupping his balls in one hand as he tried to stand naturally.

"What do you think about a tuck on the old boys, so they aren't hanging like golf balls in nylon," he asked, earnestly.

"Hmm," Michelle considered, walking up behind him and folding her fingers over his testacies while looking over his shoulder into the mirror. She bobbed them in her hand, like she was testing their weight.

At 5'6", Michelle was three inches taller than Brad.

"If you died them bright blue, then they might look like a deflated balloon animal."

"That's true," Brad replied while he pictured his

**** as a limp, half-finished, neon elephant.

"Don't change anything else, though," Michelle said, using her other hand to tousle the hair on his head. "The grey and black in your hair makes you look distinguished."

"I can't believe anyone falls for that," Brad smirked.

"Me either."

Brad's body had grown doughy with age. Not the unsightly fat that comes from consuming too much fried food, but that extra layering that comes from consuming too much time. Brad also had a thin carpet of body hair that he carefully trimmed so as not to appear to be trimming at all.

Most men of his ilk either waxed or shaved on a regular basis, but he didn't like how itchy it was and he also thought his penis would appear old and sickly.

Whatever flaws there are on Brad's body make no difference when it comes to women. His ability to pour charisma into a room like rain into the desert is more than enough to counterbalance love handles, pasty skin or even grey hair on his comically low-hanging balls.

Brad's money and power help, too.

"There is nothing sadder than aged nuts," Brad said, finally releasing his balls and slipping on his boxers. "I feel like anyone under forty that sees grey pubes will suddenly imagine me as their grandpa."

"Who knows," Michelle shrugged. "Maybe they are into that."

"You think?"

Michelle kissed Brad's shoulder, patted his butt and then walked past him into the closet to shed her robe.

"Mmm," Brad groaned, looking over her long legs, his favorite feature on her.

"Not now," Michelle snapped. "I am heading to the gym."

"I'll keep it brief and to the point," Brad grinned.

"Don't you always?"

"Touche," Brad chuckled, walking into the closet and closing the door behind him.

"Ugh, fine, just keep it quick and if you mess up my hair I'll rip off your old man nuts."

—

Thirteen and two/third days. Three hundred, twenty-eight hours. Nineteen thousand, six hundred and eighty minutes. One Million, one hundred and eight thousand, eight hundred seconds.

For decades, Michelle had put off suicide, seeing it as a failure, an admission of defeat to life and all the hassles that come with it. That was easier when their marriage was still vibrant and promising.

Brad had moved into public life just out of college, winning a state seat at twenty years old. She would spend the next twenty years as a glorified housewife. It was exhilarating at first, all the attention, all the galas, all the nice things, all the respect.

But then she realized that everything in their lives belonged to him. Michelle was not a real person, but just a placeholder as the wife of an important man.

Brad had retired seven years ago after questions arose about campaign financing and a closed door meeting with a seventeen year old, female staffer. His gubernatorial ambitions dashed, Brad decided to retire into the world of consulting and lobbying. Journalists stopped calling for interviews, their pictures no longer appeared in society magazines and she no longer felt the compulsion to live up to the image of a proper wife to one of the brightest senators in the history of the state of Oklahoma.

It seemed her life was already coming to a close. Forty-six was still young in this world, but with no children and no enduring interest in charity work, she really didn't know what to do to fill the time. There was the country club, but she'd grown bored of her high society friends whose husbands where still roaming around the political and corporate world. The women talked only of their famous friends and charmless grandchildren.

Her knees were no longer healthy enough for tennis and she couldn't stand the monotony of golf. Sex was still fun, but she didn't like that her greatest satisfaction in life came from ****ing the governor's grandson in the secretary of state's office.

There was her painting, but she knew she was a hopeless amateur. She hadn't completed anything of worth since Brad first ran for office.

And Brad would be fine. All he needed was attention from time to time and there were long lines of women willing to take Michelle's place.

Her body was still in spectacular shape, thanks to her little, Cuban personal trainer. The man was shaped like a 5 foot 11, two hundred twenty-pound solid brick triangle and slept with every bored housewife at the country club—except Michelle. He was too obvious and too easy. He was also a great motivator and she found the boiling sexual frustration kept up his vitality.

Even though her body was reaching its self-imposed expiration date, Michelle felt compelled to keep its façade tidy, firm and appealing. It was her body, after all.

Being married to a man of destiny was a full time job. Individuals charming enough to reach the upper echelons of society come with their problems, which meant that Michelle's primary challenge in life was to keep other women's hooks off her husband. That took a liberated look at monogamy.

So, where to find women to satisfy his carnal desires without having to worry about them challenging her throne or divulging their affairs to the world?

A fellow Republican's wife gave Michelle the key to publicity-free infidelity early on in Brad's political career.

"Honey, the dumbasses who get caught are the ones that sleep with interns and prostitutes," the aged woman with a harsh smoker's voice growled in a frankness that thrilled Michelle. "The smart ones are sleeping with each others' wives. That way, everyone has something to lose, and the Republicans are always going to protect their own. As long as he is getting his, you might as well get yours too, sugar."

The old woman had placed her thin, wiry hand on Michelle's knee and slid it up her thigh. Michelle had nearly jumped out of her skin in shock.

That very night, Brad and Michelle traded off on the trophy wife of a senior senator. In the days before Viagra, these old men liked to get off on the pride of watching their wives with the freshmen studs—a kind of hazing process that Brad was particularly fond of.

To Brad's knowledge, it had been Michelle's first time with another woman, and she let him believe it.

—

Thirteen and a half days. Three hundred twenty-four hours. Nineteen thousand, four hundred and forty minutes. One million, one hundred sixty-six thousand, four hundred seconds.

The communal showers were an oasis for Michelle. The country club had private showers too, but where was the fun in that?

Not that there were wild orgies going on amidst the steam, but there was always the thrill of catching a look at just the right moment. Trading glances, wondering, talking and then, perhaps, bedding. It was another challenge, finding a star in this sea of squares.

There were more vanilla members of the club than those in the know, to be sure, which was the best part of the game. There were also the liberated, but woefully unattractive wives who, once catching wind that Michelle was sexually adventurous, where hard to get rid of. Over time, Michelle had gotten adept at brushing off unwanted attention, but Michelle didn't mind them looking.

"I work hard on my body," Michelle told Brad when explaining her affinity for the locker room. "Somebody better be ****ing looking."

As she warmed under the showerhead, she let her eyes trail across the room and the only bodies she saw were perky, snotty and siliconed second wives.

She'd met some peaches in the past worth the effort, but for the most part, these young, naïve fools didn't know how to play the game yet and didn't respect the old guard wives.

They measured women like Michelle as obstacles on the social ladder, determining whether it was worth their time to maneuver around her or just pry her off the rungs altogether. These young fools believed their positions were secure, that their aged husbands would worship them forever. They didn't understand that the beauty queen shine faded quickly. If they continued to be prudes, then it was only a matter of time before they would be supplanted by third wives or humiliated amidst a nasty sex scandal.

The lucky ones were the girls with gay husbands dutifully tucked into the closet.

"If only," Michelle mumbled as she rinsed conditioner out of her hair.

These prissy bitches still slinked around the locker room with dismissive whispers and acidic giggling. When she caught one alone, she would pat the girl on the butt just to watch the jolt of shock climb up their bodies and mangle their perfect faces.

And who knows, maybe she'd get a smile. It'd happened before.

Brad had slept with a Barbie once, but when the girl started demanding gifts in exchange for silence, Michelle intervened and unleashed the full might of the old guard wives.

The women who sleep together stick together.

The poor, dumb girl was isolated in society, her husband was politely keyed in to what was happening and a conversation between the Barbie, her decrepit husband and the chairman of the state GOP wrapped up the incident quietly.

A polite letter of apology for unspecified wrongs showed up on Michelle's desk a few days later.

Throughout the affair, Brad and Michelle never discussed the situation directly, but Michelle would later refer to the incident as "the troubles," and Brad would laugh as if it had been one of their friends, not himself, that had gotten snared in another woman's vagina.

Michelle shut off the nozzle and followed the Barbies out of the showers. The girls shuffled to the other side of the lockers to change. They probably knew about the game and that's why they weren't comfortable changing in front of Michelle and other old guard wives. They probably thought it was icky and vulgar. They were probably true believers who sang from the heart at church and at baseball games.

And yet, they still showered in front of Michelle, so maybe they had a game of their own.

A loud, chirping laugh announced the imminent arrival of Michelle's closest companion amidst the old guard. Her name was Catherine and she was just abrasive enough to be interesting and just unrefined enough to be worth Michelle's time in bed.

Her humor was pointedly impolite and that raucous laugh served as a siren, warning others who wished to stay out of her way.

When Catherine walked into the locker room, she turned and playfully sneered at someone standing outside. Michelle couldn't stifle a wrinkle-inducing smile.

Catherine's strong thighs were bulging from

underneath her tennis skirt and her soft face glowed from exhaustion. Catherine was showing her age more and more these days.

She'd been the picture of the salty Southern Belle, equally as passionate about sex and booze as she was about God. That vibrant life was starting to leave its marks on her face. Michelle told her repeatedly that she smiled too much, but Catherine said she didn't mind the lines.

"I'd rather die," Michelle mumbled in response.

Catherine's husband inherited oil money and Michelle had met the couple twenty years ago through a lobbyist. Brad thought they were boring, but the pair were cuddlers, which Michelle found amusing and a nice break from the jackhammer boys that populated much of the Republican Party. Not that the judgmental and prudish Democrats were any better.

Catherine and her husband grew apart and they now secretly lived in two entirely different sides of town. That freed up Catherine to play to her heart's content, so as long as she was latched to his arm during corporate events.

Catherine glanced over at the Barbies as she walked toward Michelle.

"How was your workout, darling?" Catherine asked, opening up a locker next to Michelle's.

"Ramon is an asshole, but he gets the job done," Michelle replied.

Catherine lifted her shirt and sports bra, revealing baseball-sized breast implants that were starting to sag. Without a husband at home, Catherine didn't seem inspired to keep up the maintenance needed to ward away Father Time. As a woman,

Michelle should have been above such surface flaws, but she wasn't.

"I think I need a change, Katie," Michelle said, using her pet name for Catherine.

"A change" would be as close to admitting the impending date that Michelle would ever come. It was her subtle plea for help.

Catherine had heard this before, though.

"We all do, honey," Catherine started, watching the Barbies leave the locker room. Catherine sat down on a bench and patted the seat next to her. Michelle sat and leaned her head onto Catherine's shoulder.

"If you want to leave," Catherine cooed into Michelle's ear, "we can leave for Malibu, just you and I. We can grow old on the beach."

"Yuck. And be sun-bleached lesbians? I'd rather die."

"What's wrong with lesbians?" Catherine asked, feigning hurt feelings to hide the fact that the comment did truly sting her.

"Lesbians are too political," Michelle sighed, standing up and rummaging through her locker for clothes. "I really don't want to hear about your nose ring, your views on Marxism or the inequity between the genders. I'd rather just go on voting Republican, have someone lick my *****y once in a while and tell me how pretty I am."

Catherine stood and wrapped her arms around Michelle's waist. Michelle straightened and leaned back against Catherine's body.

"I could do that," Catherine whispered.

Michelle leaned back, tilter her head so she could peck a kiss on Catherine's lips. She then let out a soft sigh.

"I'm also not completely over males. Sometimes I just need a man to be strong and protect me. God knows Brad is worthless. He'd let me drown in the ocean rather than mess up his hair."

"I'd save you."

"And I appreciate it, Honey." Michelle kissed Catherine, lingering this time.

"I don't know why you are so grossed out by Malibu," Catherine pouted. "You go to those swinger clubs with Brad, and those things are just skeevy."

"That's why they are so fun." Michelle chuckled, turning in Catherine's arms to face her.

"Hmm," Catherine grumbled, running her hand along Michelle's back. "I tipped the towel boy to block the door for us."

It took Michelle a moment too long to respond, and Catherine noticed.

"Oh, well, if you insist."

FUN FACT: Second Wives' Club
Every Swinger Club has a contingent of trophy wives who believe that the Lifestyle is the ingredient needed to keep their high-dollar man honest. The smart woman can make it work with these two simple rules: No playing alone and no gifts.

A Charmed Life
Part 1

Lying in a warm bathtub with the water hugging one's face just above the ears but below the mouth must be similar to the isolation chambers eccentric singers and blind superheroes used to shut out the demons in their lives.

Sometimes I pretended to be that isolated, tortured superhero.

Yeah, I'm jaded, I'm scarred. I'm an antihero.

I, at thirty-two, still pretended to be a superhero and I refuse to be ashamed of that. I considered it the result of a healthy imagination.

These retreats were necessary since this parenting thing was all still new to me. Years of isolation, resulting from a persistent case of bachelorhood, was obliterated two and a half years ago when a chance meeting turned into a wedding ring five months later.

Was it a good decision? Not sure yet. The

benefits of hitching to a woman with three kids are:

    1. I leveraged a stable career and a healthy financial portfolio in order to marry up. My wife was absolutely gorgeous, a five foot five punk-chic with bright pink, spiked hair that worked as a beautician at this artsy-hip salon in the Plaza District in OKC. When we met, she had a towering pink mohawk, a nose ring and wore the sort of used clothes boutiques call vintage so they can charge an exorbitant markup. She also had tattoos dotting her body like landmarks. Even her name was badass: Elena—like this mix of Euro trash and old Hollywood. I acknowledge how completely bizarre our pairing was, as if our romance had been scripted by John Hughes.

    2. This hipster punk princess had been married to much worse than me, so I got to set my bar low. My job consisted of not beating her, earning a steady paycheck and being sweet to the kids. Done, done and getting there.

    3. Her job was then to turn me into the sexual dynamo I've always known I could be in my heart of hearts. I wasn't a virgin, but I wasn't exactly Don Juan, either. She started with my hair—apparently washing and combing is a daily thing. Then came my wardrobe, which also needed to be washed on a fairly regular basis. Who knew?

    She cleared my closet like Paul Bunyan in a rainforest, keeping only the "vintage" concert t-shirts I'd hung onto since high school. She insisted I book (and keep) regular appointments at her salon and that I start a strict regimen consisting of shaving, not picking at my zits and using moisturizer and fake tanner to offset my near translucent skin.

    She also replaced my glasses with a pair that were obscenely expensive and looked unnervingly close to what pervey rich men like to wear to show they are still hip. It was okay, though, because with every sour pill of self-improvement came a romp through the sheets that left me dazed, dumb and utterly pliable.

    Apparently, when a sexually confident woman has kids, motherhood puts a chip on her shoulder. She wants to prove to the world that she is still a virile sex kitten willing to work harder than her childless peers.

    And after a lifetime of failed gambles on cute boys, charismatic rockers and dashing intellectuals, I was a safe bet.

    This, in short, was an ideal situation for me. Low expectations, high yield.

    But that also meant that, since my career was largely undertaken at my home office, it fell on me to raise these strange children. That is why I had retreated to my isolation chamber, to return to the time when I was alone, sexually underserved and completely miserable.

    It was a refreshing break.

    Unfortunately, a tub of water centered within a house with thin walls wasn't an effective isolation chamber, but more of a filter. I could still hear the squealing of the three children in the next room, but never the context.

    Wait, wait, no, not squealing, shouting. Yes, definitely shouting. Teamwork between the middle child and the youngest had broken down in the midst of a particularly challenging obstacle of a video game.

The elder likely joined in on the shouting out of annoyance that the eldest's mainlining of whatever manufactured pop idol was being pushed on impressionable children these days had been interrupted. It was tame for a sibling squabble, as if coming from outside, from another person's child in another person's yard, where I held no sovereignty and therefore was absolved of all responsibility.

So, I soaked. I steeped in the tortured memories of murderous supervillains, a desperate city brought to its knees, and long-legged damsels whose love was lost to tragedy. You see, being a superhero meant I had this inability to trust another human being because it was only a matter of time before the dark, dark nightmares inevitably chased any good woman away.

Then I was only left with the bad women, and they were more fun anyway.

Another uproar from the next room. I waited, listened, and when the shouting subsided and no crying followed, I sank back into the isolation.

I am alone, I am jaded, I am scared. I am alone with my thoughts, my terrible, terrible thoughts.
Oh ****, I forgot to feed the kids!

I lifted out of the tub and glanced at my cell phone sitting on the closed lid of the toilet. Is that gross, that I leave it there when I take a bath in case it rings? I close the lid first and it's not like I piss on the toilet seat—or at least not since I cut back on my drinking.

Elena was uncomfortable being around drunken

men.
 Don't ask.
 Ugh, 12:30 p.m. Lunch had totally slipped my mind while waiting for my skin to go prunish in my superhero isolation chamber.
 "Hey! Have you guys eaten?"
 No answer.
 "HEY!"
 Foot stomping toward the closed door.
 "Yeah, Will?"
 "Have you eaten?"
 "No, we haven't, Will."
 "Okay, give me a second and I'll be out and I'll feed you."
 "Yes, sir!"
 Foot stomping away.
 Yes, sir.
 They're good kids, well trained. It took time to get them there, though; it took a lot of crazy to get them in line. A lot of fuses blown, a lot of crazy eyes, a lot of storming into rooms with the wrath of God despite how insignificant the matter. Because of the age difference, they all had their own uniquely nuanced issues, which arose from their mom's fairly complicated past. The youngest didn't remember much, the oldest remembered everything and the middle was lost somewhere in-between.
 They still call me Will, so I don't really feel like a full-fledged parent yet, but I kind of think I'll get there in time. It took a while for their mom to trust me watching them all day, but once she did, she gave me full reign.
 So, I was free to go ballistic without the fear the

kids would snitch on me.

I hated playing the unhinged parent. Don't tell the kids that, though. I find that, for an otherwise ill-equipped parental figure such as myself, it behooved me to leave the possibility of insanity and the subtle hint of infanticide open.

Sometimes I would spin on my heels, yell at the children when one child (usually the eldest) had taken something from the middle because the elder child was bored. It was even better when the children's annoying friends were over, because then my entirely unjustified fit of rage swept across all small humans within the half-acre of my homestead.

Also, being a stand-in dad was more ominous than a real deal dad because the kids didn't feel I was as emotionally and instinctually invested in their future.

It settled problems before they were really problems, which is critical when you're outnumbered three to one. Once peace had returned to the land, I was free to get back to my home office and attend to more pressing matters such as work-related issues, book publishing or just the passing curiosity of what prurient images would pop up on the internet search engine when I typed "cheating wives."

Disappointing really, mostly just grainy hidden camera stuff. Bleh.

Proper parenting, in my mind, emulated Rome's vast empire, where relative freedom was given to the ruled. The true might of the ruling class was only displayed when insurrections arouse, and the punishment was swift and bold.

I didn't spank the children; it seemed too formal

and predictable. I preferred a raging bellow from the other room, followed by a severe act of intimidation usually involving some crazy eye, some close quarters tirades—just enough to put everyone in the house off balance.

I learned this from a documentary I once watched on boot camp. "Ears Open, Eyes Click!" Check it out, it's like parenting 101.

So, rather than a mundane corporal punishment system where $X + Y = Z$, I liked to stoke the fear that physical punishment lurked, ever out of sight and with no respect of proportion to the crime, and therefore more frightening.

In reality, I stewed in guilt the rest of the day whenever I so much as swatted a kid (usually the youngest) in the back of the head because the child just couldn't find it in his heart to share with the siblings some random toy found under the couch that'd been lost for a year.

No, I didn't have the heart for corporal punishment, but it was okay, you see, because the kids didn't know that.

And if you tell them, I'll f****ing brain you!

I also enjoyed invoking a labored fury, rife with disappointment and a subtle hint of unhinged delirium simmering like Mount St. Helens. That would always end whatever disagreement had arisen, and hopefully unnerve neighborhood children enough that they all decided to go to their friends' houses to get away from the crazed stand-in parent.

And then I could finally get back to "cheating wives + night club." Much better.

Before you leap to conclusions about my poor

parenting skills, bear in mind that the children were not at school six hours a day, but instead imbedded in our house for the summer like a bad case of fleas.

During that time, writer's block was rampant, leaving only my terrible, terrible thoughts.

And by terrible, I mean self-doubt, questioning my lot in the world, wondering why my recent thirty-second birthday should send so much fear through me and why the hell I wasn't famous yet. Didn't they know how great my new wife thought my writing was? Did they not read the review of our last book, cleverly disguised so not to be obvious that it was written by a friend of mine?

Was Charles holding me back? Writing as a team had its conveniences—he loved all the promotional stuff that I detested—but should I strike out on my own?

Then I wondered if my puttering writing career was because I wasn't good at description, whether I made a horrible decision when, in junior high, I decided I would be a writer no matter what hurdles rose up ahead of me.

Now, a couple decades later, we still hadn't had a major publisher take our work seriously, and neither one of us knew what the hell we were doing. My career was only kept afloat by the dubious reputation I gained from "the dominant hand" and all the insanity therein.

I should have given up on this a long time ago, but the two things that kept me going were the meager success of the aforementioned book, which then led to my eventual introduction to Elena.

She admired me, and I think that's the only thing

I have that she found attractive. If I quit writing, I would lose her, and then what would I have left? No writing, no career, no woman, no family.

And really, I guess I'm doing okay. I'm eking out a living, but I can't help but feel like I'm wasting my potential.

Before Elena, I'd spent a better part of my adult life trying to adjust my life goals, find some better use of my time that was more rewarding financially, but I was utterly incapable of visualizing myself as anything other than a writer.

There was the whole Jim Jacobs fiasco where I briefly entertained the idea of being Shropshire Plaid's manager, which really, really didn't work out.

There was the time I tried out for the fire department. I know I don't look it, but I'm generally in pretty good shape, even before Elena cleaned me up and made me presentable.

Don't believe me? Come watch me play hockey sometime. I'm no Bobby Hull, but I scored sixteen goals in the last rec league up at Arctic Edge in Edmond. Granted, it's a crap league, but still, sixteen goals. How many did you score?

So, during one of my failed stabs at finding a real job, I wandered into tryouts to become a firefighter. I played hockey several times a week, lifted weights sporadically. So, I thought, in-good-shape + smart = hero material!

All went well through the physical, where I was relieved to find I was not in the bottom of the barrel, but then annoyed to find that there were a couple guys that could flip their legs over a seven-foot wall like a giant hurdle. When I tried, I got stuck and ultimately fell on my ass.

Still beat one of those guys' time because he couldn't pull a test dummy ten feet. So suck it, Leapy McLeaperton!

Then came the test. I was about as prepared as I was for most college tests, which is to say I hoped my ability to bull***** on the written essays would make up for my complete apathy for studying.

It did!

Then came the interviews. I don't like to admit it, but I'm not awful at interviews. This was because, like other writers, artists, musicians or other aspiring superstars, I compulsively interview myself while alone in the car, and not just about impending interviews for jobs, but:

1. prospective interviews with literary journalists
2. talk show hosts
3. leaders of great nations
4. dictators of rogue nations that need to be talked back into the fold and clearly I'm the only man reasonable enough to do it. I mean, who else you gonna call, Charles? **** that!

So, I sat down across from a grey-haired man who'd once been a spry and plucky recruit such as myself, but was now behind a desk as he waited for retirement to kick in. I wondered if he yelled at the younger firefighters for all their crazy antics, which no doubt involved blowing things up, perhaps lifting cars into the air via water pressure alone, and maybe duct taping someone to their bed and leaving them outside all night.

The man asked:
"Why do you want to be a firefighter if your life's ambition is to write?"

I realized at that moment that he saw through me, and I was not, as I'd assumed, more clever than they were. I was not able to pull the wool over their eyes, not able to hide the card I'd palmed during my magic trick and no poof of smoke or lovely assistant was going to save me. They knew I didn't want to be a firefighter. I just wanted the experience to offset my otherwise boring life and bolster my chance of getting published.

Instead, I went back to work in journalism.

A brief squabble between the two youngest brought me out of my isolation chamber. I should have been fixing lunch, but just wanted five more minutes. I listened, and by tone, pitch and the few words I could discern, they were unable to coordinate their efforts within the video game.

I knew this because the middle child barked commands while the youngest squealed, shrilled and whined. It was as reliable as a smoke detector.

It'll work itself out. Can't dote on them too much, that'll make them soft.

Since I'm obsessing anyway, let's talk about this book. Clearly, I think quite a bit of my own writing chops, otherwise, I wouldn't have written this book. Obviously, you agreed or were just obligated to read this because I begged you to give me your:
1. opinion
2. literary review
3. money.

In any case, I thank you.

So, to get everything out in the open, here is a brief assessment of my skills as a writer. First, my weaknesses:

1. Description-I tend to be too minimalist, and to be honest, I don't remember all the quirky little details that my literary betters pack inside their novels. For instance, I hadn't even mentioned that just before dipping into my isolation chamber, I'd been suffering from a severe stomach virus. My mind and body were drained from repetitive trips to the bathroom, some just in nick of time.

Yes, I did clean my backside thoroughly (though I wished we still kept baby wipes in the house). After the worst subsided, I decided I just needed a bath. The water was probably fine, but to think of it, it was kind of disgusting I was just soaking there.

Bleh.

2. I'm totally up my own ass. I mean, look at what I'm doing now, I just inserted myself into my own novel...again. I'm a repeat offender and even the characters that aren't based on me directly, are still some sort of confessionary allusions to something I aspired to, something I feared, or something I've already done and wanted to brag/apologize for without actually acknowledging it was me.

Writing with a partner would, in theory, allow the other person's strengths to make up for your weaknesses. Unfortunately, we mostly work independently because, despite what he tells you, we can't stand each other.

This new book was a source of great angst on Charles' part. He just wasn't sold on the value of the "swinging" angle. I, on the other side, think it is absolutely fascinating.

I do hate the word "swinger," though. Even "lifestyle" is kind of gross. They both make me think of hairy-chested men that smell like Old Spice, have thick, pampered mustaches and insist nudity is natural. So they talk about sex with the same tone as they would talk about work, sports or whatever else it is hairy-chested men who smell like Old Spice talk about.

Beer?

These men and their mustaches, as well as their unnervingly mom-ish wives are convinced that their own brand of deviant sex is okay, natural and even sophisticated. Hell, they might even introduce you to their children the same night as some twisted orgy, and you'd go along with it cause you're not particularly attracted to either of them, but you already bought the condoms and cleared the evening, so what else are you going to do?

Go home? **** that!

That kind of sex is not okay. It's unnatural and not the least bit sophisticated. Deviant sex isn't meant to be that, that's why everyone has their own brand, whether foot fetish, BDSM, group sex, golden showers, exhibitionism, light or hardcore bondage, role playing, sex games, fantasy "Lord of the Rings" cos play...its all kind of gross and beneath good-natured society, therefore irresistible to those who need a diversion from their structured and stressful lives.

And, just as an aside, I always found it funny when I met middle-America gay couples whose own sex lives should have been deviant, but had developed the same ritualistic "well, I guess we should, it's our anniversary" sex that pervades heterosexual marriages.

Deviant sex is a dessert, though. It's a luxury. It's not unlike televised sports, beauty magazines or ice cream. There are better things you could be doing with your time, but we can't always be elevating our minds, our bodies and our social standing.

Sometimes it's fun to just jump into life head first.

3. (Of my writing skills assessments, we're still on that list) I haven't really done much to be proud of. I've done a lot of stupid things, had some grand mistakes, but never suffered greatly from any of them. So, I've never really overcome anything.

Sure, I married into a family with a herd of kids, sacrificing my life of self-obsessed isolation to play father figure to a crew of strangers. But, in truth, they were like cacti that needed water and food now and again, but mostly raised themselves.

I could play the struggling artist card, having never given up on my dream of writing, but the fact that I haven't decided to move on with something more constructive is more an example of self-aggrandizing obstinance than artistic integrity.

4. I am terrible at spotting errors, whether grammatical or factual. That's why I write so much fiction, because it greatly minimizes the number of factual errors, then I just have to worry about grammar and spelling. For instance, "obstinance." I have no idea how to really spell that, and it didn't come up on spell check, so I just have to hope that Elena (former English major) catches it later and

corrects it.
 Thanks Honey!

 So, why do I write? Well, here are my virtues:
 1. I am a natural storyteller, it's the only thing I really know how to do and find interesting enough to stick with.
 2. I work hard, even if I am a shoddy fact-checker. I've written several novels, both alone and with Charles, though only published two prior to this book. I am a reliable freelancer, deadline driven and am capable of an excellent feature from time-to-time. Mostly, the editors like that I am dependable, even if not consistently spectacular.
 3. I am dedicated.

 An unnatural, curdling rumble twisted in my intestines, so I decided it was time to wrap up my bath. I emerged from my isolation chamber and was pleased that the children were not at each other's throats.
 The youngest was talking to the other characters in the video game as if it were he, not the lego-ized "Indiana Jones" roaming through a Russian mine town.
 A sample:
 "Hey, what are you doing?"
 "Oh, I'm running around the Temple of Doom. I have a whip. Wanna see?"
 "Yeah!"
 "Wupppow." (made by his voice along with the television)
 "Wow, that's a real nice whip!"

"I know, I can kill bad guys and swing on stuff."
"Cool!"

The young one had so much imagination that he is often lost inside of it, which worried me that he'd one day realize that he's thirty-two and no closer to a legitimate career than he was ten years ago in college. It was nice that I could legitimately identify with one of the children though, and there are times I honestly felt like a real-deal dad instead of a stand-in just waiting to be usurped by a more capable father figure.

Oh, and don't tell Elena about all this doubting my career crap. She hates when I talk like this.

—

So, I cooked up this really decent metaphor about why my relationship with Elena works. Here goes:

Elena and I were on two ends of a balancing board. Not like a teeter-totter, a teeter totter is kinda fun, but grows old easily and can be dismounted by merely waiting for the other person to reach the apex of their lift, then quickly jumping off so that the other person comes crashing down to Earth.

No, there was no jumping off our balance board. There was just a perpetual teeter and totter above a bottomless chasm of self-destruction. When one person shifted their weight too far, whether from depression, apathy, paranoia, self-doubt or the occasional immoral discretion, it was up to the other to adjust quickly and keep the balance board set upon its tenuous perch.

Is that good description? Maybe I should have

described the perch as rocky, or maybe it's a pin, but then what kind of pin? A safety pin? A sewing pin?

Elena and I had accomplished the balancing act to varying degrees of success for two years now. It could be argued that I benefited from the fact that her board had fallen when the father of the first child left and then a few days later she was arrested while working at a strip club and had to be bailed out of jail by her own father.

That board fell for Elena again a second time when the second man she tried to build a life with nearly beat her to death in front of her three crying children.

That is why Elena refused to argue in front of them.

But so far, we've been a good team, we've balanced the board with relative success. After a handful of months, when we first discussed marriage, she was reticent. I know five months seems pretty fast, but it was a more careful decision than it sounds.

I also benefited from the fact that I was naive, malleable, kind of boring and unthreatening. She didn't want to jump from relationship to relationship, and I could offer her stability.

I think she married me, at first, despite the fact that she didn't love me with the same abandon as she had the first two. Perhaps that's exactly why she married me.

Did she feel that now?

I didn't really care. She made me a better person, I've made her a better person and we have built a better life for ourselves and the kids.

Is that love? Is that the storybook love that every

little girl dreams of?

No.

Is it the love that Elena, a full-grown mother of three needed?

Yes, I think it is.

The process of building started for both of us before we lived together. I approached it logically, like I would build the story of a book.

I had two individuals with two varying paths in life, but, by the end, they must have one shared journey. I knew my beginning; I knew my end, so how would I construct the scenario in the middle of the story that led the two lovers to the one, right path at the end?

It helped that our weaknesses and strengths did seem to compliment each other in a way that suggested destiny.

So, in the story of Elena and I, there was one person who was logical, was adept at financial planning. One who went to work everyday without fail, one who still had dreams and aspirations, but one who worked to ensure the children wouldn't have to sacrifice again for a parent's selfishness.

And then the other (me) who remembered to cash his royalty and freelance checks and mopped behind the toilet where pee tended to splatter.

At times, one part of that complete human must compensate for the failures of the other parts of the body, such as my intestine's desperate bid to flush all the fluids in my body to make up for my immune system's failure to fight off the bacteria now set up like a flourishing metropolis in my tummy. It's got highways, it's got school systems, it's got a rudimentary form of democracy, but ultimately will fall because its prosperity is too rooted in the suffering of the rest of the body.

    Did that come off anti-American? Cause it wasn't meant to be. To be honest, I'm really not edgy and interesting enough to be unpatriotic. I still stand up for the anthem and awkwardly cover my heart while my liberal, artsy friends smirk.

    So, where were we? Ah, Elena and I. Yes, the balance board. Are we done with that?

    Yes? Okay.

—

    That night I'd finally submitted to the middle child's fourth request to aid in the building of a house of Legos. Twenty minutes passed before I found an excuse to leave the project with the roof un-built.

    You see, I'm a union worker and there are guidelines, project be damned.

    I lay down in bed next to Elena. She was working a needle and thread through jeans she was shortening by a few inches. Earlier that night I'd asked if she was making them into capri pants and she got mad and defensive. That was why I don't like to talk to her about clothes.

    Elena tends to hold her mouth slightly open when she works, not in an imbecile kind of way, but in this charmingly oblivious way that makes me happy that she can be so unaware and unguarded around me.

    She does burp out loud from time to time, for the same reason. That does bother me, but haven't figured out how to broach the subject with her yet.

I stared at a long, serpentine dragon that wound around her ankle and calf. I'd never been into tattoos, didn't have any on my body and hadn't ever gone for a tattooed girl before Elena.

But now, the tattoos fascinate me. Staring at the grey images scattered across her skin is like studying the map of her soul. They are beacons, touchstones; they are a visual representation of a life I regretted entering into so late.

If I'd only met her ten years earlier, I could have protected her. I could have been the one fathering her children, I could have been the one holding the roof up on her home and she could have been the one cheering me on as I made all the right decisions in my life.

And we would have been happy for ten more years during our painfully finite existence.

But, let's be honest. Ten years ago, she wouldn't have thought twice about me.

A rumble and churn from my belly sent me jumping off the mattress and dancing around the bed to get to the bathroom, again, just in the knick of time. I no longer felt clean from my superhero isolation chamber.

I emerged from the bathroom, uttered something about getting work done, slipped on headphones and played an album that, as a music snob, I should like, but really didn't. Elena doesn't know the difference; she was punk more in appearance than in musical tastes. Billy Idol was more of her musical guide stick than Johnny Rotten, but that no longer bothered me.

Still, I hoped she'd ask who I was listening to so I could let her know how enlightened I was.

She didn't.

I considered logging on to one of the social network websites I'd fallen into, like a desperate loner in a high school cafeteria containing millions. There, I could mention who I was listening to, and others could pretend to like that crappy band too.

Elena had e-mailed me hours ago while still at work but I hadn't noticed. The email was her attempt at adjusting her weight on the balance board, telling me things would come around, it was a good book, it would be a cult hit, how sorry she was that Charles was being a **** and she was sorry that things were so "crappy."

Heh, heh, 'cause I pooped a lot that day.

What I should have been doing while listening to music and ignoring my family:

1. The unfinished, paying, freelance gigs.

2. Working on this screenplay I was helping a friend with, though I was 90 percent sure it wouldn't ever be finished. These things never are.

3. Trying to secure an elusive review from any number of media outlets that had promised to look our book over.

Instead, I simmered with doubts, anxious creative energy and the realization that I was, in fact, too much of a ****** to write the only actual life experiences that might be of any interest to the world at large.

I. e., my recent emersion into the Lifestyle.

FUN FACT: Venereal Disease
The run of the mill swinger is generally so terrified of contracting a venereal disease that the slightest red flag can spook a prospective couple. This is one of many reasons that orgies are generally avoided by the more desirable couples. That said, Dutch researchers claim that swingers forty and older have a higher likelihood of contracting chlamydia[11] and gonorrhea than a prostitute.

The Ballad of Jerry and Carey/Cynthia/Veronica Part II

Young love is beautiful because it is tragically naïve. Underdeveloped brain chemistry, a still evolving sense of identity as well as a determined devotion to the myth of destiny all propel a simple romance beyond reason and into obsession.

And, of course, Jerry and Carry (now Cynthia), were no different.

Three developments stand out during the initial year of their relationship:

1. Their third date was when Jerry finally shed his virginity. Cynthia suddenly uttered "I love you" mid-coitus and it shocked them both. Jerry replied, "I

---

[11] What a pretty name for such an ugly condition. It should be the name of an orchid or a light, fluffy, citrus-based dessert.

love you too," because he knew it would be weird if he didn't, but also because Cynthia's surprising vulnerability touched him.
    2. Cynthia wasn't tempted to hedge her bets with other men. Though he was a clumsy lover, he was attentive and sweet, which touched her.
    3. Cynthia admitted that she had a lingering fascination with women.

    All three elements were unprecedented. Cynthia had never been particularly open with any man, but the tender way he spoke to her made her feel safe. So she slowly unfurled the complexities of her life. Jerry began to realize that Cynthia was a roller coaster that was thrilling, unpredictable and, for all its ups and downs, never boring.
    Jerry also saw Cynthia's bisexual tendency as an opportunity. On first blush, the admission was threatening, but he quickly recognized Cynthia's curiosity as a chance to expand his experience base and feed a ravenous sexual appetite that had finally been unleashed on the populous.
    After the couple was engaged, just a few months before graduation, Jerry floated the idea of letting Cynthia kiss another girl, just to see what it was like. Cynthia wasn't certain if she was being led into a trap, so just laughed and blew off the idea. She dwelled on the question, not because of her actual interest in kissing a girl, but because of the intensity of the question. It turned him on; she could tell by the awkward tremble of his voice, how his face warmed, how his fingers trembled and how animalistic the sex was later that night.

She revisited the idea a few nights later while whispering in the backseat of his car. It was a playful idea, a tease and only that.

For Jerry, the thought opened a window to a world of vice that he had only seen on fuzzy VHS tapes and late night cable programming.

It would be tempting to say the two were headed to a dark world of sin where they would lose each other under the weight of guilt and jealousy.

To the contrary, the taboo world bonded them. It was a shared interest and soon, a game.

Take for example the chauvinist rating system by which men determine the amount of alcohol that needs to be consumed by either themselves or the other party for sex to happen. For instance:

"Dude, that girl is a butter face, nice body...but her face! She's definitely a six beer and a shot of whiskey date."

Or...

"Yeah, she's pretty hot, but I bet after three shots, I could have her XXXXX my XXXX in the back of my Escort while I XXXXX her friend's XXXXX XXXXX."

Jerry and Cynthia's version went like this:

"Ugh, look at her hair and her shoes, she's a complete mess. I guess if I drank a bottle of tequila I could let her XXXX my XXXXX, but you would XXXXing owe me!"

Or...

"Okay, she doesn't look like a lesbian, but I bet if we could get four jello shots and a Long Island Ice Tea in her, then she'd go down on you to impress her boyfriend."

Then there were the parties where Jerry and

Cynthia became notorious exhibitionists. Games of Truth or Dare or I Never often led to one or both of them drunk and naked by the end of the night.

After her first experiences with women, usually dare-induced oral sex, Cynthia had three realizations that she didn't share with Jerry:

1. She could not relate with women as easily as men, especially when it came to sex.
2. It was possible that her idle fantasy was just that.
3. Men were much easier to flirt with and simpler to understand in bed.

She kept up the game because of how much Jerry loved it. So the hunt continued for a female for an elusive three-way and, over a few years, the hunt shifted from a playful hobby to a source of frustration for Jerry and for Cynthia, an open door to the darker side of her sexual identity that would lead her to another man's arms.

—

Cynthia could not be blamed for her damaged sexual identity and it would be unrealistic to think that love, no matter how earnest, could instantly heal the scars cut deep into her psyche.

The Bear still lurked in the shadows of her mind and she would find her own ways to attempt to extinguish the memories once and for all.

While in the flush of their young romance, she tried to believe that Jerry's love would chase away the fear, that he would steadfastly guard her from the beast that returned night after night in her dreams. He would stick through the mood swings and the bouts of paranoia because she deserved to be loved and protected.

It felt like a lie, though. He would reject her one day because he would eventually discover who she truly was, and she didn't believe anyone could be expected to stay after that.

When careers failed to materialize, when money became tight and when she felt Jerry slipping away, she walked through the door of a gentleman's club and applied.

Jerry resisted at first, but he was curious. They were a sophisticated and enlightened couple, after all. If athletes could make money from their strong arms and barrel chests, then why couldn't a woman make money off of her charm and beauty?

They talked of him coming to watch, of him getting a lap dance and, finally the real reason for the season, bringing a woman home with them.

He was sending his wife out to troll for other women and as he went to work, came home, watched television, played video games and read—he waited.

Cynthia went to work, came home, paid bills, cooked dinners, watched Jerry playing video games and watched him waiting. Cynthia didn't know how to talk to women, but she didn't want to disappoint him.

But she also craved attention, and the club was a place she always knew she could get it.

The club was a large facility with three stages, a VIP lounge, two bars and walls full of memorabilia of other gentlemans' clubs from the '50s when stripping was considered an art form. Cynthia's long, athletic legs and perky breasts did well, but not as Cynthia. She had to create yet another persona named Veronica, a woman crafted from Old Hollywood bombshells: refined, liberated and dangerous.

    Doctors, construction workers and lawyers loved the education in her diction, the confidence of her strong body coupled with the foul subjects she readily referenced while one-upping other salty patrons.

    When she returned home from an evening of being worshiped by strange men, she found a hapless husband who was lost in life, inattentive and no longer the sweet, tender man that she had fallen in love with.

    So, Cynthia, now Veronica, sought out that tenderness in the beds of a select group of dedicated regulars. They were:

    1. The bookworm: worked on computers, loved comic books and college football. Veronica became the most attractive woman he ever brought home, so he showered her with gifts and paid for a new set of tires for her car.

    2. The photographer: made her look like a movie star and borrowed money he never paid her back.

    3. The sugar daddy: small-time real estate tycoon who loved to show up at restaurants with young women who spoke intelligently, but who also knew when not to speak at all.

    Jerry stewed at home, knowing that something was happening when Cynthia, now Veronica, disappeared for hours at a time or never returned from work at all. She often thought of leaving Jerry, but instead just avoided spending time at home. She knew his frustration and felt sorry for him, and respected him less and less everyday, yet never stopped loving him.

At a party with other staff and dancers from the club, but no Jerry, Veronica was given a lap dance by a short, buxom blonde on a dare. The lap dance became more, as clothes were shed, drinks flowed. Then, sex.

While a room full of strangers watched, Veronica and another woman writhed, moaned and forgot about their husbands who'd urged them down this path. She was exhilarated by the experience, but the momentary pleasure of a new horizon was quickly replaced by shame.

She arrived at their apartment the next morning. Jerry pouted, but didn't fight for her. That was when the relationship should have ended, but a day later, something finally clicked in Jerry's mind. All the torturous nights finally awoke the territorial instinct and he confronted Veronica at the local mall, who he saw walking arm in arm with the bookworm.

Jerry, still muscular and imposing from his football days, stepped between the two. Ugliness ensued; the regular shrank away and disappeared from Veronica's life. She left the club, and slowly Veronica faded. Cynthia did not re-emerge, nor did Carey. For a time, the woman was merely empty and lost.

―

Marriage is like democracy in that it can only be maintained by those willing to fight for its survival. It would be simple to end Jerry and

Carey/Cynthia/Veronica's story with a tidy happily ever after bow, but this is not a book about overcoming vice. It would seem logical to end their shattered marriage with divorce, but this also isn't a story about failure.

This is about deviance, about otherwise normal individuals finding other paths toward a normal life. They would soon find that, on their path, monogamy was truly a relative term.

FUN FACT: Lubrication
With enough Astroglide, you can get virtually anything into anywhere. But that doesn't mean you should.

Superswingers
Part II

Barry and Mary disappeared from The Rumormill dance floor with an older couple. The silver-haired man seemed to be in his early fifties and had stripped down to his underwear, revealing a tanned, shaved and muscled torso. His white teeth glowed in the black lights. The man's wife was likely the same age, just as tan as her husband but with cartoonishly large artificial breasts. The two couples had slipped into a side room for half an hour before leaving the club altogether.

A text from Barry read "B back soon after we TCB." An hour later they returned to the club and sat back down next to Reginald and Fay. Reginald had nodded off to sleep, his head tilted back and to the right as his mouth gaped open. Fay gently shook his shoulder and Reginald snorted loudly as he jerked awake.

Fay – "He turned off his hearing aid. He goes

right to sleep when he does that."

Mary – "Poor thing, why didn't you go home and put him to bed?"

Fay – "Pshaw! We have an interview to do."

Reginald(yawned) – "I'm okay."

ORGIES

Barry – "They are kind of seen as the Holy Grail of the Lifestyle. Everyone wants to get one going, but no one is really sure how."

Mary – "Yeah, we've gone to a couple (used air quotes) 'orgies,' and really they are just two or three motivated people who start having sex right off, and then everyone else watches uncomfortably until you just have sex with who you came with."

Barry – "You don't want to be a rude guest."

Mary – "Right, but also, orgies are great ideas in theory, but in real life its hard to get a group of people together that:

A. like each other enough to have sex and

B. trust each other enough to have sex indiscriminately."

Barry – "Some guy could just decide to not use a condom. He might have it on initially, but will slip it off before entering."

Mary – "And we won't know, it's not like it feels that much different to us. Plus, in the back of your head, you're wondering, 'if these people are at this orgy, then they've done this before. How many orgies have they been to? What kind of funky diseases do they have?'"

Barry – "So, you just have sex with the people

you came with, which might just be her and me, and hope nobody sticks anything anywhere it doesn't belong."

Reginald – "I'm going to say this again, and I know you won't listen, but if you want a really good orgy, you start hanging out with the more unattractive or older people at the club."

Mary grimaced and Barry shrugged.

Fay – "The older you get, the less hung up on sex you become. Lord, if I had my thirty-year-old body, but knew what I do now. Whoo!"

Reginald – "We wouldn't be able to keep your legs shut with a steel chain."

Reginald and Fay laugh, Barry and Mary smile at each other.

Barry – "I did read somewhere that there has been a spike of venereal disease among seniors since the introduction of Viagra."

Reginald (apparently didn't hear Barry) – "You see, it's like a math equation. You got attractiveness on one side, you got quality of sex on the other. If you have one couple much more attractive than the other, the less attractive couple will work harder to impress the others."

Fay – "Or if the man is shorter than the woman. Lord, I do love those short boys!"

Reginald(apparently didn't hear Fay either) – "So, if you get into a group of ugly people, and you are the most attractive ones, then you're going to have yourself one heck of an orgy."

Reginald looks to Fay and she nods in agreement.

Barry – "Well, if you're not into that, then you're

probably not going to find a good orgy outside of porn."

Mary – "See, and the reason that they look so good in porn is everyone knows why they are there, the director has already set up perimeters with the actors, such as, 'she doesn't like anal,' 'he doesn't feel comfortable double teaming a girl with another guy.'"

Barry – "All the bases are covered."

Mary – "Right. If only we could do that, maybe have a questionnaire everyone filled out."

Barry – "Everyone gets to visually okay everyone else involved."

Mary – "Blood tests are run, nondisclosure agreements are signed."

Reginald (suddenly hearing again) – "Yes, but where's the spontaneity?"

Fay – "You young kids are such wet blankets. Sometimes you just want a prick in you and not know who it belongs to!"

Mary blushed and Barry chuckled, then held up his wine glass to clink against Fay's ice water.

DRAMA

Mary – "It's inevitable."

Barry – "It really is. We like to think we can separate sex from emotion. You can minimize the connection, but you can never isolate them entirely."

Fay – "The best thing to do is just to talk and know that you don't have to be right, you don't have to be logical, you just have to know that if it bothers the other person, it is important."

Barry – "Swinging is best done almost entirely on

instinct. You can try to rationalize what you're doing, but if your instincts start telling you that something is not right, then you have to listen to it. It could be you are picking up something subconsciously from the other couple that isn't kosher, or you're starting to feel jealous and don't know why."

    Mary – "It is always better to just pull out, so to speak, before it's too late. There was that one time with the couple from Kansas, remember?"

    Barry – "How could I forget?"

    Mary – "They were really cute and came with just tons and tons of toys: strap-ons, dildos, vibrators, pocket *****s, edible underwear, anything you can think of."

    Fay – "Is this the story with the shotgun and the duct tape?"

    Mary – "No, its not, but that's a good story too!"

    Barry – "Ugh, that was a rough night."

    Mary – "It was, but let me finish this story first. So, we meet them at this now defunct club up on the northwest side of Oklahoma City. They were nice, really good dancers. He was one of those guys that was a little too good at dancing."

    Reginald – "Gay?"

    Mary – "No, well, maybe, but what more put me off was that he was just too full of himself."

    Barry – "Says the woman who has a picture of herself on her phone as a screen saver."

    Mary – "I'm a chick, so it's okay."

    Barry – "Ah."

    Mary – "It is, so shut up and let me tell the story. So, he was a really, really good dancer. Really handsy too."

Reginald – "This is that young couple with the blonde girl that is a really good looker? She's almost always topless, but never dances?"

Barry – "That's them."

Mary – "Are we straight? Can I finish? Okay, so we dance with them and my "spidy" senses are tingling, but I ignore them 'cause he's telling me about this briefcase full of toys he has and what he wants to do, telling me how pretty I am. Just a slick-as-snot sweet talker."

Barry – "He'd actually got to the hotel early enough to stick some trays in the freezer so they could use ice dildos."

Mary – "Not going to lie, that was a big selling point. At any rate, I was all ready to pack up and leave when he tells us this story about another event he went to. They were playing in the room with another couple and they blindfolded a topless girl. He quietly went to the door and opened it and started inviting people in."

Barry – "This was at a swingers resort."

Mary – "Yeah, but still. So, he invites all these people in and they continue doing whatever they were doing, but now with a crowd of people watching her. So, they finish, take off her blindfold and she is humiliated."

Barry – "He didn't say that, he said she blushed but liked it."

Mary – "Gotta read between the lines on this one. I'm sure she played it off, but if you would have done that to me, I would have ripped your balls off and stuffed them down your throat."

Barry – "But you've done that kind of thing in

impressionistic take on Davinci's *Vitruvian Man*, but with warm swirls of reds, yellows and purples in the background to give the impression of otherworldliness. Her working title was *The Orgasm*, which would be punctuated by an erect penis.

In the place where a long, rigid phallus should have been was a blank space. She'd stalled and lost her nerve once she noticed that the blurred motion of the arms and legs along with the wisp near the neck as if the head had jerked back in ecstasy all seemed to mimic a gothic cross.

She'd almost painted a loincloth on the figure and renamed it *Rapture*, just to avoid any controversy. She stopped herself, began punching the wall in frustration, cried, kicked the love seat over and then spent half an hour staring out the window at a college student skimming the pool in the backyard. She flipped the love seat back over and sat back down to study the empty void where the Messiah's penis should be.

She was starting to feel urgency as she neared the big event. The first few days after the decision did mimic that weightless bliss one gets after putting in two weeks notice at a job they hate. All life's trials suddenly became easier to bear because they no longer mattered. She would be leaving soon anyway.

But then she resettled in this new reality that seemed more immediate and she decided that she couldn't simply gather moss until the end. Her reasoning being:

A. Once she was dead, the value of her artwork would spike. Perhaps there would even be a solo show organized by one of her friends or collectors. She'd prefer it to be in Brooklyn, Santa Fe or anywhere in or around LA.

It would probably just end up in Oklahoma though.

B. Also, just like putting in two weeks notice, she had a lot of loose ends to tie up before she took her final bow. The life of a pampered celebrity wife—well, semi-celebrity wife—might seem listless and effortless. It certainly could be, but to be good at it, it must be broken into two jobs. The first was the real job, the important job. That was to, no matter what happened in the public or private realm, never embarrass the husband. The other was the pretend job, such as donating time to charity organizations, church groups, literacy and arts programs, etc. Michelle had never found much joy in volunteer work, but she did have her art.

C. She couldn't stop working because she couldn't stand the thought of spending her last two weeks staring at soap operas, downing martinis, boning the pool boy and being bored.

So, she painted. She had an entire series planned where she would throw caution to the wind, paint all the ideas that she knew might embarrass Brad, and paint as if she were still just a high schooler with a chip on her shoulder.

Then she got to the penis and had been stuck ever since.

A knock at the door drew her eyes from the void. Without waiting for her response, the door eased open and Brad's head slowly leaned in. He was smiling because he was home early. He was home early because he was horny. He was horny, Michelle guessed, because someone likely came home with him. A lunch date, no doubt.

Michelle was furious that Brad would interrupt her work, especially during the countdown.

But, of course, he did not know about the countdown, and, of course, he knew that this was just her pretend job anyway.

"Can we come in?" Brad asked, glancing briefly at the canvas lying on the ground.

"By all means." Michelle smiled, standing from the love seat and brushing herself off.

Brad scooted around the painting and looked back as a man in his late forties followed. With a shaved head, deep brown tan, graying arm hair and a leathery smile, the man was obviously some sort of early retiree like Brad, someone getting an early start on spending his children's inheritance. His stocky build indicated that he had once been either military or a football player, but a layer of soft fat smoothed out the ridges of his musculature as the vices of wealth eroded the pride and integrity the man once had in his youth, when he was still hungry and driven.

"Hmm," the man grumbled, a smoker by the gravel in his throat. "It's Jesus, I like it."

Michelle smiled an empty "thank you."

"Told you she was talented." Brad beamed, though Michelle knew he had said no such thing. He probably had whispered, just before knocking on her door, "Oh yeah, she paints in here so if she shows you anything, say you like it, no matter what it looks like."

The man would have given him that leathery smile, his face flushed from the Viagra he'd popped about an hour ago.

"Oh, this is Mark," Brad said as the man reached to shake Michelle's hand. She merely held up her palm to show him the wet paint.

"A little risqué for a spiritual painting," Brad said, looking down at the canvas. "You're going to put some underwear on him, right?"

"What if I don't?" Michelle asked, her smile still present on her face if not in her voice.

Brad and the leathery man exchange uncomfortable glances.

"Well," Brad stammered. "If you just planned on keeping it at the house, then whatever is fine. But if you are going to show it to your collectors or a gallery, well…"

"I'm going to put a loin cloth on him," Michelle interrupted lightly. "I just hadn't got that far, but thanks for your concern."

Brad grinned, stepped up to her and kissed her on the forehead. He then leaned further in to whisper.

"Mark has the ear of some government contractors that might be interested in my projects."

"Good for you, baby," Michelle replied.

"So, if you could maybe get cleaned up, we'll have a little lunch…"

Michelle nodded and leaned away.

"Are you hungry, Mark?" Michelle asked.

"Starving."

"Okay, then," Michelle chirped, placing the paintbrush in a cup of water, and then motioned the men out of the room. "Let me finish up here and get cleaned up. I'll be down in a moment. Brad, go let the cook know we have a guest for lunch."

"Will do," Brad answered as he led the leathery man out the door. Then looking back at Michelle, he mouthed, "thank you!"

Michelle closed the door, walked back to the canvas and leaned down. She reached for a paintbrush and her easel, but paused. She instead grabbed a permanent marker and drew a large, cartoonish penis on the figure.

She chuckled, pulled over a wooden art case and dug inside. She found an X-acto knife. With her other hand, she lifted up the painting and studied it for a few moments, then cut an "X" through the canvas and tossed it behind the love seat.

"It was cheesy anyway." Michelle sighed.

A tear beaded at the corner of her eye as she gritted her teeth. She growled and then threw the X-acto knife across the room where it stuck into the wall.

"Wow." Michelle smiled, wiping away a tear and walking up to the imbedded knife. She raised her arms triumphantly and danced around the room like a fighter as she shadowboxed before collapsing onto the love seat laughing.

"Everything okay, honey?" her husband shouted from downstairs.

"Oh, hell yeah," Michelle mumbled, then walked to the door and opened it.

"I'll be down in a moment."

———

Nine and eleven/twelfths days. Two hundred eighteen hours. Thirteen thousand and eighty minutes. Seven hundred eighty-four thousand, eight hundred seconds.

Chattering cocktail parties and upper crust soirées were so taxing for Michelle. It wasn't just because the countdown crept along to its wonderfully morbid finality. Even during the peak of Brad's political career, Michelle had always struggled during these functions.

She'd learned how to play the game, but there was just so much talking and nothing of value ever said. If she had it her way, the two of them would arrive, make the rounds for an hour and leave. Unfortunately, Brad needed to stay and talk, loved to stay and talk and would not be pried away, no matter how miserable Michelle was as other political brides yammered on about their children, their pet projects with at-risk kids, their personal shoppers, personal trainers, etc…

Michelle was there to take care of business, to meet expectations and obligations and then move on with life. Unfortunately, politics was all about waiting, watching, biding one's time until an opportunity arrived.

She had hoped that once the political game was over, so would be the marathon stays at backyard barbeques, fundraising galas and All-Star salutes to the fad disease of the week.

When she was younger, she could talk it up with the best of them. The key was to offer at least one insight for every three topics brought up and gossip for every five topics. Never give away anything that wasn't already common knowledge, make sure that every opinion was stated so that it was educated and somewhat edgy, but at its core was completely benign.

In short, Michelle learned to sound interesting without actually being interesting.

Michelle also learned to spot other attendees struggling to hide their boredom. She would then lead them away for either:
   A. A smoke.
   B. A drink.
   C. A quick game of tennis.
   D. Sex.
   E. All of the above.

As she got older, her ability to bullshit with the best of them got better, but her tolerance for particularly obnoxious or ignorant second wives plummeted. She had once gotten into a shouting match with an oil man's big-t***ied, trailer trash, ex-stripper third wife and left the party in tears. Brad didn't notice until he tried to leave at 3 a.m. and the car was already gone.

The hookups were also losing their allure as young studs developed ridiculous affections for Michelle. The men would show up at the house, they would call relentlessly, send flowers, send letters. They were worse than the gold diggers who were trying to root Michelle out of the mansion. That was business and Michelle understood, but these man/boys honestly thought that they could win her heart.

She tried lesbians for a few years, but after one had set her car on fire, she decided to just grit her teeth and bear through women discussing their cats, grandkids at beauty pageants, hot flashes, and midnight basketball leagues.

Sure, there was Catherine, but she was always more a friend than a lover. Sex was a bonding agent rather than a primary element in their relationship.

It was hour two of a boxing night fundraiser at an old warehouse building that was being renovated into a facility for at-risk youth. The event had an open bar and a catered meal, but she had to sit at a table with other people from Brad's nonprofit foundation that gave scholarships to…someone. Michelle wasn't quite sure and didn't quite care.

It was a reasonably tolerable night, though. There was a definite beginning, a definite end and sweaty, muscled up men wailing on each other throughout. Not the worst way to spend the night, but the countdown was weighing on Michelle.

A meaty "whap" from the ring sent the crowd hollering and a mouthpiece bounced across the table and into Michelle's flan.

"Bingo!" Brad cried and the table erupted in laughter as Michelle smiled, picked up the mouth piece and walked it back to the ring. The fallen boxer's trainer was a short, Irish red head with a scar from his lip to beneath his eye and a cocky snarl.

"Appreciate it, ma'am," he smirked, taking the mouth piece and flicking the custard to the ground.

Michelle thought about what it would take to catch the man in a dark corner somewhere and whether it would be worth the risk.

"Hell yeah," she whispered to herself.

As she returned to the table, Brad led the others in a standing ovation and Michelle curtsied. The only unenthusiastic reveler was one of the tiresome boys she'd slept with at an OU watch party in a hotel in downtown Oklahoma City. He leaned back in his chair, arms folded, staring dead in her eyes.

The boy's name was Stephen and he was a college boy, f***-up from a plastics dynasty. He was intelligent, charmingly awkward and a dazzling kisser, but had grown bitter when Michelle put the brakes on their "association" after he'd pulled her into a backroom during his father's birthday party at the Petroleum Club.

They'd ended up at the same table at the boxing fundraiser because he'd joined Brad's foundation with his mother to get closer to Michelle. In turn, she'd rarely even acknowledged Stephen with a glance.

Catie soon joined the foundation to act as a buffer for Michelle, or so Catie told her. Michelle believed her old friend was reverting more and more to her lesbian tendencies. Catie was getting jealous and territorial. Though there was nothing Catie could do about Brad, she could at least beat away over-eager college boys.

"Well, that's the closest you've been to swapping spit with a young buck in a long time," Catie smirked, giving Brad a wink. Brad betrayed a slight bristle.

"Wanna bet," Michelle shot back, sending half the table into laughter and the other half into uncomfortable smiles.

"Well," Michelle sighed, looking down at the mess that was once flan. "I guess I'm done with this, anyone want to finish it for me?"

"Don't be gross," Brad snipped. He raised his hand to flag down a waiter and then held up the plate to the passing teenager.

"Sorry about that," the pimpled girl chuckled. "Can we get you another?"

"That's okay, hon," Michelle said. "Just point me to the ladies' room."

The girl motioned to double doors on the other side of the facility. Michelle excused herself and made her way through the maze of tables, waving and nodding when appropriate but quickly skirting away from conversations.

The smell of the restroom hit Michelle at least three steps from the door. Perhaps the organizers let the stale pee smell linger to punctuate the facility's need for further funding. Inside it was fairly clean. The ductwork was exposed, mops were stacked near the sink and despite being the "Ladies' Room," the bathroom had a trough-style urinal and only one toilet.

Michelle looked around for a clean spot on the floor for her purse. She turned to latch the door closed, but it opened and Stephen emerged. He grinned and then closed and latched the door.

"Ladies Room," Michelle said. "Boys go across the hall."

"I know."

Michelle wanted to stand her ground, but her feet backpedaled for her.

"What are you doing, Stephen? People will see."

"I know."

"I'm not doing this, Stephen. Just turn around and walk out."

Stephen continued approaching as Michelle made her way past the trough and toward the lone bathroom stall.

"Don't make me scream, Stephen."
"You won't scream."
"I will."
"No, you won't. I know you."

Michelle turned and dashed for the stall but felt his arm around her waist. He whipped her backwards and she rolled to the ground, feeling her knee pop out of place as she tumbled. The fountain of pain brought tears that burned through her eyelids.

She groaned slightly, but fought back the pain and used the wall to help her stand again.

"Might as well get comfortable, this won't take long," Stephen grumbled, unfastening his belt buckle and dropping his pants.

"Fine," Michelle mumbled. "But I'm not laying down on that floor. Come here."

Stephen chuckled, dropped his underwear and, with his pants around his ankles, took short steps toward Michelle.

Summoning her four years of martial arts lessons, Michelle lunged at Stephen, hooked her foot behind his ankle and pushed him backwards. They fell in a tumble and Michelle heard a *clank* as she landed on top of him.

"F***!" Stephen growled, pushing her off him and then holding his head. "F***!"

There was a streak of blood on the lip of the trough where his head hit. The image seared into her mind as adrenaline sparkled through her limbs.

Michelle smiled and stood. Her knee still burned but the pain was dulled by the rush. She grabbed her purse and turned to Stephen.

"Don't ever look at me again," she hissed.

"Go to hell!" Stephen growled as blood seeped from his scalp through his fingers and dripped down on the ground.

"Don't look at me!" Michelle screamed, taking a hobbled step toward him and raising her purse to hit him. He looked away and threw his arms up to protect his face.

"Don't look at me."

She turned and limped toward the door, unlatched it and opened it to see a crowd of men and women gathered just outside.

"None of you tried to help me?" Michelle asked the crowd.

Someone started pushing bodies out of the way and the short, redheaded trainer emerged through the herd. His defeated boxer followed with a large, purple mouse under his right eye.

"You okay?" the man asked in a growl. "What happened?"

He stepped into the bathroom, followed by his boxer, who closed the door behind them. The trainer glanced at Stephen and then stepped close to Michelle, held her cheek in his hand and gently rubbed his finger over blood splattered on her nose.

"It's not mine," she mumbled, then looked back over at Stephen who cowered and hid his eyes. She turned back to the trainer.

"Kick his ass for me."

"You got a pretty good start on it," the boxer chuckled, exposing a missing tooth in the bottom front row.

"Just warmed him up," the trainer grumbled. "That's a good girl, but now you go get a drink. We'll clean this up for ya."

The boxer opened the door for her, and once she had hobbled out, the door closed and latched.

"Get the f*** out of my way," Michelle hissed at the crowd. Catie pushed her way through and put Michelle's arm over her shoulder and helped her to the nearest table.

Over by the ring, still sitting at the foundation's table, Brad talked with Stephen's doting mother as if nothing had ever happened.

—

Eight days. One hundred ninety-two hours. Eleven thousand, five hundred twenty minutes. Sixhundred ninety-one thousand, two hundred seconds.

Michelle felt like celebrating, so convinced Catie to pop a bottle of Dom Perignon from Catie's private stash. They didn't have sex, but Michelle cuddled against Catie's chest for two hours while they talked about the future and Michelle's knee cooled under an ice pack.

Catie asked why she'd never had kids.

"Brad needs too much attention. Children would make him jealous, and he would have left me for another woman with the time to give him the pampering he thinks he deserves."

"So? Wouldn't you be better off without him?"

Michelle leaned up to grab the champagne and refilled her glass.

"No," Michelle finally answered. "Brad's not always the most easy person to live with, but I've enjoyed my time with him. He burns so brightly, it's thrilling to be around. Men like him don't make good dads, but if I'd really wanted children, I would have made it happen."

"That sounds like the past tense, 'enjoyed my time with him.'"

Michelle shrugged, took a sip and then leaned back down into Catie's arms.

FUN FACT: Committed Couples
It would seem that couples in the Lifestyle would just hop from bed to bed to bed. Not so. In fact, there is a contingent of swingers who, once they jive with one particular couple, form an extended bond, sometimes even a monogamous relationship. Male swingers have been known to carry pictures of their "other spouse" in their wallet alongside, or instead of, a picture of their actual spouse.

A Charmed Life
Part II

Houseflies must be vanquished. I understand the importance of flies outside—someone has to eat the dogs' XXXX coiled up in the backyard, and I preferred it wasn't me or the children. And you'd be surprised by the sheer volume of feces three lapdogs can produce in one day.
At any rate, to deal with the housefly problem resulting from having children and yapping dogs constantly going in and out of the house, I'd devised a clever trap. To create a visual contrast to help me track the little black bastards, I utilized my egg white bathroom with white shower curtain and mostly light colored countertops as a sort of Punji stake pit. But instead of setting up dozens of pointed bamboo

spears[12], I relied on my wicked awesome predatory skills.

I also had an electric flyswatter that could electrocute a fly when it got trapped in the wire mesh. There would be a slight, satisfying pop as the two AA batteries sent a lethal surge through the fly's body, then, if I was lucky, a small puff of smoke followed by a sizzle.

It is hard for me to adequately express how much I loved that flyswatter. It was not unlike the bond early hunter/gatherers must have shared with their spears and clubs. They'd name the weapons[13]; they'd hold their weapons close as they slept and cradle the weapons like children as they watched the plains for days. When a herd of buffalo happened along, the hunter would creep through the tall grass and track the weakest member of the herd until Zap! Pop! Sizzle.

The electrical current stopped working after I'd swung too wide and cracked the bathroom mirror. I could still swat flies out of the air, though, which was actually more satisfying because it required skill, timing, coordination, patience and ruthless precision.[14]

To set the trap, I turned off the light in the bedroom and turned on the light in the bathroom, luring the creatures to their doom.

When a humming black speck wound around the

---

[12] Not that I didn't want to use spears, mind you, but some concessions had to be made to the local governing agency, i.e. my wife.
[13] Ginger.
[14] Not unlike a ninja.

bedroom, then veered into the bathroom, its fate was sealed. I'd stand at the doorway, flyswatter at the ready, and wait for the foolish creature to swerve within my reach, then, whiff! There was only a slight "ping," made by the fly's body bouncing off the wire mesh. Then I'd search for the carcass, use toilet paper to pick it up and drop it into the toilet.

Victorious, I returned to the bedroom where Elena pretended to watch the television, but her down-turned frown and reddened eyes foreshadowed a long conversation I wasn't up for.

I asked her anyway, while in the back of my head, I was tracking another little black dot darting back and forth through the bedroom. When the revolting intruder slipped into the bathroom, I considered rising to kill it, but didn't.

Now, before we go any further, let me make one thing clear. My name is Will and I am addicted to sex. Not in that teenage way that you obsess over it because of hormones and its mysterious allure. I'm addicted in the bad way, the habitual way, the way that can destroy lives.

I wasn't always this way. Sex did have a very strong appeal since I was a child, but when I did actually have sex, it was largely disappointing. Once I met Elena, that all changed and I—well, I went a bit overboard.

Pine Grove Behavioral Health and Addiction Services[15] has a ten question assessment to help self-diagnose sexual addiction:

    1. Have you experienced difficulty resisting

---

[15] They cure celebrities!

impulses to engage in sexual behaviors?
    2. Have you tried to stop, control or reduce these behaviors?
    3. Have you thought of killing yourself because of your sexual behaviors?
    4. Have you experienced legal consequences due to your sexual behaviors?
    5. Do you spend large amounts of time trying to get sex or recover from being sexual?
    6. Do you ever feel anxious or irritable if you are unable to engage in sexual behaviors?
    7. Do you worry that others will find out about your sexual activities?
    8. Do you often find yourself preoccupied with sexual thoughts?
    9. Do you feel that your sexual behavior is not normal?
    10. Are you experiencing family problems as a result of your behaviors?

    Okay, my responses to 1, 5, 6 and 8 could apply to any heterosexual male. That's just life when you live with a set of working testacies. 2 – I've never tried to cut down on the amount of sex I have, but I have tried to curb my masturbation, which never really goes too well. There is that first week where I feel invigorated and energetic, but then, like a smoker, one stray thought or one frustrating day sends me off the wagon. And it's not like I'm just, "slappity, slappity, slap" eight hours a day sitting in front of my computer. More like just sneaking a quick one in to calm the nerves or focus the mind. Just like a smoker, I suppose.

3 – No suicidal thoughts. I'm much too narcissistic for that. What good is a world if it doesn't have me in it, right?

4 – Got busted skinny-dipping at the lake in college. Sex was only kind of involved since there were five guys and two girls. Only two of us had a real shot at getting laid that night, and I wasn't one of those guys. Yes, I'm embarrassed that I was there naked with a disproportionate amount of guys to girls. In my defense, they were two sets of tits that I had yet to see unleashed, therefore totally worth my time and eventual humiliation.

7 – Yes. I guess this is kind of what really got me thinking about my possible addiction. I've always been a very trustworthy lover, not one to blab about my exploits in the bedroom. But, my exploits were never really that noteworthy, until recently. Now, if anyone were to find out that I'm a ****ing swinger, that would just be awful. Sure, this book kind of brings that fear into fruition, but I've come to see it as my own version of confession, where I trade one pair of ears for a thousand pairs of eyes.

9 – Yes, what Elena and I have been participating in is certainly not normal, which is exactly why we've been doing it. I didn't see it as inherently destructive though, because I've known couples who've managed to undertake the Lifestyle with minimal peripheral damage. In fact, they seemed to thrive in the Lifestyle. I was sure that Elena and I would be the same.

Clearly we were not, so yes on 10. Otherwise, what would be the purpose of writing this all down?

I would add an eleventh question which would speak more directly to my experience. I know that it breaks their perfectly rounded set of questions, but I still think it is a good addition.

11– If you were to meet someone exactly like yourself at this very moment in your life, would you be able to respect that person?

11 – No.

What is truly frustrating about being addicted to sex is that I haven't had nearly enough of it to really feel like I can be addicted to sex. I only broke into double digits of sexual partners this year, and that's only if you count oral sex.

How lame is that?[16]

I didn't even really get a chance to earn my addiction. And now, I'm lumped in with other pathetic addicts who I despise because they are gross, shameless and have three to four times the number of notches on their bedposts.

****ers!

And sex addiction isn't even kind of sexy like drug addiction and alcohol addiction. There is no tragic mystique of the tortured soul. We are just disgusting deviants who should only be approached in biohazard suits.

And, if I weren't on the wrong side of this pointed opinion, I would totally agree with society's damning judgment of my kind.

So, I'm a passably attractive, sexually underserved sex addict. If only I were strikingly handsome, I would just be looked at as a loveable scamp. But no, I'm only a 5 foot nothing creep.

---

[16] Very lame.

What keeps me going if I have such a low opinion of sex addicts? It's the same as people addicted to golf. No matter how disgusted you get by continually dropping your balls in a sand trap, it's the one perfect swing of your 1 Wood that keeps you coming back for more.

Where were we? Ah, yes, I had gripped my electric flyswatter while suppressing my predatory instincts. Elena was lying next to me, not talking, and wrapped in a heaviness that I guessed related to a recent outing where she'd gotten drunk and flirted with another man.

This would seem an odd thing to cause a rift between us, given our liberated view of monogamy, but really, it shouldn't be. You see, Elena was years ahead of me. She'd discovered her sexual addiction before even meeting me, and that was why these moral trip-ups bothered her. Also, there is a bit of history you should probably know.

Just three months after we'd first moved in together, she softly unlocked the front door and slipped inside the house. It was 4 a.m.; I was watching television on the couch, the children where in bed. Her eyeliner was stained where she'd been crying. At first I looked over her face and arms for bruises from a car crash, a fight, or any other scenario that could explain away the last six hours.

There was nothing to find, of course. I didn't say anything, just stood up and walked to the bedroom.

She took a shower before coming to bed, and a cold silence shrouded our house for days. She gave me space, and while she thought I wasn't paying attention, she began packing just in case she would have to leave with the kids at a moment's notice.

I was furious, mind you, but I wasn't shocked. I'd prepared myself for it since the day we met because I'd known she was too good for me.

But, where some might see disaster, I saw opportunity.

After turning it over in my head ad nauseum, I found a clever way to resolve the situation. I called it an "unconventional solution to her need for sexual conquests." How very magnanimous of me, no?[17]

I saw my chance to catch up with her vast wealth of sexual knowledge that was both a source of fascination and intimidation.

I could also capitalize on my new sense of physical confidence. No more of this innocent flirting that would never lead to anything, I argued for a more frontal assault. That was, of course, The Lifestyle.

Here was my pitch:

"It really is okay, honey, this is just something that you will always have a problem with. I want to be with you, but I also want you to feel like you can be true to yourself. Perhaps this is an indulgence that would be better served by finding an outlet rather than prohibiting it all together. We aren't like normal couples, we never have been, so this might be a good opportunity for us to expand our horizons together."

It was an angle; it was a con; it was a Jedi mind trick. I felt myself channeling Charles at that very moment. Mr. Asshole. The charmer that can turn reporters into doe-eyed believers and skeptical

---

[17] No, not really.

shoppers into dedicated readers.[18]

At my core, I was revolted by these mind games, by the cold-blooded manipulation, but I was also incredibly turned on. And isn't that the spirit of true fetishism, spiking your depravity with a healthy dose of shame?

Elena was skeptical, but not appalled. She would be lowering herself, you see. This beauty of style and grace, this cool-as-**** hair stylist that looked like she was plucked from an LA salon and airlifted to the Heartland, how could you turn that into just another middle-American swinger?

Sensing this, I said:

"We'll sniff around and see what the scene is all about. If it doesn't work out, we'll think of something else."

She smiled, bit her lip, and said, "could be fun." She seemed to mean it, too.

So there it was. I got what I desperately craved: the hall pass that would allow me to even the score. Looking back, I recognize there is no evening the score for infidelity; there is no eye for an eye or counterbalance that will make up for one person going astray. It can only be either forgiveness and absolution or devolving into a game of one-upmanship where, no matter how many women I would sleep with, I would never win.

During that initial conversation, we set the parameters.

We only played together.
No bondage, no pain.

---

[18] His words, not mine.

No single men.
Protection was a must.
No friends.

Stepping back out into society with the new rules established, I re-imagined my world as a vast hunting ground. It was more than that, though, because no one in my real life could ever know about my liberated self. I was a secret killer, an assassin.

We first tried a swinger club. I didn't want to ease into this and waste months online talking to junior high kids posing as twenty-two-year-old single women. I wanted to jump in all at once.

It was certainly a jolting experience.

So, while sitting with a strange couple on a couch in a black-lit "play" room, I became fixated by this man's hand sliding along Elena's soft thigh. They kissed and my heart began hammering in my chest. The man's wife was nibbling at my ear; I felt my belt loosen, but I knew it was time for me to come up for air.

I pulled out my cell phone to check the time, muttered something about needing to take the babysitter home, and the moment was officially over. We exchanged phone numbers and retreated from the battlefield.

It was quiet on the ride home. I did my best to soften the mood, even springing for milkshakes. There was no babysitter, since the youngest kids were spending the night with the middle's friend and the eldest had some big sleepover birthday party. "Babysitter" was just the pre-determined safe word.

We kissed when we got home, she excused

herself to go change, and I decided to play some video games to get my mind to stop spinning. She came back in, wearing only a spectacularly tiny, black thong as she beckoned me for sex.

I didn't ignore her, but mumbled something about "finishing the level." She sat next to me, kissed me gently on the cheek and read a book while waiting for me to start yelling. After an hour, I finally turned to her and said:

"That was really, really weird."

—

I cannot describe how confusing it is to see your wife ****ing another man. Clearly, we're not talking about walking into your house after a long day at work and finding her riding the milk man like a galloping horse. No, I'm talking when you've slipped away together to a strange couple's hotel room, slipped off the clothes and, while some nameless woman has her face buried in your lap, you look over and see your wife tangled with another man.

Let me try to break down the mix of emotions and neurosis that were blended in this complex cocktail that flooded my mind at that moment:

38 percent was depraved eroticism.

42 percent was bitter territorialism.

15 percent was fear that I wouldn't get an erection.

05 percent was a desperate bid to record every piece of stimuli, knowing that I would recall this imagery for years whenever I was masturbating.

Shake and strain into a martini glass. Garnish

with shame.

It was like tasting whiskey for the first time. The searing taste was overwhelming, and more than a little bit revolting, but the way it made me burn inside was something I quickly came to love.

It was not an easy trip to that moment, though. It started with me, hours earlier, staring into the bathroom mirror of the swinger club.

"Ok," I told myself. "I can totally do this. I am intellectually superior, spiritually advanced and above the base instinct of jealousy."

And I had to be, right? I mean, have you met me? Then surely you know how intellectually superior and above things I am.

But, as it turned out, I was no more above jealousy than the rest of the human fray who also succumbed to that most unsophisticated instinct of ownership.

Elena met me as I emerged from the door, asking if I needed to leave. She'd learned a lesson from the first time around and was at my side until an hour later when I was busy sucking face with a short, older blonde. With me occupied, she turned her attention to the woman's husband.

That couple would not be the ones to bust our swinger cherries, though. When we peeled away from that encounter, I was officially warmed up and Elena and I spent a good deal of the night on different ends of the crowded room scouting, talking, flirting, and touching.

I now felt what Charles meant about stepping into "d*** mode." D*** mode is when you've stowed your pride, your integrity, and your sense of rightness and become Mr. Asshole for a short time. It is easy to enter into, but it isn't as easy to leave behind.

Mr. Asshole just has a habit of leaving his stink whenever and wherever he sits down.

We ended up attached to a buxom brunette and her talkative husband in their hotel room. It was a little awkward, but we all parted with big, ****-eating grins on our faces. I got my erection, but just barely, so I decided to look into preventative measures to ensure that next time I arrived at the big game, I didn't find out I was playing with a flat football.

By the time we stumbled through the front door of our house, Elena couldn't keep her hands off me and we ****ed like wild, vicious animals claiming their territory. I actually pulled a pectoral muscle. Crazy.

And it was like that, one night we'd be both on our games, the darlings of the ball and leave madly obsessed with each other. Then there would be times where I wanted to fight every ******* that looked at Elena for more than a passing glance.

I had no true understanding of which temperament would surface and it was a source of shame.

Elena also sensed that my sexuality was dangerously volatile, which is why she treated innocent flirtation so carefully. She knew that no matter how much she cleaned me up, how much I swaggered or how much I insisted I was enlightened, deep inside I was still a short geek with embarrassingly bright red hair that resented any woman who would want to sleep with me.

After six months into the game, it was clear that

we both loved and hated the Lifestyle. I was not ready to give it up, though. It wasn't even about settling the score anymore. The Lifestyle became a fascination, a bizarre wondrous puzzle that I just had to get my head around before we could move on with our lives.

So, back to our bedroom, little black dot buzzing around the room, Elena dreadfully quiet and me waiting for the argument to start. I knew how this would play out, word for word. She wanted to say she was getting rattled by that bizarre cocktail of emotions that came with betraying the fundamental human instinct of monogamy. She wanted to assure me that she could be loyal and she could make me happy.

She wanted me to agree to turn our backs on the Lifestyle.

But I wasn't ready, so I allowed the statements to remain unsaid. I let her stew in that misery. Hurting, alone and terrified.

Ain't addiction a bitch?

—

"Why does this beautiful, capable woman stay with a worm like you?"

Good question. There is an equally good answer. Ninety-five percent of the time, our marriage is an ideal situation for her because:

    I am financially dependable.
    I will never beat her.
    I will never leave her.
    The children love me and I love them.
    I love her, and 85 percent of the time, I do

everything I can to make sure she's happy.

So, she sees the other 15 percent as a small price to pay. She just has to occasionally suck a strange man's **** or go down on a woman while I **** her ******. It's how she balanced the board, but I knew my time was ticking. I could only get away with this bull**** for so long before she traded me in for a new model.

I did not acknowledge this as addiction. To be honest, I only recognized the addiction as I wrote the book. Only in hindsight could I see how despicable Mr. Asshole had become.

And Mr. Asshole always kicked in when Elena was ready to back out of the Lifestyle. Mr. Asshole knew that I needed to seem like I was balancing the board, so I agreed to marriage counseling, which started that Thursday.

I was not trying to balance, of course, rather I was trying to stall.

Now, before we start thinking we know how Will's story ends, lest we think that Professor Bumblebeard tweaked my psyche and sent me on my way, let me say this: **** therapy. Did you hear me in the cheap seats? **** therapy!

I know I was supposed to see it as an opportunity to change for the better and improve our relationship. Now that I'm a little more self-aware, I should see it as a haven for realization, a wonderful chance to glimpse my situation through the eyes of a reputable third party. And how happy I should be that I get to confess my darkest secrets to a judgmental, over-educated psychiatrist whose job is reliant on their ability to instill in me a sense of dependence thereby prolonging counseling and paying for the guy's next trip to Venice. Oh ho! I bet he and his significant other chuckled as they recounted the many ways I am a deficient person. Well, you know what, ***? You do not get to look through the keyhole, you have no right to pick through the gears grinding away in my head. If you want to know what's happening in my noggin, then cough up fourteen dollars and buy a ****ing book. Why should I pay you when I charge everyone else in the world? Your degree does not impress me; your tweed jacket does not impress me. Your beard does not impress me. Your thick books collecting dust on your shelves do not impress me. Your smug sense of superiority does not impress me. You will say nothing to me as insightful as the college drop out who threw down a twenty-dollar bill he couldn't afford to spend and found something I wrote worth investing in emotionally. That guy/girl who lacks your professional pedigree, sir, still has an opinion that means everything to me because he is someone who sought me out. He sought out my life, my experience, my imagination. And when he talks, I will listen. So, **** you, sir. **** your opinion and **** your beard.

    Well, wait. Maybe I am being rash.

    No, no honey, you're right! I am excited about my opportunity to pay seventy-five dollars an hour so a person I give exactly two ****s about can tell me why my vision of the world is flawed! So, let's give it up for therapy, give me three cheers for the scratching of pens and the measuring of eyes while I pour out my soul to a douchebag with a doctorate who must know more about what makes my life work because, well, look at all those books!

Hip Hip[19]
Hip Hip[20]
Hip Hip[21]

So, with that said, I went to the damn session. Twice, even, but I already knew how it was all going to play out between the wife and I based on precedence. There was an oft-repeated pattern of behavior that went thusly:

A. Lifestyle emerges in dirty talk.
B. We start joking about it in normal talk.
C. We start discussing in normal talk.
D. We start looking around online.
E. We discuss parameters.
F. We set up dates with couples.
G. We hook up and have fun.
H. We bond like mad afterwards.
I. We go to a club.
J. We hook up.
K. We bond like mad afterwards.
L. Something spooks her.
M. She cries a lot.
N. We sever relationships.
O. We are monogamous.
P. We are bored.
Rinse and repeat.

---

[19] Hooray.
[20] Hooray.
[21] Hooray.

And yes, I now recognize the similarities to drug addiction.

So, is the sex really good enough to be blasé about my wife's suffering?

No, not really. The sex can be really fun or really disappointing. But that's not really the point of all of this. That is not what kept us going back. Instead, it was that thrill of a new physical/emotional attachment. You must remember that spirit of desperate passion when you start dating someone new. It permeates every second you are together and just gets more intense when you are apart.

Well, with swinging, there is a twist. When one would think those bonding hormones would be directed at the new person in the scenario, they are actually redirected at the spouse. It's intense, it's dangerous and it is a high that comes with a pretty heavy low.

That low comes at "L" in our cycle, and we are now on "M."

So, am I cured, knowing what I know and having had this revelation? No, not at all, and here are two inescapable facts that will continue to haunt my "recovery":

1. Real life is boring.
2. Elena and I love flirting too much. Hell, I just found out how to do it properly.
3.[22] I still don't feel like I've hit bottom, and the wrong person at the right moment could fail all these good intentions. Hell, I'm having dinner with a wrong person this weekend. I see wrong people everyday. I

---

[22] Okay, the three inescapable facts...

talk to these wrong people continuously for work, promotion or while trading small talk at the grocery store checkout line. If just one of them said the wrong thing at the wrong time, then—well, addiction is a bitch.

FUN FACT: High School
Don't be fooled by pornography or men's magazines, swinger clubs are surprisingly similar to high school cafeterias. Everyone is in a clique and there is always another table where you'd rather be sitting.

The Ballad of Jerry and Carey/Cynthia/Veronica Part III

Forgive this writer's indulgence into the finer nuances of Jerry and Cynthia's tangled romance, but their winding path to marital bliss was an unusual and difficult one, so it takes time to retrace the steps that led them to the Lifestyle. Not every couple could or should be expected to follow our heroes down this twisted path. These lovers are unique, as is every sexual relationship, and as such, Jerry and Cynthia had to mark their own course.

Like all humans, their weaknesses and strengths required understanding if balance could ever be achieved.

Now, the story can proceed by picking up where it left our devastated couple.

Fate had laid its burdensome hand over the

hearts of our two young lovers, and it is without surprise that there would be no reprieve during this turbulent time.

    Cynthia made the long walk from the bathroom, through their small apartment and into the bedroom where Jerry slept after working sixteen hours split between two jobs. Cynthia crept into the doorway and stood watching. He sensed her presence, and opened his eyes narrowly. She was standing in a short nightgown, her body as toned and gorgeous as ever. Despite his fatigue, he felt desire percolate. His vision narrowed on her face, and he recognized the urgency. When carrying bad news, she often hoped that he would start the conversation, so he mumbled:

    "Everything all right?"

    She looked down toward the kitten brushing along her leg. She shook her head. Jerry sat up and rubbed his eyes.

    "What is it, honey?"

    He used the endearment softly, masking his annoyance that she was making him dig for information. In his mind he cursed:

    "She's already ****ed another man!"

    It was a bitter, vile jolt of jealousy, but upon studying her weary face, he knew that it was something else entirely.

    "Honey," he whispered, sliding off the bed and walking toward her. He took her face in his hands and led her chin up so he could look her in the eyes.

    "Have you noticed my breasts have gotten larger?" she asked, taking his hands off her face and backing away to expose her chest beneath the satin gown. He did acknowledge a slight enhancement, but had no idea where this was leading, so he shrugged noncommittally.

"I had a friend who had her breasts get larger and start to ache…it meant she was pregnant."

She looked up at him, her eyes desperate for a reaction, either positive or negative, just as long as it was definite. She needed to know where he stood; she needed to know her future. While sitting on the bed just an hour prior, listening to him sleep, she'd thought about her options and had seen few that included Jerry.

There was:

1. Abortion. As a liberated woman, she felt obligated to consider it, but was terribly afraid of what the psychological aftermath would be. Plus, she had become inexplicably attached to this pregnancy. A miscarriage would be a relief, but an abortion was impossible.

2. Adoption. It was more plausible, but it wasn't realistic.

3. Miscarriage. Of which she played no part.

4. Keeping the child.

At that moment, while she watched Jerry's face, searching for either strength or weakness, she instead received a wavering smile and:

"What are you going to do?"

And she realized that the real question in his mind was:

"Is this my child, and if it's not, what does this mean to me?"

So they discussed.

It was decided the child would be kept and

raised. Jerry made it seem like he knew he would be there after the child came, and forever thereafter as the dutiful father.

Cynthia did not believe him, and to be truthful, neither did Jerry. They were children having a child. They did not know how to love each other, so loving a third person seemed like the biggest obstacle the world could throw at the young couple.

And after a few weeks and a visit to the doctor, the pregnancy was confirmed. Jerry picked up more hours at his two jobs, and Cynthia decided she would put her aspirations of marketing on hold until the child was settled into his new world.

After a bitter fight over finances, which were really about Cynthia's inability to trust Jerry and Jerry's inability to trust Cynthia, she began wondering how best to separate from him. She decided to begin looking for a more suitable father for her child.

She still loved Jerry, and in many ways admired him. But that was inconsequential. She was now preparing to live for someone else, whereas he still only lived for himself.

Jerry was adequate, though somewhat distant, as an expectant father. He never asked questions to the OBGYN. When looking at ultrasound images, he seemed slightly more curious then he would be had Cynthia instead shown him her favorite Barbie doll from childhood. He studied it, only because he knew he was expected to.

Even during the most intense moments of the pregnancy, he never allowed himself to be pulled into a screaming match, but instead trod through the nine months like a sanguine and serene monk.

Once labor pains started, Jerry served as a placeholder, being where he needed to, doing what was asked of him. When the baby came, he looked at it curiously, held it when he had to, but then, days later, Cynthia said:

"The baby needs to be changed."

She rested on the couch of their small apartment. Jerry sat at the computer, typing at something unimportant and, she thought, pretending he didn't hear.

She knew at that moment he would need to leave, and he had a similar idea. He was filling out an online application for a temporary job on the distant Oklahoma oil fields. There, he could earn good money, work beyond normal human limits as he had back on the farm, and be away from the confusing responsibilities of his Oklahoma City life.

It took two months for the job to come through and for him to be summoned. Those two months were the most volatile time of their relationship, yet he made the promise he would return. Cynthia believed him, but she wasn't sure she would make herself available for him to return to. She only knew that their life would have to change, he would have to change, and more importantly, she would have to change before she could consider this relationship ever again.

She determined that they were not good influences on each other, and that it might just be better to end the marriage before more damage could be done.

———

The oil fields were everything he'd expected: the long days, the exhausting chores and the long stretches where Jerry would not, for even a second, think about his wife and the mysterious lump of flesh he was supposed to love more than himself. In actuality, the baby was little more than an annoyance, a detail that he would appreciate when it came time to collect the tax credit.

This might seem like an escape where he was the coward and she was the shrew. But this, though they did not know it, was a firing process. Like the bricks hardened to build a house, the last impurities of childhood were being burned away and replaced by the hardened resolve of maturity.

After the first two weeks, Jerry had successfully avoided any time off, any breaks in work, and any chance to be given a moment to collect himself. But he finally submitted to a night out with the crew, and while sitting at a dive bar populated by oil workers and lonely women, another father came to sit at Jerry's side. The man was older than Jerry by several years, and this would be the only time the two men would trade words.

"You're the one with the new kid, huh?"

To which Jerry could only shrug, lift the beer to his mouth and stare straight ahead at a bottle of liquor shaped like a monk that, in Jerry's drunken stupor, mystified him. Undeterred, the older man asked,

"How old is your kid?"

"Almost three months."

"Ooh, that sucks, man."

Jerry harbored a shame that he was not a doting father and found hardly anything in the child that was any more amusing then a chewed up tennis ball. To hear another person agree surprised Jerry, specifically since he'd seen the man show off pictures of his two- and five-year-old children to every table in the bar. The man had the warm devotion that Jerry, to this point, was incapable of.

"Why does that suck?"

The man laughed, pulled out his wallet unprovoked and laid it open to reveal pictures of his two children. Jerry skimmed over the pictures and nodded his head to verify that he'd looked. The man left the wallet on the bar with the two children smiling up at Jerry as the man patted him on the shoulder and settled into the barstool.

"The first months are the hardest. The kid is little more than a doorstop that ****s in its clothes and cries constantly. The mom is an emotional wreck who is crazy for this small pile of slime, and expects you to be too. And when you aren't, she is furious. Am I right?"

Jerry shrugged.

"Yeah, I'm right. God knows I'm right."

Jerry smiled, hiding a wave of relief that flooded through his mind. He'd tried to stifle the torture and the fear that he would never be a good father and husband because he knew nothing of marriage and felt very little for parenting. The man must have seen this in Jerry's face, because he ordered another round, tapped on the pictures of his kids and said:

"It gets easier."

"When?"

The man took his beer, slid the other to Jerry. He threw cash on the bar, folded his wallet and slid it into his back pocket. He took a few moments to stare at the bottles crowding the shelves of the bars.

"Wait until that first moment where the kid looks up at you, and he isn't looking at you as just another person who feeds him, but as one of only two individuals he really needs in his life. At that moment, man, it's still not easy, but you never really think about how hard it is again. Plus, makes changing their nasty diapers much easier."

Jerry smiled, lowered his eyes to his beer and mumbled:

"I never changed a diaper."

"Well, when you go home, make sure that is the first thing you do. Go change the diaper, then hold the child, even if you don't want to. Then, when that kid starts playing, starts crawling and chooses you over everyone else in the room, you'll know what it's all about."

Jerry grinned and nodded, determined to do just that.

Back in Oklahoma City, Cynthia hadn't slept a full night in weeks. She was taking online courses on graphic design and she was caring for the child all on her own. She used the money that Jerry sent her to pay the bills and shoved the rest in a savings account. She didn't know how much longer he would send money, so she hoarded. She'd lost all the excess weight from the pregnancy because she rarely ate, and when she did it was only to keep her energy up so she could care for the child and keep her hair from falling out.

The self-imposed starvation was a source of pride to Cynthia. Her time was not hers, her space was not hers, her sleep was not hers, but her body—

nobody could tell her what to do with her body and nobody could tell her when to eat.

More than anything, she felt a protective instinct burn within her, a strident desire to protect her child from her own childhood. Whatever the cost, this child would not suffer.

She considered returning to stripping, returning to Veronica. But then she would say to herself:

"No, never again."

And she meant it. It made her laugh when she thought about Jerry wondering if she was sleeping around. She had no time for men; she had no time for bars, for alcohol, for anything. Her life was her child and her future. She perpetually felt like a tire worn of its tread and that at any moment, she could roll over the smallest nail and:

BLAM!

And at times she craved the disaster, the release. She rarely thought of sex, but often thought of how to replace the male figure in her life, not because she needed a ****, but because she needed stability

But, as it is with life and the desperate, fate knew when it was time to ease its suffocating grip on a human life so that it could grow, so as long as it grew in the right direction. And, with the child asleep and her gazing at the television in the living room, surrounded by a sea of toys and the smell of vomit, she began to understand happiness.

And for Jerry, covered in filth, dirt and oil and staring out toward the horizon in a brief moment of rest, he only thought about returning home to change diapers, play with the child and wait for his moment when the child understood that it needed him. And as

Jerry began to feel the intense longing for his young family, he too began to understand happiness.

It would be easy to want this story to resolve with Jerry running home to Cynthia and his child. Everyone finding their place in the world and no other complications would ever arise, but this is not a story about that. Too much had passed between Cynthia and Jerry for such a simple ending to be plausible, and there was so much left for the young couple to face.

Jerry's curiosity would stir again and Cynthia's Bear would one day reawaken from hibernation.

This was merely a moment of reprieve, a time for them to finally catch their breath. Fate was not done testing them, but then, it never really is.

FUN FACT: How to Spot a Swinger
Two women making out while their husbands watch would seem like a sure signifier of swingers, but not necessarily. Being regular attendees at erotic events should be a good indicator, but in reality means nothing. There are a number of subtle clues, like a form of Gay-dar, that help point out swingers, but ultimately there is only one way to know for sure. The question is how bad do you want to find out?

Superswingers
Part III

A twenty-minute section of the interview was unusable as a drunk woman, apparently unaware the conversation was being taped, kept on interrupting Barry and Mary. The woman was possibly in her early forties, but had an artificially hardened face typical of meth users, so could have actually been ten to fifteen years younger.

The woman's comments ranged from "woohoo, that's sexy as f***," "Did I tell you this is my first time here" and in a louder than necessary whisper "what are those old people doing here? Are they dead or just asleep?"

Fortunately, both Reginald and Fay were just asleep, and Barry and Mary had decided to let them sleep rather than nag them further to go to their hotel room.

Finally, the drunk woman staggered off to fall

into another conversation at the next table. Soon thereafter, the doorman walked up to the woman, sat her down, and he and the Rumormill owner started pushing coffee and water in front of her while they looked for the man she came with.

    Mary – "Poor thing, it's her first time here. I remember mine. It really is very nerve-wracking and easy to get waaaay too drunk."

    Barry – "One or two drinks is fine, but you really have to moderate yourself, otherwise you are likely to drink quicker and quicker as the night goes on."

    Mary – "I remember that one time at the (Club Name Removed) by the airport, the first one they had in that small aluminum building."

    Barry – "Oh, God, yeah. That was not my most shining hour."

    Mary – "Well, it was partly my fault, 'cause I didn't try to slow you down either."

    Barry – "Well, lesson learned. I was worthless that night. I couldn't have got it up for a Playmate of the Year, let alone that couple we ended up hooking up with that night."

    Mary – "What? They were nice."

    Barry – "Well, then there was that other time at our house, and I really regret that one because that couple was hot, but me and my two bottles of wine really shut the door on that option. We still see them around from time to time."

    Mary – "Well, as a woman, you just can't make a big deal about it. You can't take it personally. Guys just aren't always Johnny-on-the-Spot with the hard-ons, and if you start getting weird about it, then it'll just make the situation worse."

Barry – "And I hate it when they say 'What's wrong?' You know just as well as I do what's wrong, my trusty steed has stage fright. Just give him a minute or two and he'll be fine, just pretend like nothing is going wrong."

Mary – "Kind of like the reverse of icing a kicker. The longer you wait, the less pressure there is."

Barry – "Nice football allusion."

Mary – "Well, I have to watch your stupid Cowboys play every damn Sunday. It was just a matter of time before I picked up a few things by osmosis."

Barry – "And I appreciate it."

VIAGRA

Barry – "Ugh, I guess I knew this was going to come up."

Mary (traded a long look with Barry, he finally nodded.) – "You're not using our real names right? Ok, well, Barry doesn't use Viagra, he uses one of the other brands, the one that lasts all weekend."

Barry – "Really, every swinger should have a prescription. It's a pretty simple decision. You can either go into a night of activities and have the danger of stage fright lingering in the back of your head, or you can pop a pill and not have to worry about it at all. Plus, you really can f*** like a rock star as long as you want."

Mary – "Now that I know what both ways feel like, with and without, I can always tell the difference between a guy who uses it and a guy who doesn't. A guy that does gets hard at the drop of a hat, a guy that doesn't kinda struggles once the condom goes on. I prefer them to pop something, it's just simpler and much more fun."

Barry – "It basically gives you full control over the night. It doesn't mean you'll orgasm more, but even if you aren't going to be able to cum, you can still get hard to play around a bit."

Mary – "Which can be a problem if you are with the wrong guy. Sometimes you'll have guys that just don't know when to give up. They will just pound and pound and pound and pound and pound. By the end, everyone is bored and waiting around for this guy to wrap it up. My poor little ***** will be in traction for days."

Barry – "Yeah, we aren't making a porno, so it's not like we are waiting for the money shot. Sometimes you just need to know when to cut bait and fake an orgasm. You're wearing a condom anyway, so it's not like anyone will notice the difference."

Mary – "I can tell the difference."

Barry – "Sure you can, honey."

HOW LONG IS TOO LONG?

Barry – "That's a bit of a moving target."

Mary – "It is. It really depends on your sexual style."

Barry – "Well, if you are using a 'male enhancement product,' and aren't worried about using your powerball, then the first one probably shouldn't last more than 15-20 minutes."

Mary - "Powerball?"

Barry - "Your second testicle. When you orgasm the first time, that's your first testicle and is a bit harder to control because you have all those hormones coursing through your body. But the second one is a bit easier to control and will take a longer time to…unload…as it were."

    Mary – "Ah. Gross."

    Barry – "The first time you have sex with a new person, it will usually, and should be, intense and kind of awkward. You're having to learn a new body, a new personality and figure out how to push these new buttons."

    Mary – "That first time is still fun, but there is a bit of 'oh, that's what you like to do,' and 'nope, you can't stick your finger there, sir.'"

    Barry – "And everybody is nervous anyway, so you kind of just want to get it out of the way, so the next round you can really take your time to get to know the person sexually."

    Mary – "But it's the second round where you can get into trouble. You can get a guy that just ground and pounds."

    Barry – "Nice UFC reference!"

    Mary – "Thanks, I'm all about the sweaty men beating the hell out of each other. Anyway, if he's a ground and pounder, just pumping away, eyes closed and thinking of England, then once you pass the ten-minute mark, I'm done with him. Barry, he's more of a foreplay guy and isn't jack hammering me into the mattress springs. He can make sex last longer, it's not all about the oil derrick action."

    Barry – "It's more playing than just f***ing. Lots of petting, slower movements, switching positions, but you still have to pay attention to the other person to see when their attention is fading. When it does, if you can cum, then go ahead and do it. If not, quit while you're ahead."

Mary – "And sometimes I do just want to be jack hammered into the mattress springs. Just so you know."

FAKING AN ORGASM

Barry – "I assume that any female orgasm I see while we're swinging is fake. Maybe there are some women that can pull off an 'O,' but I'm a little suspect."

Mary – "I don't think so either, I don't want to tell a woman 'oh, quit it, you're not fooling anyone.' I'll fake an orgasm every once in a while, especially if the guy is taking his sweet time and I'm ready to wrap it up, get dressed and go get some Boba Tea."

Barry – "She loves Boba Tea and sushi after a night of sex."

Mary – "It's just a nice closing ceremony."

Barry – "It is. But, yeah, some girls need to see the guy orgasm or they will get their feelings hurt, so you just sort of tense up, kind of spasm a bit. Then you slap her on the butt and trash the condom before she can tell you faked it."

Mary – "We have a bit more leeway as girls. It's kinda hard to overdo a fake orgasm since guys have this ridiculous porn star fantasy flicking away in their head anyway."

Barry – "Yeah, I've never seen a fake orgasm and thought, 'okay, tone it down there, miss.'"

Mary – "What do you think when you see a fake orgasm?"

Barry (chuckled) – "By that point? I'm not thinking of much at all."

Mary – "Well, I consider myself an artisan of the fake orgasm. It's all about balancing the two tendencies. One is to undersell it, shudder a little bit and then be done. The other tendency is to go all 'Exorcist' with the screaming, shivering, groaning, wiggling. I've had orgasms that make me do that for real, but for the most part, they are more quiet and contained. If you're doing exhibitionist stuff, then you can get away with a cartoonish orgasm because most people in the room assume you are faking it for their viewing pleasure anyway. You're more an actress at that point."

Barry – "So maybe I should grunt more?"

Mary – "Yeah, maybe do that deep thrust and shiver thing you normally do, make that retard face."

Barry – "I make a retard face?"

RETURNING TO NORMALCY

Barry – "This is actually the hardest part of swinging."

Mary – "It took us five or six years to really get the hang of this, and it is still something we struggle with time and again. The problem is, most people who have been married as long as we have are having trouble maintaining the sexual satisfaction of their marriage, and one or both partners will start cheating to feel sexy again. Swingers, or at least the good ones, are pretty satisfied sexually. It's the emotional part that is often short-changed."

Barry – "Yes, I've come to understand that I'm

not great at the listening and understanding thing."

Mary – "But you try, and that's what's important. He'll tell me how pretty I am, but not in the reflexive "you're hot" kind of way, just more elaborate ways, using some metaphors. Basically putting effort into it."

Barry – "She, in turn, will go with me to see all my dorky sci-fi movies."

Mary – "It's about being a good boyfriend and girlfriend. Keeping the intensity of our emotional bond in line with the intensity of our sexual bond."

Barry – "Hmm. I am lucky that you are as smart as you are pretty."

Mary (patted Barry's hand) – "That's a good boy."

FUN FACT: Swinger Chic
Society's comfort level with swinging and sexuality in general is a cyclical thing. Once taboo lifestyles will suddenly permeate mainstream culture, but then be driven back underground only a few years later. Ironically, restrictive cultures are where most fetishes thrive because the element of danger is a large part of the appeal, and the Lifestyle is no different.

The Fishbowl
Part III

Seven days. One hundred sixty-eight hours. Ten thousand and eighty minutes. Six hundred and four thousand, eight hundred seconds.

Long-nailed and brutishly awkward fingers stumbled and tripped around Michelle's vagina as she feigned orgasmic joy just to give some finality to her entanglement with the wrinkled and orange-tanned woman who'd trapped her in the backseat of Brad's Lexus.

Michelle was certain the fumbling faux-lesbian was causing a urinary tract infection and couldn't tell if the woman was mad at her ***** or just had no idea what to do now that she was three knuckles deep.

But Michelle still groaned in the backseat as they wound through the dark streets of her gated community. It was three a.m. and an orgy was collecting at Brad and Michelle's front steps. Michelle was trying to go to her happy place while the bitch was buried in her crotch and the woman's husband watched from the passenger seat. Michelle was tempted to use her foot to open the car door and then kick the woman out into the street.

Perhaps she would even smack into a passing mailbox, which would be brilliant.

When the car finally, and mercifully, pulled to a stop inside the garage, the tanned woman unlatched from Michelle's vagina and gave Michelle a sloppy kiss.

"Your good at that," Michelle lied.

"I know," the woman purred. "There's plenty more where that came from."

"Mmm!"

Michelle pealed away from the woman and stood up out of the car, slipped back on her panties and quickly scooted into the house with a slight hobble from her still aching knee. Brad jogged to follow, giving Michelle just enough time to throw him a bitter glare.

"That bad?" he grimaced and she nodded.

"Okay, well," Brad said as he swiveled to walk to the refrigerator. "I'll get them a drink while we wait for the others to arrive. Want some cranberry juice?"

"I want to go to bed," Michelle hissed. The couple walked into the kitchen a moment later.

Michelle wondered if they'd heard her, hoped they had.

The woman strode over to Michelle, picked her up and planted her on the counter. She began to spread Michelle's legs, but Michelle gently pushed her away.

"I have to go to the bathroom," Michelle apologized, taking the cranberry juice from Brad's hand. She pecked a kiss on the blond woman's lips and then disappeared through the kitchen door.

"Christ," Michelle mumbled as she limped up the stairs, walked into the bedroom and shed her high heels. She sat on the bed, downed her cranberry juice and rubbed her knee. It was a little swollen, nothing gross.

Michelle slid across the bed to the side-table and took off her earrings and put them in the jewelry box. Wedged between the box and her vibrator was her tazer.

Brad had only seen it once, when he was blind drunk and had thrown her across the room. Brad hit Michelle rarely and it was usually over after the first blow when either regret or fear of police intervention ended the argument.

But the night that Michelle zapped Brad had been bad. He'd been embarrassed during a town hall debate by a homosexual, Unitarian pastor who was arguing for gay marriage. Brad decided to take it out on Michelle, but it was Brad who ended up on the floor. He was so drunk that he pissed himself after getting hit with three milliamperes of electricity and then passed out. As far as Michelle knew, he never remembered how he ended up facedown in a puddle.

Footsteps approached and Michelle was worried it was the tan woman stalking her.

Michelle wondered what Brad would do to her if she tazed the woman. It would, at the very least, put a damper on the orgy.

The door opened and it was Brad, so Michelle

slid the drawer shut again.

"Hey, let's game-plan," Brad said, closing the door behind him. "How's your knee?"

"A little sore. Needs some rest."

"Okay, well why don't you get a good night's sleep, don't worry about housework tomorrow. Just rest up."

"Oh, well, okay, thank you," Michelle said, surprised that Brad gave her a pass so readily.

"But as far as tonight goes," Brad continued, and Michelle sighed.

"What?" Brad asked.

"Nothing. You were saying?"

"Well, almost everyone is here. We should have about ten people and most of them have been here before, but we have a few newbies."

"Okay," Michelle sighed as she hobbled to the bathroom to get some water. "Just keep that woman away from me and my p****. If she gives me a UTI, I'm going to castrate you."

"Okay," Brad chuckled. "How about you go after the newbies, that younger couple? The guy's a lawyer and she's a secretary at his firm."

"Angela and Tommy."

"Right, you go sit between them and maybe start playing with her first," Brad said. "I'll maybe stick close to you, make out with Cindy a bit, and if the crispy chick starts getting close to you, I'll grab her and maybe lead her over to someone else."

"Okay, thanks," Michelle said, knowing that Brad would just end up forgetting about her as soon as they got downstairs. He was trying to lure her downstairs and knew that she would feel too insecure to leave the orgy once it started.

"Ted, the older guy, he said he wanted to tag team you with me, so we need to make that happen tonight, okay?"

"Gotcha."

"And, I don't think Lewis brought any coke, but if he did, make sure he keeps it away from me because you know I'm just going to do some if I see it."

Michelle nodded. Brad walked up to her and kissed her forehead.

"You're a champ."

Michelle gave him a strained smile. He patted her on the shoulder, kissed her sore knee and walked to the door.

"Brad," Michelle called.

"Yeah," Brad replied, not turning around.

"Does this make us happy?"

Brad put on a smile, then turned to face her.

"Of course it does, it's fun. It's a great stress reliever. That's what you told me, right?"

Michelle didn't answer. Brad walked up to Michelle, gave her a light peck on her lips and then hugged her. He let go and raised up her chin to look into her eyes.

"Do you want some ibuprofen for your knee?" Brad asked, but Michelle shook her head. "Okay, well, come down when you're ready."

He rose up and walked to the door. Just before he disappeared, he paused long enough to say, "Don't take too long."

―

"I was just waiting in line at the concession stand talking about my investment in this start up company in Austin and this guy taps me on the shoulder. I turn around ready to rip into the ****er for touching me, cause I'm a bit lit, if you know what I mean, and you know who it was?"

"Who?" asked an older man with bright white hair, bright white teeth and an unnervingly muscled torso. He sat next to Brad as women were sucking both their d****.

"Billy ****ing Corgan," Brad beamed.

"Who?" the man asked.

"Billy Corgan, the singer," Brad said. "He's from, oh ****, some band. Oh, hey Michelle, welcome to the party!"

Around the living room, naked or near naked bodies lounged on couches or coiled together on the floor. The tanned woman was with a tangle of women near the fireplace and she had her hand deep into another woman, a travel agent named Anita. Anita was thinly masking pain as pleasure, but the stupid males didn't know the difference.

Michelle felt sorry for Linda, but not quite enough to risk getting caught up in the mess.

"Hey, baby?" Brad asked while he ran his hands through the woman's hair who was buried in his lap. "What band was Billy Corgan in? You know, that bald guy we met at the music festival a few years back?"

"Smashing Pumpkins," Michelle said.

It wasn't Billy Corgan, the kid just said he was to see if Brad would believe him. Michelle knew all along but never told Brad.

"Ooh," the woman said, taking Brad's d*** out of

her mouth just long enough to say, "I love them!"

"Yup, Billy ****ing Corgan," Brad smirked down at her.

"So, why did he tap you on the shoulder?" the white haired man asked.

"He had thought about investing with the company I was talking about and wanted to know what I thought," Brad said, then looked at Michelle. "You're a little overdressed, honey."

Michelle eased off the straps of her dress and lifted it up over her head and dropped it down to the floor. The tanned woman quickly stood and began to walk toward Michelle, so Michelle skirted away toward the young, dark-haired newbie whose wife was now kissing Linda on the floor.

Michelle mounted the newbie and began kissing him. Her knee ached, but she thought this position would deter the bitch from going after her *****.

The newbie was new to this because he nervously jammed his tongue into her throat, apparently looking for her G spot between her tonsils. It was still preferable to the tanned woman and she could tell the boy was teachable.

Michelle felt hands grip her hips and pull her backward. She glanced behind her to see the tanned woman trying to slide underneath and wedge her head between the newbie's lap and Michelle. Michelle shifted off his lap, leaned back on the couch and pulled the newbie on top of her.

Undeterred, the tanned woman slid her hand between them to reach for Michelle's vagina. Michelle shifted her hips away from the woman's mannish fingers.

"Come on, let me in," the tanned woman purred, pulling at Michelle's hips.

"Not right now, honey," Michelle murmured, turning her attention back to the newbie.

"But I want it right now," the tanned woman insisted, pulling at Michelle's hips again.

"I said not now!" Michelle growled, shoving the woman's hands off her. "Take a ****ing hint and leave me the **** alone, you shriveled up whore!"

The room froze, the tanned woman flushed to an orange red. Michelle was tempted to backtrack, but then looked over at Brad who was too busy ****ing a woman on the other couch to even notice Michelle's outburst.

"I'm done with this," Michelle grunted, pushing the newbie off her, standing and then hobbling out of the room.

Brad followed Michelle upstairs thirty minutes later, after the majority of the disappointed and uncomfortable swingers had shuffled out the door.

Michelle kept the tazer under the sheets, just in case. She wouldn't need it. Brad patted her on the butt as he lowered under the sheets.

"Don't worry about it, honey," he said, kissing her on the shoulder. "We'll have that couple over to make nice. I'm sure if you just apologize and let her go down on you, she'll be fine. I know that's asking a lot, but they have a lot of oil money in their family and they might invest in my foundation."

"Oh," Michelle said. "I guess it would be for the best. Just..."

"Yes?"

"Can we make it after next Sunday? I have

something important to do that day."

"Whatever you want, baby," Brad whispered, leaning in close to her and wrapping his arms around her waist. She new he still hoped to get laid. She thought about tazing him, just for the fun of it.

Instead, she just gave in. Why pick a fight now when there was so little time left?

FUN FACT: Swinger Etiquette
Even Lifestyle Clubs follow the norms of traditional dating. For instance, going to a club with a particular couple, but then leaving them for a more attractive couple is considered gauche. This is why it is better to "meet up at the club," which avoids being tied down to one couple all night long.

A Charmed Life
Part III

Music snobbery is a bit of a double-edged sword. It offers a quick way to bond with strangers, is a great tool to out-obscure young, pretentious hipsters and it is an easy way to make people feel out of touch and inferior.

And I do love making people feel out of touch and inferior.

The problem comes when your carefully forged and precisely pompous tastes get in the way of regular life. Take a recent situation. I was clinging onto to the hips of a bombshell blonde. She had a tight, muscular body, a pretty smile and beguiling green eyes that just seemed so surprised and entertained at the novelty of having sex with the first new man in her thirteen years of marriage.

Her husband was on the other side of the couple's bed, getting blown by my wife. I think he was having problems achieving an erection, but I didn't want to look because it makes it worse. I know from personal experience.

So, I was having just an entirely wonderful time until I hear, from the couple's MP3 player, the first few notes of a Dave Matthews Band song.

Dave ****ing Matthews. Are you kidding me?

I instantly dislike anyone who owns even one Dave Matthews Band album[23] and detest with a blinding rage anyone who refers to the band as "DMB."

I'm usually pretty forgiving of poor musical taste when the offending party is naked, but this really jolted me. And the revolting song was not even one of those kind of creepy, backwoods Louisiana tracks that is okay for sex because it's kind of disturbing and angry (or as disturbing and angry as Dave Matthews Band ever gets). Instead, it was one of those really sappy prom songs that completely ruined it for me.

Okay, for wannabe swingers out there, here is a brief primer of Lifestyle background music:

1. No love songs. This act has nothing to do with love. This is about fun and nasty. The more fun and the more nasty, the better. If I wanted to make love, then I would have stayed home with the Mrs.

2. No Britney Spears, no Backstreet Boys, no Michael Jackson, no Journey, no Garth Brooks. Even if you feel like you shouldn't be embarrassed by it, don't play it. It will take everyone out of the mood because they will either laugh and bond about the awful music or they will secretly start second-guessing their

---

[23] I'm looking at you, Charles!

decision to go home with you. Whichever way you go, the new couple is no longer thinking about sex.

    3. Nothing too weird or heavy. And by too weird or too heavy, I mean nothing so psychedelic and inaccessible that it is pretentious. Don't get me wrong, I love pretentious and weird. I love the "Soft Bulletin" era Flaming Lips and before-they-became-a-thing Animal Collective, but also acknowledge that neither band makes for good panty-dropping music. And by too heavy, I mean anything with screaming, shouting, etc. Unless you know for a fact that the other couple is way into that kind of music, it could be intimidating.

    4. You want music that can fade into the background and is overtly sexual, but not cartoonishly so. Blues is good, but can be silly, clichéd and a bit too Harley Davidson. Soul is good. Party rap can work, but trip hop is better. Country is hard to pull off, so should be avoided. Drum and bass can be a bit migraine-inducing. Classical is fine, but perhaps a bit too staid unless turned way down low. Trance is perhaps the best option as a modern, hipper equivalent to the 70s porn track.

    5. If all else fails, put on the classics: Prince, Lou Rawls, dirty, back country blues, Ray Charles (nothing too familiar though), Billie Holiday (when it's not too Billie Holiday) or Of Montreal (when they were in their Prince superfreak phase).

    6. No hair metal! Though the chicks love a good glam ballad, the last thing you want is for them to stop mid-coitous so they can clap their hands and squeel, "I

love this song!"[24]

7. You don't have to stay away from your favorite bands, necessarily. Just pick the tracks with great care. I like to groove to some early nineties hip hop like Digable Planets, Das FX and Leaders of the New School, and Elena generally opts for punkabilly like Flametrick Subs, nouveau soul or even a few select Clash songs. It was okay because she knew to pick atmospheric tracks that represent her musical soul but don't distract her from sucking my d***.

A sampling of good-for-any-occasion Lifestyle tracks:
1. The Beatles "She's so Heavy"
2. Deep Purple "Hush"
3. Clap Your Hands Say Yeah "Satan Said Dance"
4. R.E.M. "Nightswimming"
5. The National "Fake Empire"
6. Van Morrison "Into the Mystic"
7. Cold War Kids "Hang Me Out to Dry"
8. Sons and Daughters "Rama Lama"
9. The White Stripes "The Union Forever"
10. Yeah Yeah Yeahs "Cheated Hearts"-Though a bit on the nose.

All "bowa-chica-wow-wow" music should be played at a low level so that it can fade quickly into the background and keeps the mind focused on the task at hand.

And, while we're on the subject, you want to

---

[24] Once had a girl use my **** as a microphone when she sang along with Warrant's "Cherry Pie." Just ghastly.

know what else is distracting? Ringing cell phones. It was my phone, though, so no one to blame but myself.

So, as Elena toiled away on Skippy-Soft-Penis, I dismounted the blonde and danced over to my pants to find my cell phone. The worst part was that I had to touch it before I got a chance to wash my hands, so it ended up smelling like rubbers for the rest of the night.

Bleh.

I dug through the pile of clothes to find my jeans and pulled the cell phone out of the front pocket. It was the middle child calling.

"Dammit, hold on, I have to get this."

I slipped out of the room and closed the door behind me.

"What's up?"

"Hey, Will," the child said.

"Is everything okay?" I replied, trying not to sound as annoyed.

"Where are you guys?"

"At a friend's house—listening to music."

"What are you listening to?"

I lowered the phone, rubbed my temples and then lifted the phone back up to my ear.

"Is there a specific reason you are calling? Is something wrong?"

"Yeah, I threw up, but I think I'm okay. The babysitter said to call anyway."

"Oh, um, ok. Tell her we're on our way home."

"Ok, bye."

"By the way..." I tried to get out, but the phone went dead.

I sighed, closed my phone and moped back to the

bedroom. Mötley Crüe was raging through the speakers. "Dr. Feelgood," of course. Elena and the other girl were singing into the guy's semi-erect penis. He was dismayed by the turn of events, and I just wanted to say, "Dude, it's your MP3 player, you should have known better."

"Everything okay?" Elena asked once the chorus wrapped up.

"We had a small issue and probably should head back."

Quick goodbyes were exchanged along with a few tongue-heavy kisses and promises to meet up again. It never happened, but I did secretly want to have them over just to show them what real music was all about.

God, I'm such a pretentious twat.

—

The night wasn't a complete wash. The interrupted bout was our third go around and we were probably going to leave soon anyway. I did get left with a disturbing thought tickling the back of my cranium.

It tied in with the first visit to the marriage therapist, which had only been a week prior.

We had discussed personality types. My wife is an ISTJ, which means she's a compulsive organizer that is practical and trustworthy.

I, on the other hand, had my choice of four categories, INTJ = independent thinker, INTP = conceptual air-head, ENTP = inventive but flaky or

ENTJ = gregarious alpha male.[25]

So, if the test is correct, I apparently have no distinct personality, which was comforting.

We also discussed being emotionally supportive, or rather Elena discussed it and the therapist discussed it and I nodded my head at the appropriate times as I watched the minutes tick off the clock.

The only truly informative moment of the session was when a teary-eyed Elena confessed that she sometimes fantasized about other men. We had not discussed the Lifestyle in the session, so this took me off guard. Fortunately our time ran out before the therapist could dig into the admission, but it just sort of lingered like a hangnail.

Fast-forward a week as we pushed the babysitter out the door, cleaned dried vomit off the carpet and finally slid into bed. Elena clarified her admission, saying that her fantasies had nothing to do with sex. She instead pined for men who would be really sweet to her.

This is troublesome, and I know that might sound hypocritical considering what we'd been doing earlier in the night. There is a very real difference between craving another person sexually and craving them emotionally.

Odd as it may seem, I never really worried about Elena leaving me for a sexier man, but I could see an emotionally attentive man as a considerable threat.

Later that night, I'd begun replaying in my head some of the moments from past dalliances with other couples. There were the awkward first times that

---

[25] I asked to check the therapist's math, but he thought I was kidding.

were often spastic, kind of painful but all and all, fun. There were the copious amounts of girl/girl play and then the tangled messes where it was just body parts and giggles.

What stuck with me first was a moment earlier that night when we where playing on separate sides of the room. I looked over to see Elena cuddling with the man as he whispered someting to her. She smiled in a different kind of ecstasy. It didn't mean anything at the moment, but when coupled Elena's admission, it became much more significant.

Then I remembered how guilty she had been after flirting with another man. I had written it off as innocent initially, but now saw why she made it such a big deal. I'd been so distracted by the book, the kids, concerts and those ****ing flies that I didn't realize that she wasn't looking for another lay, she just wanted someone to pay attention to her.

I was suddenly jealous and I had no idea what to do with it, because it really is hard to tell your wife she can **** anyone, but no one but me can tell her she's pretty.

So, I had two routes:
1. Throw a fit and then set up an even more troublesome trip to the marriage therapist.
2. Try to figure out this whole sweet, attentive husband thing.

Honestly, "1" seemed like a lot less trouble.

FUN FACT: Toys
When selecting an array of toys to use with new partners, it is best to start small, particularly when presenting an object meant to be inserted into any kind of orifice. Not only are there deviations in personal elasticity, but the overall message sent when breaking the ice by busting out a baseball–bat sized dong can be off-putting, to say the least.

The Ballad of Jerry and Carey/Cynthia/Veronica Part IV

Successful marriages survive by momentum, a tide created over time that becomes stronger than any individualism lingering from childhood. This current needs to be so powerful that it can force the couple into and then beyond tribulation, across the vast expanse of time and ever onward for the rest of their lives.

Momentum cannot be created by intentions alone. The most earnest aspirations equal nothing without repetition. It is a long series of decisions and small battles against one's weaker, selfish instincts. That is where one truly gets a firm grasp on maturity and creates an inertia that will hold their course true even when their hearts begin to wander.

Jerry and Carey, now Cynthia, both had the ambition to be parents, but they had yet to shed the thin, soft skin of adolescence and develop the rough, impermeable hide of adulthood. Childhood is an easy thing to outgrow physically, but it is a laborious process to outgrow mentally.

Even though the trials of pregnancy and childbirth had instilled Cynthia with the resolution to be a woman, she still needed direction to know what womanhood truly meant.

In her defense, what role models did she have? The women in magazines and the Barbies in her toy box where the only female figures that she had ever admired. Neither were based on reality, though, rather just airbrushing and plastic molds.

Stumbling was inevitable and stumble she did. Collectors called on unpaid medical bills. Fines mounted for expired insurance verification forms. Her hair began to mat into the bristles of her brush because of nutritional deficiencies and stress. A mountain of dirty laundry covered the corner of her room and stank like rotten milk. The litter box went untended; cabinets were bare of everything but baby formula.

But she responded with the mantra:
"As long as the baby is healthy and happy.
As long as the baby is healthy and happy.
As long as the baby is healthy and happy."

And let us not forget an often-overlooked mental blow of every mother. For a year, Carey's body was not hers. It was being stretched, kicked and twisted by another human. It was being prodded and poked by doctors, every decision she made from what she ate to how often she went for walks was analyzed by the judgmental eyes of strangers.

After childbirth, the body was left ravaged and scarred. Her hips loosened and weakened, her stomach was etched with a web of stretch marks. The child latched at her breasts would leave cuts and scabs because of his vigorous nursing, and she didn't remember the last time she'd felt pretty.

And when she quit breastfeeding because the pain was too intense and she couldn't keep her nipples from bleeding, strangers would attribute the baby bottles to a breakdown in her mothering skills.

After six months, the hormones subsided and her body had healed enough that she looked like herself again, albeit with wider hips and stubborn pockets of fat left over from the pregnancy. She was still constantly tired, her blood pressure pulsed like a bass drum, but she could feel that the waters were leveling. Ahead of her was a chance to begin building a life, if she only knew how.

Jerry was not faring any better. He went from the simple but lucrative livelihood of the oil fields to slinging drinks at a neighborhood bar.

When he'd been isolated in the countryside, his muscles torn to shreds and exhausted, there was a weathered satisfaction, a sense of completion that never came while hustling to fill the glasses of an endless train of thirsty souls. There were no answers in a beer tap, there were no moments of peace to find the solutions to his problems when everyone in the world was asking him to solve theirs.

And there was no real home.

Cynthia held onto the same apartment where

Jerry had abandoned her nearly six months ago. It was a small, one bedroom prison where the mistakes of the past were mixed in with the piles of baby toys, hanging in the air and poisoning the water. The couple's flawed history crawled under the door when she soaked in the bath and slithered into the bed sheets to haunt her dreams.

For Jerry, "home" was a rattrap in southwest Oklahoma City near the airport. Home was the silence where a child's crying should be. It was the empty sofa where Cynthia should be lounging while she read beauty magazines, wearing nothing but a bath towel. It was the bed where they should have been making love, but instead was occupied by a waitress that Jerry ****ed because he was desperate for a woman's touch.

But even the waitress knew she was a placeholder until Jerry figured out how to win Cynthia back.

Cynthia and Jerry did agree that home was not a place that they could share, at least not yet.

This belief was punctuated by Jerry's arrival from the oilfield when he returned to his wife and child.

The long, suffocating moments had been strange and forced. Jerry desperately wanted a connection to this child, he wanted what the doting father from the bar had described. But the child did not know him, and soon cried until it was returned to its mother.

The void between Jerry and his child was a deep, sickening hunger that drove Jerry to be a better man and to be a better father.

Jerry and Cynthia had sex twice in the months following his return. Both times were as alien and cold as Jerry's interaction with the child. He did not blame Cynthia; he was now just a visitor to her cold apartment.

So, he called his parents. They understood more about the troubled lovers than they let on and had stepped up their involvement with the grandchild. They were forging a permanent bond with the baby even if its parents were destined to split.

They brought a crib and a stroller, took the young mother out to eat at least once a week and provided babysitting, sometimes arriving unannounced and pushing Cynthia out the door so she could get a break from the child.

They would insist she dress up and go out and eat. They would shove cash in her hand, but she would only walk out to the park and watch the ducks swim. She would then use the cash to pay down bills or buy a toy for the child.

When Jerry called his parents to discuss a plan to reunite the family, they were willing to do anything to help. He knew they had very little to give; Jerry's family had always hovered just above the poverty level.

But they did have land.

"What do you think about El Reno?" Jerry asked as they both watched the child gnaw on a plastic block, slobber coating the toy like ectoplasm.

"Not sure, I've never been there," Cynthia replied. "Why?"

"My parents offered me some of the family acreage out there that used to belong to my mom's cousin. They also offered some of their farming equipment. My parents are going to retire soon, and I really don't want to move all the way out to their land, but there is plenty of good land in El Reno that nobody has done anything with for a generation."

Cynthia took a deep breath, slid off the couch and knelt down by the child. It rolled over onto its stomach and wobbled its legs back and forth in a slow crawl to the mother. She sat it up on her lap and retrieved its slime-covered block.

"There's also a community college out there," Jerry furthered. "You could go to school, and I was thinking about taking a few classes on growing grapes, maybe section out some of the land for a vineyard."

"For a winery?"

"No, just a vineyard for now," Jerry said. "There are more wineries out there than vineyards to grow the grapes. It'll take us about five years to get it going, but..."

"Five years is a long time."

"I know, but I can work another job. The other crops will produce sooner than that as we get the land back into shape. It will be hard for a few years, but it will turn around."

"Jerry, I just don't..."

Jerry sat down next to her and the baby. He lifted up his hand to the baby's scalp, stroked its hair until the baby grabbed his hand and began gnawing on it. He didn't move his hand, even as saliva dripped down his wrist.

"Listen," Jerry whispered, using his other hand to brush the hair out of Cynthia's eyes. "You don't have to answer right now, but I am going to propose to you again. It isn't some kind of renewal of vows or anything like that. It is a promise."

Cynthia chuckled and then took a deep breath while wiping a tear off her cheek.

"I'm listening."

"Life will be very hard for five years," Jerry began. "We will be poor for five years. We will work like mules for five years. But at the end of those five years, I guarantee we will see our future. It will be out in front of us, visible, set in stone. I will give you stability, I will work this land and will give everything I have to make sure that the soil, the roots and this family will be healthy and prosperous."

Cynthia was crying, silently at first, then in heaves. The child was unnerved, rustled slightly and then clung to the mother. She held the child tight, wanted to stand and walk away from Jerry, but also wanted to fall into his arms.

"I know what I've done to you and to the baby," Jerry said. "But I also know what I need to do now. El Reno isn't so far away. You can come up to the city and work or just get away on the weekends. I won't isolate you, I won't leave you, and after these next five years, you will see that I can protect you and provide for this family. And after five years, when he is older and in school, you can work anywhere you want. You can start your career, whatever you want to do. This is my proposal. A five year plan and at the end of that time, we will have land, we will have crops and you will both have the lives you deserve."

Cynthia looked up from the child and into Jerry's eyes. For the first time in years, she saw the future. Her deep sobs were warm and cleansing, as if the toxins from her poisoned childhood were finally dripping away.

Cynthia spent hours listening to financial talk radio at home with the baby, partly as a substitute for adult interaction, partly because the commentator was a reassuring male presence. Once negotiations began on how to find the financing to get the farm started, loans were the major sticking point. Grants were nowhere to be found, but there were programs available to help with startup costs.

Low interest loans and government-backed loans meant debt, which scared Cynthia.

"You are wanting a Cadillac, baby, but all we can afford is a Pinto," Cynthia told Jerry, trying to be playful as she drew her line in the sand. "So, figure out what is the best way for us to use that Pinto."

The bare essentials were then agreed upon. It would start with the soil, irrigation, and minor but necessary repairs on the shotgun shack, which hadn't housed humans in fifteen years. Jerry, his parents and a few extended relatives cleaned the house thoroughly. Then Jerry and Cynthia painted and furnished the inside the best they could and, for the first year, ignored the outside. As long as the roof held out water, everything else could wait.

Five acres were reserved for the vineyard. It was five acres that would not yield a true cash crop for five years. The rest of the land they could grow wheat and barley to sell, fruit and vegetables to eat. The rest of the land could be developed to pay off immediately, but those five acres were a promise.

A promise to be patient as the roots got hold of

the land in the first year. A promise to let the trunks build their strength in year two. A promise to not overburden the vines in year three. A promise to maintain discipline and curb their disappointment in year four when the crops weren't what they'd hoped for.

But year five? Year five would be when the vineyard would finally reach its potential.

The first winter was spent with one space heater and a fireplace, the following summer with one window air conditioning unit. The siding was replaced a section at a time as Jerry could find extra pieces from the various construction teams he worked on.

Jerry and Cynthia worked the land and steadily rebuilt the house. Work began after he came home from his job and continued until they went to bed. Work would continue throughout the waking hours of the weekend. Jerry had to rewire the entire house just so Cynthia could use a second hand computer to begin online classes through the painfully slow dial-up modem.

The land was overrun with weeds; the equipment supplied by Jerry's parents only had a few years left, despite Jerry's patch jobs. Their life looked like it was all held together by the thinnest of strings. If that string broke at any one point, it would all unravel.

And yet, it never did.

There was the tornado that ripped off half their roof.

There was the drought that wiped out all their first crops except the radishes they planted in the worst of the land.

There was the child's pneumonia.

There was the wrenched back that kept Jerry on the couch for two weeks when he wasn't at work.

There was the leaking radiator.

There were the bounced checks.

There was the empty bank account.

But the string never broke.

Somehow, no matter how implausible, the string held, and during their second spring, the dried, dead rows of wheat sprang back to life. They shot up tall and proud. In the vineyard, small tentacles climbed, intertwined, twisted and fought to live.

The second year they got an additional space heater, a ceiling fan and finished repairing the plumbing. It was an unseasonably wet season, that ruined half the wheat. Disease killed their two apple trees and there were no grapes.

"Five years," Jerry whispered to his beleaguered wife.

There would be days when Cynthia would stare out over the barren land and feel as if the life was draining out of her. She would remember the pictures of dustbowl era women, dried, shriveled and lifeless.

Then there would be days when Jerry taught the child to throw a plastic ball. The child would stand for a few moments, toss the ball wildly up in the air as he stumbled backward, his fall cushioned by the diaper. The plastic ball would plummet back to Earth, bounce off the child's head and all three of them would laugh hysterically.

It was a life of extremes those first few years, but there was a security in their desperation. She and the child had jumped into this new life with no ripcord, no safety net. She had thrown in her lot, betting that this man curled up next to her in their cold bed could carry the weight of their family until the land started bursting with life.

And after five years, with healthy crops for as far as the eye could see, she could send the child to school and begin her own career. It was so far away, but it was there. She could almost see it.

Jerry felt oddly unburdened by the new existence. His heart ached when he saw his wife worry for money. He was ashamed that he could not give the family more than the absolute basic staples needed to survive and that it took government assistance to feed their child.

But he never stopped fighting. He was either working on the land, working to earn money or sleeping. The absolute simplicity of his life made him feel as if he could breath again. The path was straight, no matter how rugged it might be.

And they limped into the third season. Cynthia began taking the child to the farmers' market to sell what they could. Being young didn't help as the older, "wiser" farmers jealously guarded their regulars. A surprise run-in with an ex-customer from one of the strip clubs resulted in Cynthia's first break. The customer had worked his way up to chef at a restaurant, and after surveying the tomatoes, vowed to buy from Cynthia and gave her leads for a few other restaurants in the area.

It was not much money, it was a small victory, but it was a desperately needed victory.

That night, the child tussled in his bed and the parents prayed that he stayed put for the night rather than toddling into their room again. When they heard him settle, they closed their door and made love.

The couple had reached a turning point and they knew it. The five-year plan was, finally, beginning to work.

Just two more years of pain.
Two more years of crock-pot beans.
Two more years of ugly, patchwork siding.
Two more years of Goodwill clothing.
Two more years of under-producing vineyards.

They were hungry, tired and substantially happy in a way that yielded few smiles, but was producing a tangible hope for better times.

During a panic, Cynthia burst into a teary confession that their first customer was a man that she danced for at a strip club. Jerry just laughed.

"God, do you really have the energy to cheat on me?"

"No," she sighed.

He then pulled her close, rubbed his nose to hers and whispered, "I trust you."

With the fourth year came bountiful crops with record yields for the farm and a sliver of financial breathing room. Jerry could now work the land full time, Cynthia could attend classes in person as she worked toward a career in advertising and their child was now ready for kindergarten.

In celebration, Jerry and Cynthia were preparing for a night away from the farm, away from work and away from parenting. It was the first taste of freedom they'd had since moving to the farm.

As Jerry's parents shooed the couple out the door, Jerry and Cynthia realized they had no idea what to do with their time and meager wad of disposable cash.

They drove to a nearby bar, sat down and drank. They joked with the regulars. Jerry played pool, but they bored quickly and left. They drove around the countryside aimlessly, talking about leaving poverty behind once and for all and what they wanted from the next phase of their lives.

Jerry wanted Cynthia to be happy; he wanted to reward the faith she had in him. He knew that she still dreamed of forging an elegant, sophisticated life in the city and he wanted to give it to her. She wanted urbane dinner parties with hip, stylish friends, but he didn't know where to find this chic, new life. He only knew that it couldn't be found in dusty country bars or small town farmers' markets.

The more their burdens eased, the more restless they both became. They now felt they had earned the chance to enjoy their lives, but neither could have known that the darkest times still lay ahead.

FUN FACT: Breaking the Ice
It is best to think of each new encounter with a swinger as a job interview. A little self-deprecating humor is appreciated, but never lead with your weaknesses. If a new couple has approached your table, it means the job is already yours to lose, so don't give them a reason to change their minds.

Superswingers
Part IV

The Rumormill closed and the interview relocated to a Denny's. Barry and Mary curled up in a booth while pecking kisses and giggling at jokes whispered back and forth. A few other couples from the club sat in separate areas of the restaurant as if afraid to be seen in a pack and arouse the waitress' suspicions.

The revelry shared by the swingers was not unlike the smirking satisfaction of black-clad high schoolers huddled in a corner booth nursing a pot of coffee and up well past curfew. Everyone in the restaurant, it seemed, was proud they were getting away with something.

ADDICTION
Barry – "Huh, haven't ever thought about it like

that. I don't feel addicted, do you?"

Mary – "No, not really. I don't think it affects our lives like being addicted to meth or alcohol would be. I think we'd be naïve to say we don't have some sort of addiction to sex, but I think this is a relatively healthy way to deal with that addiction."

Barry – "There are certainly some similarities though. You have your triggers just like any other addiction, you have your withdrawal too."

Mary – "Oh yeah, that's true. There is sometimes a pretty heavy come down from the Lifestyle, especially when the experience is really spectacular. The more high the high, the more low the low."

Barry – "That's really true, you're right."

Mary – "Gawd, that makes us seem kind of pathetic, doesn't it?"

Barry – "Oh, I don't know, I don't think it's that much different than being really into sports. It's like my brother who lives and dies by an NFL team. Every time they win, he is just the happiest, lightest guy on the planet. When they lose, it is like someone shot his dog. When the season is over, you can tell he is suffering from withdrawal because he is just so apathetic and listless."

Mary – "I'm not sure if I'd rather be compared more to a junkie or your brother."

Barry – "He's not that bad."

Mary – "Really? Do you remember that conversation where he told me how good I looked in a skirt and he wished his wife looked more like me?"

Barry – "Oh, yeah, I kind of blocked that out of my memory bank."

Mary – "And they call us perverts."

Barry – "So, um, getting back to it. I think you could call the Lifestyle a habit which some people let develop into an addiction. Like any other habit or even hobby, it consumes as much of your life as you let it. For us, yeah, we spend a good deal of time and money on our habit if you lump in the cruises we take, the weekends we spend at clubs or with other couples, but its money we would spend on other pastimes if it weren't the Lifestyle. Its nothing I would see as inordinate."

Mary – "But we do have to keep each other in check. That rush you get from scoring with a new couple can be very alluring, so it's easy to become obsessed."

DRAWBACKS

Barry – "There are definitely some. I assume you're not just talking about getting found out by friends of family, right?"

Mary – "Well, going back to the habit/addiction thing, the Lifestyle is something that your body really becomes reliant on. Sex is a natural process of the body, so if it becomes trained to see the Lifestyle as a necessary element in your sex lives, you become dependent."

Barry – "And you do see that a lot, couples that are going to Lifestyle events or meeting with couples two to three times a week. They go to different clubs every weekend; they are at every house party. I feel sort of bad for them."

Mary – "People don't look at us like that, do they?"

Barry – "I guess they might; you can't really tell what other people think."

Mary – "No, you aren't suppose to say that! You're supposed to say, 'no, honey, of course they don't. We're awesome and everyone wants to be like us.'"

Barry – "Oh, yeah. (Clears throat) No, honey, of course they don't. We're awesome and everyone wants to **** us or be like us."

Mary – "Ooh. Good ad-libbing."

Barry – "Thanks."

TRIGGERS

Barry – "One thing we've struggled with is that you can get into a rut, even in the Lifestyle. You fall into the same group of friends. You will have sex with the same people just because you didn't want to go away empty handed. So, it's good to back away from it all from time to time."

Mary – "Turnover is kind of high too, so if you're gone six months, then about 40 percent of the faces at any club are brand new."

Barry – "Right, and you are more excited by the prospect. So, we try to wait until it feels right to go back into the Lifestyle."

Mary – "Which is usually when one of us is really stressed at work or we're just getting bored of the suburban nuclear family thing. Maybe one of us is depressed and needs a pick-me-up, or we're just plain horny."

Barry – "I will sometimes take on big projects like re-shingling the roof or working on the car, and I

will use the Lifestyle as a reward for finished work."
    Mary – "Kind of like a carrot on a stick?"
    Barry – "Yeah, but instead of a carrot, its *****."
    Mary – (Laughed) "Gross."

OBSESSION

    Mary – "There are plenty of drama couples out there, just way too desperate to hook up. They send out these mass emails to everyone on God's green Earth to see who might want to hook up that weekend."
    Barry – "Who would say 'yes' to that? I'm more selective than that when putting together a softball team."
    Mary – "And you don't exchange bodily fluid with those guys."
    Barry – "Right. Well, depends."
    Mary – "What?"
    Barry – "Nothing." (Smiled)

PROPISITIONING

    Barry – "It's actually pretty easy—much easier than the real world where you are more selective because you are looking for a life mate rather than a **** buddy. If you see someone you might like, you go up and talk to them. If you see their profile online, you send them an email. Pretty simple."
    Mary – "You can tell by their response whether you have a shot. It's either, 'Sounds like fun, when will you be available,' or 'Perhaps. We're kind of busy right now, so its hard to say, but if you see us at such and

such club, come by and say 'hello.'"

Barry – "We all know why we are here, so if you are vibing someone, you just need to ask, 'do we want to take this somewhere else?' It's really straightforward and some people say 'no,' some say 'yes.' It's more like finding tennis partners than lovers."

Mary (in austere British accent) – "Pardon me, but I was ever so curious if you would like to be my luu-vah."

REJECTION

Barry – "Not really a big deal, usually. If it's someone you've hooked up with before, than that stings because you aren't sure why they are saying 'no'."

Mary – "Sometimes they get that silly ass puppy love for another couple and 'oh, we don't want to offend them.' Whatever."

Barry – "Yeah, but also the dynamics in these types of situations are just so complex that it makes it easier to say, 'it's not us, it's them,' because that is actually the case more often than not. There are some couples that just can't handle the Lifestyle, but they like the friends they make, so they just go to the events to socialize."

Mary – "So, you can't worry about it because there is no way of knowing what's really going on in another couple's head."

Barry – "And, the really good thing about the Lifestyle is there are always more fish in the sea."

Mary – "Yup, always a couple new kids just

stepping off the bus into Sex town."

(Barry and Mary laughed.)

Mary – "Speaking of which, have we heard from them?"

Barry – "The farmer couple? Yeah, they texted about ten minutes ago while you were in the bathroom."

Mary – "Score!"

FUN FACT: Breaking the Ice: Addendum
For God sake, stop blabbering on about your children!

The Fishbowl
Part IV

Four and one-quarters days. One hundred and two hours. Six thousand, one hundred twenty Minutes. Three hundred sixty-seven thousand, two hundred seconds.

Michelle loved gas stations. It was an odd thing for her to admit, but there was something cleansing about stopping off at a gas station while in the midst of running from fundraisers to galas to dinner parties where she was forced to snob around with the rest of the wretched elite.

But at a gas station, she got to sift through the entirety of the human condition, albeit briefly. She would insist, every time they stopped, on going inside and buying a pack of gum, getting a bottled water, and maybe, if she really wanted to be crass, getting an Icee, a Slurpy, or whatever frozen concoction that station served.

While inside, she watched the children darting from the candy section to the pastries and back again. She listened to the graveled voice of a long-haul trucker leaning against the coffee pot and discussing the Oklahoma Sooners with a policeman. She smelled the menthol from a pack of cigarettes that a single mother ripped open as soon as the clerk slid them across the counter. As the mother waited for the clerk to run her credit card, she put one cigarette between her lips and let it rest there unlit, a promise to herself.

Michelle wasn't so naïve as to believe that these people had simpler and more beautiful lives than hers. The poor and the middle class had their own complications, but regardless of what her friends in politics and industry believed, the lives of the lower classes were the true foundation of Western civilization.

What happened on the stock market, what did or didn't pass in the Senate, all of that meant less in the grand design than the trials and tribulations of a blue-collar family pouring every ounce of energy into keeping their homes intact until the next payday.

In the end, what happened in the capitol and what the mighty men of commerce decided in closed boardrooms, all of that could be reversed when a new group of rich white men came to power.

What happened to these people who shambled around the gas station aisles could never be undone and their mistakes had no safety nets. Their successes and failures would ripple for generations.

She saw the immediacy all around her, the construction worker who talked about the ***hole who coached his son's baseball team, the grandmother buying candy for her grandsons who were staying over because their mother was in county for unpaid traffic tickets…it all made Michelle's life seem meaningless.

Which was why Michelle loved gas stations.

Well, that and she loved how much Brad hated them, which is why he stood outside, hovering over his roadster as he waited for her to return.

Brad loved the poor when he was asking for a political donation. He was sympathetic with their plight when a camera was around and he deeply understood their pain when he was about to sleep with one of them. But at a gas station he was off the clock, and he liked it that way.

"Michelle!" a voice called from the chip aisle.

Michelle turned from the Slushy machine as if she'd been caught stealing. Mary's face emerged behind bags of Doritos and Funyons.

"Hey, girl, how are you?" Mary chirped, then looked toward a child hidden behind a Doritos display. "Stay there, I will be right back."

"Okay," the child replied wearily, echoed by another child in the candy aisle.

Mary skipped across the store and hugged Michelle, who politely patted Mary's back. Mary's breasts felt like they'd gotten bigger since the last time they'd been together.

"We've missed you," Mary whispered into Michelle's ears.

"We've missed you too."

Mary pealed away and looked on the counter where Michelle had abandoned an empty cup.

"Ooh, you're getting a Slushee?" Mary purred.

"That sounds good, I think I'll get one too."

Oddly relieved to be found out, Michelle took the cup and followed Mary to the whirring machine.

"Brad always gets mad when he sees me with one of these, but Pink Lemonade just sounds so good right now," Michelle said as she pulled the handle. The machine's nozzle pooped coiled pink froth into her cup.

"I'm a Mountain Dew girl," Mary shrugged.

"You don't say," Michelle smirked, to which Mary slugged Michelle in the shoulder and whispered, "Bitch."

"You look nice, by the way," Mary continued as she topped off her drink. "Where are you headed?"

"A fundraiser at the Oklahoma City Museum of Art," Michelle answered, waiting until Mary had turned her back before she mixed Watermelon into the Slushee. A "suicide Slushee" was just much more declassee than a regular Slushee.

"Really, is it a new exhibit?"

"No, it's this beer thing they do every year," Michelle said, quickly stirring up the two colors so no one could tell. "You get to drink beer all night and look at fine art."

"Ooh, that sounds fun. Wish I didn't have Thing One and Thing Two over there, otherwise I'd come with you."

"Mom, he just hit me," a voice howled from the chip aisle.

"Oh my God, I don't care!" Mary howled back. "Just stop being retarded for a few minutes and we will go in a little bit."

"Told you," another child's voice murmured.

"So," Mary purred, then leaned in close. "Are you guys going to the Rumormill this weekend?"

Michelle shrugged as she took a sip of the Slushee.

"Well, even if you don't, we should get together again," Mary continued. "It's been too long."

"You know," Michelle smiled. "It has. I'll see if we can make it out on Saturday. It would be nice to catch up."

"Good." Mary beamed and then kissed Michelle on the cheek.

She held up her Slushee and Michelle tapped her Slushee against it.

"To liberation!"

"To liberation," Michelle echoed with a blushing smile.

"All right, you heathens," Mary called to the children. "We're going home. Whoever is not in the car in thirty seconds rides home in the trunk."

"Cool, really?" a child exclaimed.

Michelle listened to the flip-flopped feet clap their way to the counter as Mary paid, and then clap out the side entrance. On the front side of the station by the pumps, Brad was holding his wrist up in the air and pointing at it, indicating they were running late.

Mary held up her Slushee and then took a drink, indicating that she didn't care.

"Is that all for you?" the clerk asked behind the register. "Maybe some chips to go with that?"

"You know, I think I will."

Michelle was already crunching away on generic salt and vinegar chips when she returned to the car where Brad waited, impatiently drumming his thumbs on the steering wheel.

He reached over the side consol and pushed opened the passenger side door for her.

"Thank you."

"Just hurry," Brad grumbled. "I have a lot of people I have to glad hand tonight."

"Sexy."

Brad inadvertently chuckled, but frowned again as he glanced over at the chips and Slushee.

"Really? Couldn't wait until we got real food at the museum?"

"Nope," she replied, then crunched on another chip. "Did you see Mary of Barry and Mary? She was in the store with her kids. She says 'hi.'"

"How's she?" Brad asked, half-listening as he whipped through the parking lot and out onto the road.

"Good. I think her boobs got bigger. She invited us out to the Rumormill this weekend and I think we should go."

"Hmm."

"What? You love clubs."

"I do, but if we want to hook up, we really should hook up with the couple you offended at the party. I think they'll be at the museum tonight."

Michelle's skin crawled and anger brimmed, but she managed to lower it to a simmer.

"We can always do that later, maybe after Sunday," Michelle said, managing a light tone. "But I'd really like to catch up with Mary, see who all is still kicking around that place. Can we go—please?"

Brad sighed, glanced over and then patted her on the thigh.

"I spoil you."

—

Four and one-sixth days. One hundred hours. Six thousand minutes. Three hundred sixty thousand seconds.

What amused Michelle the most about the annual beer function were the faces on all the pampered upper-crusters that hadn't tasted beer since last year's event. Whether craft beer or fine art, they understood that they were expected to appreciate the nuances, the different tastes, the sensations. In reality, it all tasted like Milwaukee's Best to them.

They sipped on their plastic cup, cringed for a millisecond before they instinctually returned to a plastic smile. They looked down at the beer contemplatively and let other people explain why they liked the beer they just drank.

It wasn't just the proper women in their thousand-dollar cocktail dresses, either. It was the old men in their expensive sweaters who only drank single malt scotch at the country club. It was the baby bird attorneys who weren't sure how to act in civilized society yet, so instead mirrored everyone else around them.

There were also hipsters, which was the function's saving grace in Michelle's opinion. People gave the hipsters such a hard time these days, but Michelle loved them.

True, they tended to be pretentious assholes and reformed nerds who use obscurity as a class distinction, but Michelle loved to listen to them talk about art and music the way rich people talk about business and politics. She loved that they wore interesting t-shirts and shoes painted by weird and exciting young artists.

They were who she could have been had she not married into politics. And they genuinely tried to understand beer. True, they did this because craft beer is fashionable, but Michelle still liked listening to them talk about the stouts, the Belgian wheats, and the origins of the IPA. She liked how they tried to out-do each other with obscure facts and trivia.

She liked how they didn't at all fit in, but didn't care.

Perhaps those cute girls in the tight jeans and dozens of small buttons on their jackets would grow into the same calculating women as their mothers, but at that moment, they were young, vital, and beautiful.

Sadly, hipsters generally can't **** to save their lives, but it can't always boil down to sex.

"So, what do you think?" a redheaded hipster asked her while they loitered by the table of a local brewery.

He smiled in an awkward, toothy way indicative of a man who's just learned how to be cocky. He was still not entirely comfortable striking up conversations with beautiful women, but was toying with his newfound sense of moderate attractiveness and relative cool.

She found men like him kind of precious, which then made her feel old.

She studied his vintage t-shirt, his fitted over-shirt, and his designer jeans; they all seemed a little too coordinated. There was a woman out there somewhere who dressed him tonight.

It was charmingly juvenile.

Michelle raised her half-full cup of a hefenweiser, took another drink and swished it around her mouth.

"It's complex for something as light as it is," Michelle said. "It has a bit of a honey finish on it, but still savory. I like it."

He smiled thoughtfully, perhaps surprised that she had an answer. She began to think that they'd met before.

"Somewhere in the other room, there is this Kaiser beer from Avery that is just insanely hoppy," the man replied. "It was almost painful, but I've had the same beer after it's been aged for a year, and it turns into this gorgeously smooth beer with hints of lemon. The alcohol content is still pretty crazy, but the hops have really settled."

"Really? Sounds good," Michelle replied.

"It was."

On cue, Brad emerged with his trademark smile that had flashed on political mailers for decades.

"What are we drinking?" Brad asked as he finished off the last of his ale.

"Hefenweiser from over there," the man replied, nodding.

Also on cue, a strikingly beautiful brunette with tattoos peaking out the sleeves of her cocktail dress approached and slipped her arm through the man's.

"Hey, honey, there is a chocolate stout over there that is awesome," the brunette said, punctuating "awesome" with devil horns in the hand not holding the dark beer.

"Nice, I'll make my way around."
"We've met, haven't we?" Brad asked.
"Maybe, my name is Will. This is my wife, Elena. I'm a writer and she's a hair stylist, and we tend to get around to a lot of the art events."
"No, I don't think that's it." Brad smirked as he traded a knowing look with Will, who in turn just seemed confused.
The confusion melted away as embarrassed recognition replaced it. He rebounded quickly.
"You were at the table with the OU fans; I think the guy coached a football team or something?" Will said.
The brunette wife caught on and laughed as she reddened slightly.
"Gary and Lynn," Michelle said. "Gary coaches for a semi-pro team as a hobby."
"Well, there you go." Will smirked, holding up his cup and they tapped their glasses together.
Michelle still didn't remember Will and his mystifyingly beautiful wife. She could tell by the way Brad was measuring up Elena that he hadn't slept with her yet, so clearly she hadn't missed much.
"Don't worry," Brad whispered, leaning in. "We won't let on. We've got more to lose than you, I assure you."
"Peace through mutually assured destruction is a wonderful thing," the wife said, and Michelle could tell by Brad's gaze that he was in love.
Fortunately for Michelle, Brad's love lasted from the moment he met someone to the point that he orgasmed, so Michelle had nothing to worry about as long as the tattooed girl put out.

But this was not the place for Brad's bedroom eyes, and Brad knew it too. So, after tasting a few beers, Brad pulled a few strings and got a security guard to let them go up onto the museum roof terrace.

"They've never been up here before," Brad boasted to the disinterested guard while they rode the elevator to the top floor. "It's so beautiful that it's worth getting a little chilly to see, don't you think?"

"Sure," the guard yawned as the doors slid open. "But I'm needed back downstairs. Will you be okay?"

Brad was already halfway out the door when he turned and pressed a hundred-dollar bill in the guard's hand.

"We'll be fine, but I'm not sure if it'll be a good idea to let anyone else up," Brad warned, and the guard smiled in agreement.

The terrace had one long bar, which only operated during the more temperate months. The museum had built the overlook the length of the outside wall to pack in contributors.

Wind whipped along the terrace as a hazy mist began settling on the city. The lights were off, leaving plenty of shadows for the two couples to hide in.

As if it were choreographed, the group paired off with Brad leading the tattooed wife over to the railing and Will sitting down on a bench hidden from the wind. Michelle sat appropriately far away, waiting for Brad to make his move before she made hers.

The young couple was a curious pairing in Michelle's estimation. For someone as striking and interesting as Elena to fall for someone like Will, the man must have plenty of money or she may have kids and judging by how fresh the paint seemed on Will's new persona, the kids likely weren't his. Trophy wives were nothing new, of course, but Will didn't strike her as the type.

Brad already had his finger tracing along the woman's back as he studied a tattoo on her shoulder. He hated tattoos on women, but was also good at faking interest.

"Do you paint?" Will asked.

The question took her completely off guard and she stammered for a response.

"Yes," she finally smirked. "Why do you ask?"

"I think I remember seeing you at an opening," Will replied. "It was at the IAO Gallery, but we didn't talk. You were there with some portraiture work. I wanted to compliment you at the show, your lines specifically, but I couldn't ever catch you alone."

Michelle warmed, slightly embarrassed, as if she'd just been exposed, but also satisfied that someone remembered her work. She often feared her work was sorely forgettable.

"You liked the lines?"

She was surprised at how fragile her voice sounded.

"You have good technique, nice and clean. I was a little surprised that you only had portraiture there. Is it your primary format?"

"Why do you ask?" Again, a slight tremble. She felt so childish.

"There seems to be a bit of a self-conscious edge to the way you draw faces," Will responded. "I'd like to see what you did with something a bit more meaty…well, not meaty in a vulgar way, but…you know what I mean?"

Michelle smiled and ducked her face away.

"Thank you. I can't believe I don't remember you."

"We haven't actually talked. I met your husband at one of the clubs, but don't remember you being there. A shame..."

He touched her lips with his index finger. "But here's for making up for lost time."

They kissed. A soft, electric kiss. She wasn't expecting this approach from him, and maybe he knew that. Maybe he was a bit more slick than she'd anticipated.

"You're pretty good at reading people," Michelle said, bringing her eyes back on Will.

"Do you think I'm manipulating you?" Will asked.

"Yes."

Will smirked. "Do you like it?"

"Yes."

—

After the initial burst, the group had huddled together on a bench. Will and his wife were very attentive to Michelle. They were cuddlers, lots of talking, lots of petting, lots of kissing. Will and his wife kept talking about her art, kept asking to see more. If it weren't for Brad and his stupid fundraising, Michelle would have taken the couple home to show them the work Brad wouldn't let her show to anyone else.

To ensure that no one would stumble upon the scene unfolding on the roof, the security guard had turned off the elevator. Unfortunately, he'd also forgotten about them.

    Will and his tattooed wife volunteered to take the fall and called up the museum to admit they'd snuck onto the roof and needed someone to send up the elevator. Brad and Michelle would hide in the shadows and wait for the elevator to be sent back up for them so they could discreetly sneak back into the party.

    No headlines, no rumors.

    It was decided that in return for their favor, the two couples would meet up on Saturday for dinner, drinks and a trip out to the Rumormill.

    It didn't initially register that it would likely be Michelle's very last night of sexual escapades, but when she thought about it later, it seemed a nice culmination.

    "I like them," Brad said while they hid in the shadows. His hand ran between her legs and up her thigh.

    "I do too. I'm really looking forward to Saturday."

    "I like our life," Brad whispered, and then kissed her on the neck.

    "It has its moments."

FUN FACT: Poaching
Because danger is a central ingredient to the allure of the Lifestyle, it is tempting for couples to poach within their normal lives. Starting a fling with a single male or female is particularly destructive since the new playmate might not be capable of putting the relationship into proper prospective, and that's when rabbits begin appearing in boiling pots of water.[26]

A Charmed Life
Part IV

I kept my eyes on the road as my hand wandered across the middle consol of the car, and then reached a fingernail to trace, from memory, the pin-up tattoo on Elena's forearm. Goosebumps immediately rose on her skin as she shivered and giggled.

"God, I'm just so keyed up right now," Elena gasped. "I cannot wait to get you home to do dirty things to you."

"That was fun. How was he?"

Note to prospective Lifestylers:
This is the first question after any experience, and it is not an honest request for information, but a test. Knowing how to navigate the truth is critical.

Examples of a proper answer:

---

[26] *Fatal Attraction* reference. Required viewing for would-be poachers.

"Memorable, but not mind blowing."
"The first time is always awkward, but not bad overall."
"He tried to stick his pinky in the no-go hole, but other than that, it was fun."
These answers are positive enough to leave open the possibility of return customers, but are not too glowing.
Examples of improper answers:
"You better be careful or he might just steal me away."
"I wish you'd **** me like that once in my damn life!"
"He reminds me of my dad a little."
"It's like your penis, just bigger."
"If you kissed me like that, I wouldn't have blown your cousin at Thanksgiving last year."
"Finally, a man that knows the difference between a ****** and a hole in the ground!"

So, liken "How was he?" to a bear trap, in that one false step and the aftermath will likely involve you chewing your own leg off.
Elena answered:
"Well, we did have sex on the roof of a major cultural landmark, so it was bound to be great, but he kind of screws like a rich guy. That might be because he is rich, or that it was kind of cold and he was trying to finish quickly."
Well played, ma'am.
"So, how does a rich man screw?"
"Cocky, lots of pounding porno action and not much awareness of whether or not I'm enjoying it.

Plus, if they start getting soft, then they get really defensive like it's your fault."

"Did he?" I asked, hoping for a yes.

"No, rock hard throughout. But I think he takes Levitra or something because he stayed hard afterward too."

She's so good at this.

"Soooo, how was she? She seemed really into the cuddly sex."

The one proper answer:

"Well, she's not as hot as you, but she was fun."

This answer can be tweaked a little, but must always include "not as hot/pretty/beautiful as you."

Improper answers:

"Did you see the size of her ***s? And they felt as great as they looked!"

"It's been so long since I've had a decent blowjob that I almost forgot what it felt like."

"So that's what a vagina feels like before squeezing out two kids."

"She kind of reminds me of my mom."

I went with:

"When I sleep with someone like that, it makes me realize how lucky I am to have you. She's pretty and interesting, but she's just not as gorgeous as you or as fascinating as you and she isn't as self-confident as you are sexually."

See that? I spent one whole paragraph describing how great Elena is so I could follow up with this:

"I think she would be more fun in a bed when I have a little more time to get to know her body and what she likes. I also think she's holding out on her art too. I bet she's got some stuff packed away that she doesn't want anyone to ever see, but is probably pretty interesting."

"Maybe. We'll see if we can dig it out of her," Elena replied as we exchanged a fist bump. "I think Brad would be more fun in a club situation. He seems to be an exhibitionist, so maybe limiting prolonged exposure might be the best way to handle him."

"Saturday should be interesting then."

See, this is the reason we were in the Lifestyle. These times were just so great. We were Bonnie and Clyde, roaming the countryside, robbing banks and running off with the farmers' daughters.

We were a team and it was exhilarating.

We hit a dive bar on the way home and shot a few games of pool. I noticed her goosebumps return a few times without her even being touched. She flirted with the bartender and leaned over further than she had too when she lined up her cue stick. That made a pair of college guys fumble for quarters as they quickly claimed the pool table next to ours.

It was cute and Elena was eating it up. She was so fun like this that I'd quickly forgotten about the previous therapy session were she accused me of shutting down emotionally. If only we could just freeze the relationship at this moment, then it would be perfect.

I could be here with this goddess, showing her off to the world, showing that Will Weinke was capable of landing this marvelous prize. She was so fun when she was my trophy, my status symbol, my proof that I was no longer the nerd that ducked my head in high school and sped through the hallways as quickly as I could so bullies didn't have a chance to corner me.

But Elena was not a trophy, she was a woman. She was complicated, and even though she was riding a high right now, that tide would settle back into the ocean. When it did, she would be left with all the wreckage that been washed ashore.

We paid our tab and stopped off at an all night sushi place near our house.

"You know, I think Brad used to be a politician," I said as we surveyed the various fish, shrimp and octopus on display.

"I thought so too, but wasn't really sure and didn't want to ask."

"I think I remember that at the exhibition where I'd seen her work, someone had said he'd been a senator or something. I think he retired a while back," I said. "There was something about taking kickbacks or something."

"Not really that plugged into local politics, but maybe I'd recognize his last name if we knew it."

I bumped her in the shoulder and then leaned into whisper in her ear.

"Ha, you had sex with someone whose last name you don't know."

"Like that would surprise anyone," she smirked.

"And he's retired. Did he have old man balls?"

"Nah, they were like yours, just bigger."

———

Happiness is stumbling through the front door, kicking the babysitter out, slipping off your shoes, grabbing your kids' bowl of leftover Halloween candy and then finding a zombie movie on television you've never seen before.

Good zombie movies are broken down into three categories:

1. Gloriously campy and thoroughly self-aware. Examples: *Shaun of the Dead*, "*Zombieland, Night of the Living Dead Part 2*, and *Dead Snow*.[27]

2. Intense, serious and with a message. Examples: *Night of the Living Dead*, and *28 Days Later*.

3. Gloriously campy, completely unaware of how awful it is and tethered to a half-baked message. Example: *Plan 9 from Outer Space*.[28]

The zombie movies that go wrong often try to balance between those worlds. "Hey, look how silly we're being, but seriously, listen to our anti-anti-terrorism message."

And how can you go wrong with Dennis Hopper as an ideological dictator of a fortress city surrounded by a zombie hellscape? Well, apparently you can when the ax you have to grind with the Bush administration is bigger than the ax you're using on the zombies threatening your city/state.

So, we cozy up with piles of fun-sized candybars and single-serving Twizzlers to watch some brain-chomping goodness. Only problem is I understand

---

[27] Foreign flick about Nazi zombies!
[28] Though what that message was, the world will never know…unless Ed Wood came back to life as a zombie! Get on it, Hollywood!

that the formula is working against me tonight. The formula is a simple way to determine proximity of a come down from a particular swinging escapade.

In this formula, X represents the time that the initial affects of the come down can be identified. Y is the normal time it takes for a comedown to occur = two nights after said event. I represents the intensity of the event. D represents the danger level of the event.

So:

$X = (I + D) - Y.$

The intensity level was fairly high, but there wasn't much build up. It was very quick from meeting to orgasm, so won't count the same way as a more drawn out, but equally intense experience.

The danger level was pretty spectacular. Thus, by my calculations, Elena would begin fretting about the night's adventures before we even got to bed. So, I needed to head it off before that train got a chance to really start rolling and then plow through any chance of me catching round two before we call it a night.

Zombie movies help, but only for so long, and from the looks of it, the heavy handed delivery and preachy metaphors mean I need to get a hustle on damage control.

"So, it's a good thing we went to the roof," I ventured.

"Why's that?"

"Well, it was 9:00 p.m. on a weekday downtown, the building is too tall to see the roof from the street and there definitely wasn't anyone in the surrounding office spaces, so it was a relatively safe place for something like that."

"Huh, maybe you're right."

Her tone was lighter than I anticipated. Maybe my calculations were off.

"Kind of liked that he was Johnny on the Spot with the condoms too," I continued. "Makes me think they're just as worried about the crotch rot as we are."

"Or they do this so much they just assume they'll get laid wherever they go. Then God knows what they're carrying around with them."

Dammit! Walked right into that. Stupid Will!

"I don't know. If he is a politician, he's probably pretty cautious about just slinging his **** around in public."

"Oh yeah, 'cause you never hear about politicians and sex scandals."

Strike two. Maybe I'm just making things worse.

Elena smiled at me.

"I really am okay, Will, but I appreciate what you're trying to do."

"OK."

We fell asleep with the television on, but I heard her rustle in her sheets at 3:00 a.m. She took a few deep breaths, rustled some more and then:

"Are you awake?"

"Sure."

"You don't think they'll try to have us silenced or anything do you?"

"What do you mean, like rubbed out gangsta-style?"

"I'm serious."

I rolled over and lay my arm over her, kissed her on the cheek.

"No, I don't believe we are going to have our

door busted down by secret service because we ****ed an obscure politician and his wife on the top of a museum tonight. You're being silly."

"Really?"

"Yes, oh my God, yes."

"Sorry I'm so crazy."

I kissed her on the lips, squeezed her body and chuckled.

"You're worth every second of it."

I eventually rolled back over to go to sleep. She rustled, sighed.

"Are we bad people?"

—

Getting through the next few days would be a perilous balancing act for me. We'd promised the mysterious couple from the museum rooftop that we'd be meeting them again on Saturday. I did want to know more about the woman. I wanted to give her body a more leisurely drive to see how it handled when we weren't balancing awkwardly on a cement bench.

Elena, on the other hand, was still rattled from the come down and clearly sleep-deprived that morning. Her smile was tight, twisted slightly to show me that she was coping. I hugged her, but she was stiff and impatiently shrugged me off as she walked to the kitchen to get some coffee.

I waited until she returned to the bedroom.

"Do you want me to get a babysitter for Saturday or would you rather we stay home?"

"Let me think about it. We'll discuss when I get

home today, okay?"

"Of course."

She let me hug her momentarily, but then pecked a kiss on my lips and scurried out of the house and off to work.

It's all so fragile, just like dating in high school. Any small tremor could make the whole thing collapse.

A simple, generic email appeared from the anonymous address, "Boatlovers2001." It read:

"Had a great time, thought we connected ;), would love to see you again this Saturday. Let us know if you can make it."

I let the e-mail simmer for a few hours while I worked, but finally the nagging need to respond won out. I typed:

"Should be able to make it about 10:00 p.m. but hinges on babysitting. If we can't, we'll let you know."

That doesn't obligate us. We can still wiggle out if Elena is struggling.

I really do want another crack at the woman, and here is where the Lifestyle gets complicated for younger swingers. There is an allure to new meat that feels a lot like early love, but isn't. It's just a natural obsession that will fade over time, no matter who it is.

Perhaps the obsession with swinging in general will fade as well and my addiction will ease. I am probably just being naïve, though.

And then, around two in the afternoon, Elena texts me this:

"Go ahead and check around for babysitting, but I'd like to talk more about this before we decide to go."

To which I reply:

"OK. By the way, saw a photograph of you from the beer thing at the museum and you looked incredible!"
Twenty minutes later:
"Wasn't taken from the rooftop was it? :)"

FUN FACT: Naked by Nine
House parties are like any other gathering of people: the larger the crowd, the more likely something unfortunate will go down. Sex increases these odds exponentially.

The Ballad of Jerry and Carey/Cynthia/Veronica Part V

    A weightlessness settled on the farm as the child slept soundly miles and miles away at its grandparents' house, leaving Jerry and Cynthia adrift. It was an unnerving restlessness that stirred in both of them, with no sense of urgency, no sense of purpose. They were untethered, at least for one night, and stood like a dog that's slipped its leash, confused and overwhelmed with this new freedom.
    So they lounged back against the porch swing, Cynthia curled into Jerry's arms as the swing creaked listlessly in the wind. The couple had asked for babysitting so they could go to an art exhibit at a gallery in downtown Oklahoma City, have dinner at a restaurant renowned for a discerning wine menu and spend the rest of the night sniffing out the big city society that Cynthia sought to silt herself into.

To do that, they needed to leave the farm by 6:00 p.m., but it was now 8:00 p.m. When Cynthia had started counting up financial expenditures it would take to make the evening go off as planned, she buckled at a final price tag hovering around one hundred dollars.

So, instead of sipping on a full-bodied Argentinean malbec, her fingers were laced around the stem of a plastic wine glass filled with her very own wine, dubbed Film Noir. It was a dark, gentle and dry pinot that wasn't quite ready for its public debut, but fine for a lazy night on the farm.

The bottle sat next to the porch swing, nearly empty. At the moment the bottle had no label, but Cynthia was talking to various artists about commissioning a design. She'd envisioned an illustration of a grizzled detective embracing a smoldering femme fatale, a not-to-subtle reference to Humphrey Bogart and Lauren Bacall.

Elegant and classic, that's how she saw the future of her little winery. Many Oklahoma palates weren't quite refined enough for a dry wine, so the instructor at the community college suggested to also produce a sweeter wine like a blush or a moscato, which he jokingly called, "Chateaux Cashflow."

Cynthia bristled at the idea and refused to produce anything she wouldn't drink. Jerry wasn't terribly concerned either way. He was just relieved she had a sense of purpose to her life and he had never really counted on the winery making money. He planted the grapes for her.

She took another sip and let the wine roll around her mouth for a few seconds before swallowing.

"Just another year, I think," she said, licking her lips.

"Are you sure we don't even want to give a few bottles away as gifts?" Jerry asked while grabbing the bottle and topping off his glass.

"Not yet. I want it to be perfect before anyone else gets their hands on it. A lot of Oklahoma wines have a bad rep, so if we are going to change minds, this wine needs to be perfect so we can just blow people away."

"Makes sense."

Jerry nudged the ground with his foot to rock the swing. Cynthia nestled closer, chuckled and then leaned off of Jerry.

"Mmm, someone is feeling naughty," Cynthia smirked as she reached behind her to rub her hand over Jerry's erection.

"Sorry," Jerry shrugged.

"Oh, that's quite all right. Let's finish our wine and then I'll see what I can do for you."

Jerry gulped down the last of his wine, took Cynthia's glass and downed hers. He then hopped off the swing and jerked her up into his arms as she giggled. He cradled her and carried her across the porch. Cynthia reached behind her and pulled open the door, and Jerry shuffled inside with her giggling and kissing his ear and neck.

He wound through the house to the bedroom, laying her gently on the bed and then kicking off his shoes and unbuttoning his shirt.

"Close the door, please," Cynthia said as she pulled off her shirt.

"Why? We're alone."

"Just…please."

Jerry chuckled and closed the bedroom door, but his hand lingered on the doorknob.

"What's wrong?" Cynthia asked.

Jerry smirked. He felt it too, an air of domesticity, a stifling wholesomeness. There was a mist that sifted through every room and left a trail from their porch all the way across Oklahoma to his parents' house where the child slept. Even when the farm was silent, the child's voice still echoed in their heads.

They were being haunted, not only by their responsibilities as parents, but also by the years of crippling poverty they'd weathered, by the fields and all the million little jobs waiting to be finished and the general unease of serving as Atlases, holding this tenuous world upon their shoulders.

Jerry swiveled back to Cynthia, who was naked and perched on the bed.

"We're leaving," Jerry said with a grin. "I've got a plan."

—

Young parents dread surprise and spontaneity, which is reliably expensive and inconvenient. Every unplanned moment, every unexpected turn of events inevitably results in something negative. This is only compounded by poverty, thus the only surprises are those that involve bills, doctor visits, loss of income, broken transmissions, leaking roofs or late frosts.

But Cynthia and Jerry were no longer young parents clawing for every spare penny, tightening their budget just to find money to repair cars or equipment. Their savings account was respectable, their crops were bursting and their child was approaching relative self-sufficiency.

It was difficult for the pair to make the mental transition though, and that was why Jerry drove his Jeep into the heart of Oklahoma City. Cynthia's finger twiddled nervously as she looked out ahead toward the tall buildings crowding downtown. He hadn't told Cynthia where they were going or what to expect. He'd slipped outside to make a few phone calls and then told her to wear something "nice, but not too slutty."

She flipped him her long, thin, middle finger, but was invigorated by the veiled gesture, almost giddy. She could not remember the last time they'd done something spontaneous without the child. They'd had a few nights in the past year where they'd dropped the child with the grandparents, but the nights were always planned out, nearly to the minute and dreadfully disappointing.

There was the wine bar in Dallas to meet some of their college friends, but everyone else backed out at the last moment and Jerry and Cynthia were left to discuss the child and the farm until they finally made the long track back home.

They'd tried to go to a few wine tasting events, but the conversations they got into were generally uninteresting and the people were old and pretentious.

There had been an erotic art exhibition, which was kind of fun, but they didn't know anyone and had a hard time finding a place to fit in amidst the crowd of artists, scenesters and rich men trolling for young girls with loose morals.

After a few drinks, Cynthia hit the dance floor and a drunk Asian woman emerged from the crowd and latched onto her. For three songs, an audience quickly gathered as they watched the women grow progressively more handsy.

Jerry had that dumb grin on his face, which was cute and reminded her of the little moments she enjoyed at the strip club. She liked it when men looked at her like that, particularly when it was Jerry.

The drunk woman tried to pull Cynthia's shirt over her head, but Cynthia resisted. The woman pouted, then wandered off into the crowd. Jerry and Cynthia lingered while talking to a few different couples who were suddenly very interested in hearing their opinion on the art, and a photographer who wanted Cynthia to model for him. They left the show with their bodies lit up by endorphins.

But that long drive back into the country at night was always sobering, and by the time they hit the front door, the dance floor was just a distant memory and Jerry and Cynthia's thoughts instead turned to the irrigation ditches that had flooded during a rainstorm that hit earlier that evening.

So, to keep another night from being ruined by the haunting responsibilities on the farm, Jerry drove the Jeep deeper into downtown.

―

"We can't afford this," Cynthia gasped as she looked up at the Skirvin Hotel.

The one hundred-year-old building was an

architectural work of art with fourteen floors, three wings and stylized flourishes that looked like a resilient anachronism while flanked by parking towers and glass skyscrapers. The building had been the pet project of an oil tycoon, then had fallen into disrepair before being salvaged during the revitalization of Oklahoma City following the bombing of the federal building.

That violent act seemed to shake the city leaders out of a fog and the city sprang to life afterward. The hotel's bold, art deco design emerged as a symbol of the city leaders' oath to forge onward toward better times.

Jerry saw it as a fitting start to their new life.

The valet opened Cynthia's door and she glanced over at Jerry. Her look was pleading and guilty. She wanted to follow headlong into Jerry's romantic gesture, but the spending fear that lingered from their years of poverty stood between her and the hotel like a judgmental father.

"Baby, I've already paid for the room and there are no refunds," Jerry smirked. "And we don't waste money in this family."

She laughed nervously, took a breath and then stepped out of the Jeep. She thanked the valet and skipped over to Jerry and clutched her arms over his shoulders and kissed him on the cheek.

"I've always wanted to stay here," she whispered.

"Yeah, I know."

The couple walked into the imposing lobby, which had ornate woodcarvings and a towering ceiling that reminded Jerry of the hotel in *The Shining*.

A concierge who correctly guessed that the

couple was new to the hotel led them to the registration desk to check in, and then gave them the grand tour of the hotel. He told them about the fourteen floors, the renovation, and when out of ear shot of management, about the ghost of a maid who'd been impregnated by the first owner of the hotel. She'd been locked on the top floor before jumping to her death and haunting the hotel ever since.

Jerry and Cynthia only spent a few moments in the hotel room before Jerry pulled her back downstairs to get desert from the restaurant and then drinks from the bar.

"We can't afford this," Cynthia insisted while the elevator crept to the bottom floor.

"Money is already spent."

"No, it's not, I'm just..."

Jerry spun toward her, picked her up and pressed her against the wall of the elevator. He kissed her feverishly. He eased her back down to the floor just before the elevator pinged.

She took a few deep breaths and primped her hair as the doors slid open.

"What were we talking about?" she sighed.

"About how great this night's going to be."

She took his hand and squeezed. The world froze as their eyes settled on each other. She let the moment linger before finally whispering:

"Yeah, that sounds right."

—

Jerry told the waiter not to give Cynthia a menu or bring the bill. He didn't want her thinking about money, and he'd already done the math in his head and knew exactly how much money they could comfortably spend.

After leaving the desert plate empty and draining her third glass of wine, the nagging voice was adequately muffled and Cynthia was liberated. The voice would return in the morning after the thrill abated and the alcohol had left her system, but for now, she was floating and Jerry beamed with pride.

They moved to the bar and sat next to a lipstick-red grand piano. Jerry fell into a conversation with a couple around their age. The man talked quickly, almost nervously, but was fun to listen to. He reminded her of the first person she'd slept with and how that man's brain had been so full of ideas that his mouth couldn't work quickly enough to get the flood of words out.

The woman had a girlish bounce to her. They were both teachers and it seemed oddly appropriate that even their names matched.

Barry and Mary, she thought. *So ridiculous it is just cute.*

They discussed politics, then the men argued sports while Mary and Cynthia discussed fashion and wine. They wanted to know about Cynthia's winery. Starved for adult conversation, Cynthia talked for longer than she'd intended. They politely, even eagerly, listened. It felt glorious to be able to boast about something, even if it was her silly little vineyard and one batch of drinkable wine.

"But next year is the year," she said. "I can feel it."

"Well, you need to get us a bottle when they are

ready, I'd really like to give it a try," Mary said with a smile.

"Yeah, we should have you over," Cynthia burst, then motioning to the bartender for a refill on her wine. "Jerry, we should have them over. Oh wait, it'd be Jerry, Barry and Mary!"

Cynthia laughed.

"I'll go by Carey and we'll be a matching set!"

The couple laughed politely, traded knowing glances. Jerry caught the exchange, but Cynthia, still laughing as the bartender tried to fill her shaking glass, was oblivious.

Cynthia finally settled, looked at her now full glass of wine and leaned back in the chair.

"Honey, you're going to need to kill this," Cynthia said. "I've officially had too much."

She leaned forward and put her hand over Mary's.

"I'm sorry if I'm being obnoxious, but seriously, we'll have you over sometime," she said, then squeezing Mary's hand and letting it linger.

"Absolutely, sweetie," Mary smiled.

A thick silence swept over the group as Jerry finished the glass of wine and then walked to the bar to tab out. Barry followed and the pair chatted about sports as they settled the bill.

"Are you guys staying in the hotel?" Cynthia finally asked Mary.

"Oh no, we couldn't afford a room here," Mary laughed, finishing her cocktail and then chewing on a piece of ice.

"Neither can we, but we are splurging since we have babysitting tonight."

"Good for you," Mary replied, then crunching on the ice. "How are the rooms?"

"Oh, wonderful! Just exquisite. Do you wanna see?"

"Um, sure," Mary said, then looking over to Barry. "Hey, honey, do we have time to look at their room?"

"We've got plenty of time," Barry called back while stuffing his wallet back in his pocket.

"That settles it, darling," Cynthia chirped. She stood, took Mary by the hand and tugged her to her feet.

The evening suddenly flowed in one direction as if fated. The couples assembled into the elevator with the two girls clutching hands and flanked on either side by the opposite husband.

They filed into the room and perched on the bed, chatting about progressively more risqué subjects until, inevitably, strip clubs arose. Flushed with wine and endorphins, Cynthia admitted to spending a few months spinning on poles. Mary and Barry promptly perked up. Mary insisted on a demonstration.

Silence settled in the room. Cynthia bit her lip and traded a smile with Jerry. Jerry nodded his head.

"Do you mind if I use your man?" Cynthia asked.

Mary blushed and smiled wide.

"Be my guest."

Cynthia gently nudged Barry's knees apart.

Mary took the cue and walked over to Jerry and sat on his lap while they watched Cynthia slowly strip down to her bra and panties. She wound her body all around Barry, and after briefly pausing to exchange a silent agreement with Jerry, she took off her bra.

—

Barry and Mary left a few hours later, condom wrappers strewn in their wake. Fortunately Mary had enough in her purse for both men to use two each, which unnerved Jerry in hindsight.

Cynthia's body was still warm as she curled against him. She would shiver every few minutes, purr and squeeze against him.

"I can't believe how fun that was," Cynthia finally whispered.

They made love and Cynthia's body seized in the midst of a powerful orgasm. She quickly fell asleep afterward and when the couple finally emerged from their hotel room at noon, just in time for check out, they were latched arm in arm and Cynthia only let go when the valet opened the passenger side door for her.

They raced home to the farm to have one last romp in their bed and then shower before the grandparents would arrive with the kid.

As Jerry stood in the bathroom, naked with a face-full of shaving cream, Cynthia hugged around his back. She kissed his shoulder and then leaned her lips to his ears.

"Please, please, please can we do that again?"

FUN FACT: The Life of a Lifestyle Club
Like a small music venue, Lifestyle clubs are born and flourish through the will power of one or two dedicated individuals. Because few clubs are money-making endeavors, the venue will only survive so long as its figurehead endures.

Superswingers
Part V

Three days after the first interview at the Rumormill, Barry and Mary resumed the interview at their home in a bedroom community tucked into northwest Oklahoma City. Due to time constraints, the couple could only section out time after the kids had come home for school, so the conversations were often interrupted as they listened for footsteps approaching and then passing the door of the game room where we talked.

Barry kept the television turned to a football game with surround sound speakers blasting to drown our voices. While playing pool, Barry's hands seemed to shake from nerves.

Unlike her husband, Mary seemed oddly at peace discussing the Lifestyle in their home, even ignoring Barry as he hushed her until the kids' footsteps faded to the other side of the house.

FIRST TIME

Mary – "Blech! It was just as bad as my actual first time, no offense."

Barry – "None taken."

Mary – "And really, neither time was Barry's fault, and he knows that. You know that right?"

Barry – (Struck the cue ball to break, waiting for the balls to stop clacking together) "Yup."

Mary – "The real problem was me, both times. You see, Barry was my first and only for a really long time. When he took my virginity, it hurt like it's supposed to, I guess, but I was really trying to pretend I was really enjoying it. I wanted him to think I was sexually sophisticated."

Barry – "I'd had a few sexual partners before her; I'm a little older than her. We waited for six months before we had sex."

Mary – "Right, so I really wanted to make it worth his time. So I watched a couple of those softcore pornos you can get at the video store. So, here I am, my ***** hurts, but I'm trying to power through and trying to change positions like they did on the pornos. Only problem is, those positions weren't really the actors having sex, it was them pretending to have sex so the angles were all wrong. I thought it was weird because my vagina wasn't in the middle of my back, but I also wasn't entirely sure what the penis was all about, either."

Barry – "So she was yanking at me like she was milking a cow, trying to bend me around like a bendee straw. (Shot again, missed and cussed under his breath.) Eventually I just had enough."

Mary – "Poor guy. So, I didn't know what was going wrong, but I knew it was my fault and I just started crying. And when I say 'crying,' I mean totally breaking down, and by the way, we're in his car. So, I'm trying to do all these impossible positions while also trying to squeeze around his Ford Escort."

Barry – "It was pretty atrocious."

Mary (Laughing) – "So, then I'm just sitting there, sobbing and naked as a newborn baby."

Barry (not laughing) – "And then."

Mary (laughing harder) – "And then who shows up? The police."

Barry – "We'd parked at this clearing off the road where I used to go drinking when I was a kid. It was about 2:30 a.m."

Mary (laughing to the point tears are dripping from her eyes) – "And, and, and you were twenty-one and I was eighteen."

Barry – "Naked and crying."

Mary (tried to settle, but begins laughing again)

Barry – "I tried to get her dressed before the officer got to the window, but it just wasn't happening."

Mary – "And it only gets worse now, because I'm freaking out because I really know I have to stop crying because I don't want Barry to go to jail, which makes me cry more."

Barry – "He took me back to his car, called a female cop, and we're there talking to the cops until 4:00 a.m. when they finally drive her to her dorm room, call her parents and then take me to the station to fingerprint me."

Mary – "Thank God they didn't charge you with

anything."
 Barry – "Not a good night."
 Mary – "Poor baby."
 Barry – "So, fast forward two years."
 Mary (dried her eyes and took deep breaths to keep from laughing.) – "Right, two years later, I'd gotten much better at sex. We'd been talking about the Lifestyle pretty much from the start and decided to try a swing club."
 Barry – "We'd actually gone to strip clubs together. We'd go to one club so she could fondle men and then another so women could fondle me. It was fun."
 Mary – "But expensive and really just a tease, so we decided to try swinging."
 Barry – "We went to a club first off, like the next night after deciding we were going to try it. Really fast."
 Mary – "Too fast, really."
 Barry – "Yeah."
 Mary – "So, we're there and things are going well. I'm dancing, other women come over and dance up against me. I'm not into women, but I like that other men are watching. So, we're really getting into it. I end up blowing a guy in a back room while Barry goes down on the guy's wife."
 Barry – "Should have just ****ed—"
 (Footsteps approached the door. Knocked.)
 Barry – "Yeah?"
 Boy's voice – "What are you doing?"
 Barry – "Playing pool, why?"
 Boy's voice – "Can I play?"
 Barry and Mary – "No!"

Mary – "Go play video games or something honey, we're talking about stuff in here."

Boy's voice – "Fine, whatever."

Barry (Waited for footsteps to fade) – "Should have just ****ed them right there, would have made life easier."

Mary – "But we didn't. We went back to their room."

Barry – "It was actually fun for the first bit. She went down on me and the guy was getting off on watching her."

Mary – "But…"

Barry – "Yeah, but…"

Mary – "He was having problems getting ready, which happens. I know that now, but you have to remember, I'd only been with Barry and he never had those issues unless he was really drunk."

Barry – "But I've had issues while in the Lifestyle too from time to time. Every guy does."

Mary – "Yes, but I didn't know that. I just thought this guy didn't think I was sexy. I was just a few years removed from being an awkward girl that dressed awful. Sure, I had a rockin' body, but I'd only just then started to know what to do with it. So, I thought he couldn't get hard because he didn't like me."

Barry – "So she started crying, which didn't exactly help the situation."

Mary – "So then everyone in the room is trying to calm me down. Barry actually had to stop before he was done."

Barry – "Couldn't exactly carry on while my wife was having an emotional breakdown."

Mary – "Naked and crying. Story of my life."

Barry – "And we moved. Not just from the hotel room, but we packed up, found jobs in a new city and moved entirely."

Mary – "Perhaps an overreaction, but yes, we moved. Fast forward a few years, we are now happy and well-adjusted swingers."

Barry – "But we go out of our way to make sure every newbie we run into has a good time, even if they can't get their flag to raise."

SALVAGING

Barry – "There really isn't much you can do aside from make do. If a guy can't maintain an erection, then he probably can't use a condom, and if he can't use a condom then he isn't getting anywhere near my wife's vagina."

Mary – "I'll spend a good deal of time going down on him, cause he really has to be drunk or nervous to not get an erection during oral sex. So, he'll still get his even if I don't get mine."

Barry – "And if you're the guy having the issues, you just make it seem like nothing is happening too."

Mary – "Which isn't too far from the truth."

Barry – "Yeah. You just have to know that sometimes it doesn't happen. No amount of fluffing is going to solve that. But, you go through that once and then you are at the urologist the next week to make sure it doesn't happen again. I have a renewable prescription of the all-weekend pill and it is just a huge load off."

Barry's pocket binged and he retrieved a cell phone. He tilted it so he could see the name on the

screen.
    Barry – "Speaking of devils."
    Mary – "Who is it?"
    Barry raised his hand to his mouth to conceal the name he was mouthing to her. He then lifted the phone to his ear.
    Barry (into phone) – "Hey, how are you?"
    Mary – "Say 'hi' for me."
    Barry nodded and then walked to the door, opened it and disappeared into the hall.
    Mary – "So, what do we want to do now? Wanna see my tits?"
    Mary laughed and stood to walk to the fridge.
    Mary – "Want anything to drink?"
    Barry re-emerged from the hall, closed the door behind him and then walked to Mary. He whispered in her ear.
    Mary – "My God. When?"
    Barry whispered again and then they hugged. They were silent for at least two minutes. Mary began to cry. She wiped the tears from her eyes and sat down.
    Mary – "Sorry."
    Barry and Mary sat down next to each other, their fingers laced in each other's hands. Mary tried to smile, but they were both visibly shaken.
    Mary – "Sorry, sorry. Is there anything else?"
    Barry – "We just found out that we lost one of our friends."
    Interviewer – "One of your friends from the Lifestyle? Would you like to talk about it?"
    Barry and Mary exchanged glances.
    Barry – "Perhaps we should finish the interview

another time."

FUN FACT: Freelancing
Freelancing is when one member of a couple plays independent of the spouse. Policies of freelancing vary. Many couples prohibit freelancing entirely, but even couples that allow extracurricular activities still monitor freelancing activities very closely.

The Fishbowl
Part V

Three and three-quarters days. Ninety hours. Five thousand, four hundred minutes. Three hundred twenty-four thousand seconds.

Vigor shone in Michelle's eyes when she woke the next morning. The surge of vitality wasn't a prolonged afterglow so much as a realization that, with only a handful of days left in her mortal existence, there was simply nothing left to hold her back.

Sure, the sex from the museum was fine. The hipster whose name she'd already forgotten was surprisingly good. He had a big chip on his shoulder, so he went above and beyond to attend to her. A little too desperate to please, but still good. Very teachable.

Oddly, it was the man's shirt that got her renewed sense of purpose bubbling. The shirt said "The Evangelicals," and she had no idea who that was aside from just another obscure band she wished she knew.

So, she decided it would be her mission to find out who The Evangelicals were, acquire an album and listen to it repeatedly to figure out why the man felt it necessary to wear the t-shirt to the museum. She vowed to do this before she died.

Then she realized she also had time to delve into other things. She probably had time to find some pot somewhere. Brad had been the junkie of the marriage, always uppers like cocaine and speed. She never had much use for a drug that made the world go faster, but was curious about a drug that made things quiet for once. So, that was Mission Number Two.

And, she could paint whatever she wanted. Problem was, she had no idea what she wanted to paint in the next three days. That was Mission Number Three.

In addition to these primary missions came several curiosities that her newfound sense of freedom finally opened up.

She could go to any dive bar she drove by. She could purchase and drive a motorcycle. She could ride a roller coaster. She could skydive. Hell, she could go to confession if the urge caught her right.

She had hundreds of thousands of dollars at her disposal and over three days to live. There was nothing left to stop her.

This was why she woke with a smile on her face as Brad lay facedown, drool soaked into the covers with his naked and pimpled ass exposed to the world.

She could also take a picture of that, because she thought it was funny and he was sleeping too deeply to know the difference.

Michelle slid out of bed, tiptoed to her purse and

pulled out her cell phone, which had a camera function.

Click.

The image came out well enough, but camera phones were so unreliable.

That's another thing she could do, buy a real camera and document everything she did during her farewell tour.

Mission Number Four: create a travel log to the afterlife.

She disappeared into the walk-in closet and sat down as she stared at the rows of blouses, slacks, shoes and dresses.

"What does one wear when they have three days left?" Michelle whispered to herself. "Nothing too drab, nothing too bright. Something sexy?"

Michelle stood and walked to a black cocktail dress that always hugged her butt perfectly. Sure, she would seem out of place walking around town in a cocktail dress, but what did she care?

But she put the dress back. She stepped back, surveyed the clothes once again and then smiled. She then retrieved her favorite pair of jeans and matching pink bra and panties.

Brad still slept like a cardiac victim at a brothel, so she snapped another picture before leaving the room.

On the way out the front door, she grabbed a light jacket and put it on over her bra. Her chest was reserved for a hipster t-shirt which she would find today. Until then, it was only a bra and a jacket.

—

The camera store would have intimidated Michelle a month ago. So much equipment, so many options, so much that she didn't know.

But today, she had an agenda and she had a deep pool of disposable cash.

Twenty minutes later, with eight thousand dollars worth of camera slung on her shoulder and another ten thousand dollars worth of peripheral equipment in the passenger seat of the car, Michelle pulled up to the official starting line on her quest for mortality.

Record stores had seemed archaic when she was a teenager, something destined to be gobbled up first by big box retailers, then by digital music formats, and yet they still stood and endured as the traditional music industry collapsed all around them.

She chose Guestroom Records in OKC because it was where the pretentious rock girl from Brad's charity had said she shopped. Therefore, it was ideal for an out-of-touch rich woman desperate to immerse into all things Bohemian.

The store seemed like cheating as soon as she pulled up. On the front window was a poster for an Evangelicals show later that night.

Amidst the tapestry of other concert posters scattered across the window, she recognized a couple band names that she'd encountered at a fundraising show for the Academy of Contemporary Music. She didn't know anything else about the bands aside from their names since Brad had insisted on leaving seconds after the first band struck the first note of their first song.

"I'd rather hear a cat being raped by a pineapple," Brad grunted as he pulled Michelle back to the car.

The door to the record shop pinged as it opened. A young kid with a mangy beard smiled vacantly, barely looking up from a copy of the *Gazette*.

Michelle raised her camera.

"Can I take your picture?"

"Knock yourself out," he replied gruffly.

She took a picture of the clerk who wore the same wooden expression found on natives who believed the camera was going to steal their souls.

She smiled a "thank you," and then looked across the rows and rows of music. She scanned the walls covered with paintings of album covers, shelves filled with concert documentaries and stickers plastered all over the counter. So many names and she had no idea where to start.

She took a picture.

"Can I help you find something?" the mangy kid yawned.

"The Evangelicals?"

"CDs are on the second aisle, vinyl is in the back."

Michelle liked the thought of vinyl, but wanted something she could listen to in the car. She wound around the aisle and thumbed through the CDs until she finally found three different albums by the band.

"Um?" Michelle called to the mangy kid, who exhaled slightly, lowered the *Gazette* and looked over at her with a labored smile.

"Which album would you recommend?"

"Start with *The Evening Descends*, it's a bit more approachable."

"Okay." Michelle nodded, winked and then grabbed the disc. She took a picture and then walked to the counter. She glanced over at a rack of Guestroom t-shirts and gabbed a lime green small.

"That it?" the mangy kid asked.

"Yes. Well, um," Michelle stammered and the kid gave her the labored smile again. "Sorry, I don't know much about music, but am trying to learn."

"Good for you."

"Yeah, thank you, but I'm not really sure where to start."

The mangy kid leaned back in his chair, laid the newspaper aside and studied Michelle.

"What do you like?" he asked, his mood starting to brighten.

"I don't know."

"Mmm."

"But if you could pick me out five albums that came out in the last couple years that you think are really good places to begin, I'd really appreciate it," Michelle said, giving the kid a warm, girlish smile.

"Are you just going to return them after half a listen, or are you all in?" the man asked.

"I'm all in," Michelle smirked. "More than you'll ever know."

The mangy kid grinned, grunted and stood up without a word. He shuffled around the counter and walked along the aisles, surveying the CDs, picking up a few here and there. She raised the camera to her eye and he flashed an absent thumbs up as he dug through the CD bin with his other hand.

He returned with ten albums and placed them in two stacks on the counter.

"These five are on the louder end with some psychedelic, some dance rock and some really experimental noise. These five are on the softer, coffeehouse end with some indie pop, new wave, that sort of thing," the mangy kid grumbled.

"Wow, okay, I'll take them," Michelle said as she glanced through the CDs.

"All of them?"

"Yes, please."

The kid shrugged and began punching numbers on the register. Michelle placed the camera on the counter, unzipped her jacket and took it off, revealing the pink bra underneath. The mangy kid lifted a subtle eyebrow as she slipped the shirt on. She stood back from the counter.

"How do I look?" she asked.

"Pretty good," he mumbled, returning his focus to the register. "I'd try on the brown though."

"Really?" Michelle asked, walking to the rack of shirts.

"You never know until you try, right?"

"Guess not, you don't mind?"

"Knock yourself out," he grumbled, but stealing a glance as Michelle shed the green shirt and pulled a brown small off the rack. She held it up for a minute, catching the kid's reflection in the window as he stared at her. She smirked and then pulled the shirt on.

"Mind taking my picture?" Michelle asked.

The kid shrugged, grabbed the camera and clicked.

"So, better?" she asked as she swiveled around while he continued to shoot.

"Pretty good, but we have a white shirt too, you should try that on, just to be sure."

"Hmm," Michelle smirked. "I think you just want to see me in my bra."

The mangy kid smirked and looked up from the camera.

"Yes ma'am, I do."

—

With a new lime green t-shirt, eleven albums from ten bands she'd never heard of and one band she only knew of because of the man from the rooftop, Michelle was off to her next emersion into the life of a hipster.

On the way out of Guestroom, she snagged a copy of the *Gazette* to figure out her next stop. She wanted to see some art, but not museum art. She also didn't want to go Paseo to see the work of artists her own age. She wanted to see what the kids were up to.

She pulled off at a park as the Evangelicals spun in her CD player. She stepped out and took photos of children playing on swing sets, but then felt like a stalker so she sat back in her car to listen to *Evening Descends*.

The songs were shimmery and loud, with lots of reverb and echoes. They seemed crazy in a beautiful kind of way. She decided that Mission Number Five would be to see the band play live tonight.

But for now, she thumbed through the newspaper looking for anything interesting she could see right now and it seemed that her next stop would be on 16th Street at The Plaza.

The strip of small galleries, retail shops and cafes had sprouted up around the Lyric Theater as dozens of entrepreneurs flooded the area in hopes that new blood might revitalize the depressed area.
    And one of the stores, DNA Galleries, was featuring a show with painted up longboards.
    "Perfect," Michelle whispered, and she was off.

—

    Three and one-third days. Eighty hours. Four thousand, eight hundred minutes. Two hundred eighty-eight thousand seconds.
    At 4:00 p.m., the dam broke and Michelle curled up in the bathroom of a small storefront gallery, shaken by vicious waves of sobbing tears. Outside, the gallery owner folded her tattooed arms, watched the door warily and wondered if an ambulance would soon be blighting her doorway.
    And it was a song that set her off. "Sometimes," by James, a song she'd heard to the point of exhaustion years ago while she'd had a brief fling with a well-dressed British boy who was waiting out his student visa in Oklahoma.
    As opposed to so many consensual flings where Brad chuckled with amusement as Michelle recounted secretive dates with other married men and hotel escapades with pie-eyed interns from Brad's campaign, Michelle kept this one a secret.
    The kid was a songwriter and claimed that "Sometimes," a song about a boy's refusal to let a rainstorm force him off a rooftop, as well as The Velvet Underground's "Heroine" were the two most

emotive pieces of music in the modern world.

Michelle thought that "Heroine" was droning and pretentious and that "Sometimes" was powerful at points, but overly long.

But when the song had piped through the gallery's speakers, the song captured the lost years of promise that could have been spent lying in the boy's arms and arguing music.

If she had stayed in that bed, she would have been poor, but she wouldn't be staring down the last days of her life.

But she did leave, and now she only had a little time left to clear the moss from decades of inactivity.

The clouds cleared, her tears dried, and she stood and took a picture of the trails of mascara melting from her eyes.

It took a few minutes to clean up, but she felt light and invigorated. And she was off again for Mission Number Three: find her artistic voice before she died.

Outside the bathroom, the punky gallery owner chewed on her lip piercing as Michelle opened the door.

"Are you okay, honey?" the girl asked.

"Yes," Michelle chuckled with a shrug. "Sometimes you just need a good cry to clear the cobwebs."

But there was more frustration ahead. She was fascinated by the tattoo- and graffiti-inspired art proliferating many of the small galleries. She loved the rockabilly throwback pin-ups and was impressed by the subtle artistry of DIY sewing shops, but none of it really spoke to her on the level she'd hoped. It felt like she was winding around the highways of a city, knowing she was close to her destination, but just couldn't find the right turnoff.

She did have Brad's credit card, so she made sure to pile merchandise by the register and never leave a shop empty handed.

Her favorite items thus far had been a longboard with a hand-painted humanoid with a hoody on the deck, a knitted penis-warmer and a toaster with a pin-up homemaker painted on the side covering her breasts with oven mitts. Written underneath was: "Caution: Hot while operating."

The penis-warmer was particularly delicious since she found it in a second hand store, which not only meant that someone had previously owned this and presumably used it, but also was also shameless enough to sell it to a consignment shop.

There was an ick factor, of course, but the elderly woman who owned the thrift store sealed the deal for her. While Michelle was staring at the rainbow-striped warmer on a cabinet full of Catholic-themed knick-knacks, the woman with snow white hair, a gaudy crucifix hanging from her neck, and an oxygen breather in her nose looked over Michelle's shoulder.

"Gee, I just don't know how someone would fit their hand in that thing, but I just thought it was the cutest thing," the old woman said. "I just can't imagine what happened to their fingers. It's just so sad, but I'm glad someone cared enough to make them a mitten."

Michelle stifled the laugh, barely, but did manage to ask if it had been washed.

Still, Michelle felt like she was circling.

Now wearing her latest t-shirt find, which read:

"Oklahoma: we're not all like that," Michelle waited for the old woman to ring up her rainbow-striped specialty mitten when her attention turned to the owner's six-year-old grandson sitting in the corner, nose buried in a comic book. Her eyes lingered on the cover image of a group of zombies with arms reaching out to the viewer, blood trickling down from the sides of their mouths.

After walking out, Michelle dumped the merchandise into the front seat and did a quick search on her phone for "comic book stores."

———

Michelle was always a little embarrassed to admit how much she liked the look of the single-panel comic styled art that flooded the market in the '80s. When given the choice between a master work of abstract or cubist painting, or a send up to the Sunday soap opera comics, she'd take the soap opera every time.

She also acknowledged that she was about two decades late, so if she wanted to try something like that, she would have to figure out how to make it relevant again. The kids loved the '80s these days, for some bizarre reason, so maybe now was the time.

She pushed through the front door of New World Comics and was met by vast rows comic bins. Like the camera store where the overwhelming selection intimidated some, she had an agenda, and her mind was focused like a huntress.

She took a picture.

"Can I help you?" a heavy set man with a

brimming smile called from the counter.

"Yeah, I'm looking for a couple comics," Michelle said. She raised the camera and the man picked up two action figures next to him and pretended to make them fight as she took the picture.

"Well," the man said, while carefully placing the figurines back down on the counter. "We have a few."

The man had a high, raspy laugh. As if he just remembered that his laugh was ridiculous, he swallowed the noise and cleared his throat.

"What are you looking for?"

"I don't know," Michelle grimaced. "I'm actually a painter, and I'd kind of like to play around with comic book format, but not exactly sure what I want to do yet. I'm kind of hoping to get a variety so I can see what all is out there."

The man's mouth twisted as he thought. He stood and walked around the counter and surveyed the rows.

"Come with me," he muttered, and she did. "So, are you going to be doing graphic novels?"

"No, probably just a painting, so I'm looking for really striking artwork."

"Ah."

The man began shuffling around the store as she trailed behind.

"Do you want some anthologies, or just single comics?" the man called.

"I put my faith entirely in your hands."

"Good girl." The man smirked as he walked to racks on the walls.

He scanned the walls, sometimes selecting books decisively, sometimes picking up a book and agonizing before either placing it with the growing stack or putting it back on the shelf.

He worked quickly though, something like a squirrel sifting through a carpet of acorns in hopes of finding the perfect nut.

He finally scooted back to the register, nodding for Michelle to follow. He slapped the stack of comic books and graphic novels on the counter.

"Okay," he chuckled, sifting through the books. "I've got a lot of a little bit of everything. A few classics by Alan Moore and Frank Miller, some Art Baltazaar, *Sandman*, this zombie book called *The Walking Dead*. which I think is just great, a couple indies and then some *Dark Horse*."

"Wow." Michelle smirked as she looked through the comics. "Very thorough."

"Well, this is actually just kind of a springboard." The man shrugged. "I kind of wanted to see what you were into and then maybe really cater to that. There is just so much good stuff out there that we could be here all day."

"I just want a thorough starter kit."

"Yes, ma'am."

The man stepped out from behind the register and sauntered back out to the far wall. Rather than following him again, Michelle veered over to a small rack of shirts and found a child's large Superman shirt. She thumbed through the others in hopes of finding a Wonder Woman or at least Supergirl, but no luck.

She took her Guestroom shirt off and slid the child's shirt on which stretched down just above her belly button.

She looked at her reflection in the window.

Raised the camera and took a picture.
"Perfect."
The man returned with a deep purple blush, and after a few moments of silence, mumbled "looks good on you" as an awkward smile stumbled across his face.

—

Three and one-quarter days. Seventy-eight hours. Four thousand, six hundred eighty minutes. Two hundred eighty thousand, eight hundred seconds.

She tossed her painted canvases out into the hallway. The portraits, her "edgy" nudes, the half-finished sketches, all of it. She would, before she died, burn it all so that her closing statement to the planet would be defined by what she created in those final three days.

Her phone hummed as a call came in, but she ignored it as she had ignored every other call and text message that day. She imagined they were mostly from Catherine, wondering why she wasn't waiting for her in the showers. Maybe it was the Cuban trainer, annoyed his 10:30 hadn't shown up. Perhaps it was Brad, hoping to get a quick **** in before heading to the golf course.

He was in the house when she'd returned home and met her on the staircase. She merely pushed past him as she toted her bags up to her art room and locked the door behind her.

The comics, graphic novels and anthologies were strewn all around her. The penis warmer was sitting in the windowsill as if it was waving to the world. The longboard rested in a corner, and she was determined that she would ride it before her final breath.

The way her agenda was filling up, she needed to come up with a list so she could keep track of it all. She found an empty canvas and in red paint, she wrote:

"Brad, if you touch this, swear to God I will castrate you!

Mission # 1, listen to Evangelicals. Done!
Mission # 2 Chronic
Mission # 3 Paint
Mission # 4 Photojournal
Mission # 5 See Evangelicals tonight
Goals, time allowing:
Divebars
Motorcycle
Longboard
Confession"

She found a hammer and nail in the garage and affixed the sign on the outside of her art room door. Brad walked over, read the first line and quickly shuffled back to his home office and closed the door.

She had two hours before the concert. Two hours to read and formulate what her farewell to the world would look like.

So, she took a photo of the door and then disappeared inside.

FUN FACT: Sustainability
There are no reliable studies into the sustainability of the Lifestyle or its ability to save/destroy a marriage. The average stretch of time a couple remains active in the Lifestyle is roughly eighteen months, making the Lifestyle three times more sustainable then a gym membership.

A Charmed Life
Part V

Is it weird that I pluck the hairs on my back? It would be simpler to shave, I suppose, but I keep coming back to an episode of "Seinfeld" where, according to Kramer, shaving one's torso only spurred wilder hair growth.

I gotta think that genetics plays into that more than shaving, but even so, I take a long-handled pair of tweezers to my back once a week just to stem the advancing hair line approaching northward from my butt.

I figure once my pants are off, then a little excess body hair below the belt line won't make a difference. I even try to fade the hairline so it doesn't just look like I was dipped in wax headfirst, stopping abruptly before my bathing suit area.

I've become increasingly vain since entering the Lifestyle. Before, Elena hounded me on maintaining my appearance. Once the prospect of being seen naked by strange women entered the scenario, I took it upon myself to sculpt the best possible version of myself. Charm only gets you so far when your back looks like a dog with mange.

It started with some self-tanner to dim my blindingly pale skin, then a concerted effort to hit the gym on a regular basis. I didn't want to get huge, just tone up a bit. Then came wardrobe maintenance, meaning if a pair of jeans had a hole in them or a noticeable stain, they must be thrown away. It broke my heart every time, but I must keep a firm line on this, according to Elena.

Finally, I must sculpt a character to play. I based this character on the traits I came to understand as more attractive to the female persuasion. So, rather than being this:

I must figure out a way to convince myself that I actually look like this:

Quite a transformation, no? Of course, the result was a douche bag. I developed short man syndrome and I knew it. Yet, it worked, and suddenly women started reacting to me in a way that was thrilling. They batted their eyes, they quivered when I touched them, they laughed when I knew they didn't really think I was funny.

It was revolting, to be honest, but terribly exciting all the same.

This is why I stopped popping zits and used some medicated moisturizer instead. This is why I begrudgingly submitted to a household ban on ice cream in favor of smoothies and yogurt. This is how I trained myself to scale back on video game play and spend more time outside with the kids. I even play tennis with Charles every once in a while.

The catch is that as I invest all this effort becoming the exact kind of person I made fun of in high school, I also find myself fading from the music scene. I spend less time tracking the growth and death of pop culture trends, I tune out news and current events, and worst of all, I spend less time writing.

I probably would have cut out writing all together if it weren't my job and if I didn't have Charles continually hounding me about deadlines for the next novel.

So this was inherently temporary. It was a distraction; it was an indulgence; it was an experience to write about.

There were many times when I'd convinced myself that I was done with the Lifestyle, I was done being Mr. Asshole and I wanted to go back to being Will Weinke. I missed my old skin, I missed my integrity and I didn't want to be this person any longer.

And at that moment of clarity, I would come across something like this:

It was an illustration Charles's wife had done a couple years back. Elena was the brunette. She'd modeled for it just after I'd met her. I know this will sound sexist, but so be it. The fact that I now had a girlfriend who could model for something that wasn't on the wrong end of a "Before and After" ad campaign was a stunning victory for me.

So, the effect of rediscovering that image was similar to someone cutting a line of cocaine on the coffee table of a recovering drug addict.

This is how I still envisioned Elena—as this glorious sex goddess who couldn't be confined by an archaic institution like marriage. Picturing her as a mom in a committed monogamous relationship just doesn't do it for me. It wasn't what I signed up for.

Now, even as I realize the damage that this fantasy is having on our relationship and how far I've devolved from the man I was just a few years ago, I still feel that desire tickling the back of my mind.

Because, it's just all so ****ing fascinating, isn't it?

—

The swinger mentality can best be likened to homosexuals before the gay rights movement. Swingers aren't interested in making the world okay with their sexual proclivities. They aren't concerned about changing minds. They just want to be left alone and to crouch beneath the watchful eye of moral institutions.

Unlike homosexuals, swingers have the option to have a relatively fulfilling sexual life in the normal, vanilla world. And, unlike homosexuals, swinger sex is inherently deviant and dangerous, so most in the Lifestyle understand on some level why the rest of the world looks down on them.

It is fun, it can be a positive experience, but is merely a distraction, just like any other vice worth its salt.

With this in mind, I am always careful to stow my deviance before heading out for a night with civilians. This is not as simple as a vow of abstinence. There are a series of subtle behaviors I must constantly ward off such as:

1. Looking women in the eye or allowing my gaze to fall on a woman for more than two heartbeats.

2. Overt casual contact with women.

3. Intentional or unintentional lurid comments.

4. Drinking more than two beers thereby

weakening my resolve to monitor the previous three behaviors.

It also helps that I rarely run into a swinger during office hours, which is why I was taken aback when I saw the woman from the museum leaning against the graffitied wall of the Conservatory with no one talking to her, not sure how to act and a Superman t-shirt stretched gorgeously across her chest.

This woman was a politician's wife, all prim, proper, and despite me bagging her in a public place, way too reserved to be in Oklahoma City's landmark for anyone that loves their rock shows loud, dirty and honest.

Did she think I would be here?

If so, that would be kinda weird. It complicated things.

Michelle? Yeah, that was her name. Reminded me of the first lady. Certainly wasn't Laura, Barbara or Nancy, so gotta be Michelle.

I had to talk to her; there was no ignoring her. I reminded myself of the four doctrines, particularly #2 – no casual contact.

Not that I was avoiding an encore, per se, I just had to handle it delicately. I have too many friends here.

I started by texting Elena, just to give her the heads up.

Truth and openness, always. There was no other way to survive in the Lifestyle.

"Girl from rooftop at concert. Looks lonely. Not sure how this will shake out."

A few seconds later: "K, have fun. Love you."
"Love you too."
Then I was off.

I'd considered the possibility that she did know I was there and had avoided me. Some people are like that; they won't even raise an eye to someone they know in the Lifestyle.

As the opening band sent squealing feedback through the speakers during a soundcheck, I wound through the crowd toward Michelle.

She saw me and waved with a surprised but relieved grin. My body perked up.

"Well, hello there, stranger," I called, giving her a half-hug, giving myself only a heartbeat to enjoy the way her breasts pressed into me before pulling away. "Nice shirt."

"Thanks, just bought it today," she answered, leaning her head against my shoulder and looking up at me.

Too much.

I released and took a half-step back, but retained my casual grin.

"So, you're here. How unexpected," I said.

"Well, you were wearing the band's t-shirt and I wanted to see who they were," she shrugged, embarrassed. "I went to Guestroom and saw they were playing tonight, so I thought, 'what the hell!'"

"'What the hell.' indeed," I replied, putting my hands in my pocket and checking to ensure I'd remembered to bring condoms.

Always be prepared.

I'd decided that I would try to have sex with her tonight, perhaps invite her out to breakfast after the show. But then I saw the way her smile quivered, the way she kept edging close to me like an intimidated child. It was clear she was feeling very vulnerable in this strange, new environment.

Emotionally brittle women are no-go areas for me, but she did look great in that t-shirt.

"So," I said, leaning in. "I'm not exactly out. For the record, we met and talked briefly at the beer thing at the museum."

"Got it," she chuckled.

"Okay, then."

I stepped next to her and then scanned the crowd.

"Are you going to start coming to shows or is this just a once in a lifetime thing?"

She turned to look at me with a clever upturned grin and an arching eyebrow.

"It's never too late to try something new, right?" she shrugged.

There it was again, the vulnerability. She masked it, but I could tell the girl was dealing with something heavy.

My modus operandi shifted from sexual to protective. Believe it or not, my default setting was Good Guy. Though it was dreadfully boring, I could tell that Michelle needed a little coddling tonight, so the nervous energy radiating from my loins settled and was replaced by the Will of six years ago.

I returned to the Will that every girl liked, but no girl wanted to sleep with.

Well, aside from Elena. Still not sure how that math worked out in my favor.

"Okay, if you want to get into the scene, then you

need to know some of the major players and a few rules of the game."

She nods, seriously.

"One: Do you like U2?"

"Yes."

"Try again."

"No?"

"Correct," I snap. "I would have also accepted 'I gave up on them after I heard *Joshua Tree*.' Two: Where do you like to shop?"

"The Plaza?"

"Not bad," I murmur. "You might consider tacking on 'and sometimes I just find stuff at garage sales and thrift stores and then alter it at home.' Three: Where did you get that t-shirt?"

"A comic book store."

"You're learning, grasshopper," I grumble with an encouraging nod. "You might just pass after all. Shall we?"

I motion for her to follow me into the crowd and can feel her reach up to lace her arm around mine.

Too much.

—

She's a pro; I was a little intimidated, to be honest. After just an hour and a half of trailing behind me, letting me introduce her to scenesters, musicians, music journalists and record store owners, she was jumping from conversation to conversation and was, in short, the toast of the room.

She bought shots, friends hovered, and I was impressed at how quickly she dived into a scene with people at least a decade younger.

I guess the rock scene isn't so far removed from the country club circles; it's all about inducing people to talk.

If you listen, they love you. Always.

A little hurt that I was no longer the star she hovered around, I retreated and watched the second opener. It was a one-man band named El Paso Hot Button. He was five feet three inches of rock sensuality, a brilliant thing to watch.

I desperately wished I could get away with the jaded, libertine, rock idol shtick, but I would just look like a low-rent, over-the-hill, goth boy with a fetish for eyeliner.

We can't all be Jim Jacobs, I suppose.

I chatted with a chipper scenester pecking away on her cell phone as she talked music. The girl was cute and a notorious flirt, but also one of the birds that was firmly fixed into the "off-limits" category. She came to my readings from time to time, knew all the bands in town and was a true believer when it came to supporting the arts.

Too nice, too loyal to the scene and to me. Can't mess with that.

Michelle saddled up next to me, our arms brushing against each other. The scenester didn't notice, but I suddenly felt very ashamed, so I excused myself to get a beer.

Michelle followed and we leaned side by side on the bar, waiting our turn as the bartender sifted through the mob of thirsty patrons.

"Thank you so much," Michelle said, bumping her shoulder against mine.

"For what?"

"I really needed this. I needed to get out," she replied, staring down at the bar top as she traced her fingers across a coaster. "I should have never fallen so out of touch with this kind of thing, but, well..."

"Being important is time consuming?"

"Yeah," she sighed, then laughed. "We were in politics and it just wouldn't be seemly if I were seen in rock clubs dressed like a sixteen-year-old."

"But," and I surveyed our surrounding before whispering, "you go to swinger clubs?"

"Well, it's not the same. That's supposed to be secret."

I nodded in agreement, waved at the bartender.

"Two PBRs!" I called over the music.

Seconds later, we were treading through the crowd to a back corner of the club, away from the music, away from my friends.

"What do you think so far?" I asked as we sat on a black couch with rips scattered across the cushion.

"It's awesome. I really do feel so much better."

"Was the museum that awful?"

She rolled her eyes and patted me on the leg.

"That was also great," she whispered. "I'm just feeling a bit out of sorts these days, but things are looking up."

"Well, I'm glad you made it out," I responded, holding up my beer can. She clinked hers against mine. We drank.

———

"Everyone was very nice," Michelle said as we

walked across the parking lot, her arm laced around my elbow as I carried three t-shirts and four CDs she'd bought at the show.

    The physical contact was dangerous, but I let it pass. I could just tell anyone that asked me about it that she had broken a heel and I was helping her to her car.

    "I felt out of place," she continued. "The crowd was just so young. I felt like a chaperone."

    "Don't worry about it too much," I replied. "The scene really benefits when they have a more diverse crowd. The young kids are great, have lots of energy, but don't have a lot of money to spend. You, on the other hand, just made it possible for the bands to eat at IHOP after the show."

    "True."

We reached her car and my body quickly reverted back into douche bag mode upon the realization that I hadn't actually seen her breasts yet. This was inexplicably frustrating.

    She opened her car door and I handed her the merch. She tossed them in the passenger side and then turned to look at me.

    "Thank you again, it was great."

    I leaned in, she leaned in, but passed by my lips and pulled me into a friendly hug. As she peeled away, I turned my face to meet her lips on the way out, but she turned and lowered into her car.

    Weird.

―

    "That is weird," Elena replied the next morning

as she got ready for work.

"I'm not exactly sure what that means for this weekend. Maybe she's not down anymore?"

"Not the only fish in the sea," Elena shrugged as she poured herself a mug of coffee. "She's clearly got some issues to work out. Don't take it personally. It's her loss if she doesn't see that we're the bee's knees."

"True. Though, it just goes to show you that no one wants to sleep with nice guy Will."

"I do."

Elena leaned in and pressed her soft lips against mine. She took my hand, led me out of the kitchen, passed the living room where the two of the kids watched television while the third giggled into a cell phone, and then to the bedroom. She closed the door behind me.

I wasn't sure if I was going to be yelled at or given a ****job. It was kind of exciting.

"I wanted to thank you again for being willing to continue with therapy."

"Of course," I said, as my body sagged.

I really could have used a ****job.

"I mean it, I know that you don't like it, but I feel like it's helping me," she continued. "I'm glad that you seem to be swimming in girls all of a sudden and I want you to sow your oats, but..."

She was pleading me to finish her sentence.

"But I'm working on borrowed time?" I submitted.

"Well, not really," Elena said, taking a sip of coffee. "I don't want you to feel like you have to beat the clock, but I can't see us doing this when we are forty. This is certainly not what I pictured I'd be doing

at this point in my life."
Ouch.
"I understand how lucky I am right now," I said, stepping close to her and taking her hands.
"Thank you," she replied with a relieved smile. "I'm sorry to lay this on you first thing in the morning, and I really am happy for you."
Elena pecked a kiss on my cheek and handed me her coffee cup.
"I gotta get to work," she said while she cleared tears from her eyes.
She then opened the door and was gone.
Well played, ma'am. I suddenly felt like the single biggest douche on the planet. Regardless of what she said, the clock was ticking on Mr. Asshole. I've officially been given my notice and my time in the Lifestyle was quickly coming to a close.
I needed to formulate a to-do list to make the most of the time I had left.
Michelle was the first question mark, and I wasn't sure if she would just be wasted effort. It was not unprecedented for me to stumble into the friend zone post-coitus, and it made me wonder what I was doing wrong. Was it just her and her issues she was dealing with, or was I not the spectacular, mind-altering sexual dynamo I'd thought?
No, of course I'm an irrepressible dynamo, a modern day Casanova, a libidinous maestro of the female body.
Aren't I?
Elena seemed to enjoy it, but since I do pay the mortgage on the house, I guess she's obligated to at least pretend.

The self-doubt was certainly an element of the Lifestyle I wouldn't miss.

And it did feel good to be old Will from time to time. I wasn't sure if I wanted to return to this:

But maybe there's a middle ground. If I can just split the difference between the predatory Mr. Asshole and Will, the lovable loser, then I can find a version of myself I can finally call home. Maybe that's where I should have been all along.

FUN FACT: Lifestyle Resorts/Cruises
Though research for this book was exhaustive, funds were not available for first-hand study of resorts or sea cruises. Should you be interested in donating to the advancement of our examination on these matters, please contact the publisher.[29]

The Ballad of Jerry and Carey/Cynthia/Veronica Part VI

    True to her word, an invitation to the farm was extended later that week and babysitting was arranged with friends down the road. Halfway into an un-labeled bottle of "Film Noir," the couples were already naked and entangled. This round lacked the same spark of excitement, didn't have the novelty and was more matter of fact than thrilling and dangerous.
    Cynthia wondered if it was the farm that was the problem, or that it was planned rather than spontaneous.
    Still, by the time the couple kissed their "goodbyes" and their taillights faded way into the country night, Cynthia felt revived. Instead of ending the night with feverish sex as they had in the hotel,

---

[29] Cabo San Lucas, here I come!

Jerry and Cynthia finished off the bottle of wine and sat in the porch swing.

"Did you hear us talking about the club they go to?" Cynthia asked.

"Yeah, I did. Are you interested?"

"I think I am."

No specific dates were discussed though, and schedules never lined up to meet Barry and Mary again. A dry spell ensured as dates with other possible candidates also failed to materialize, and life's other complications began to intrude.

It was fine, though. With the harvest coming, Jerry and Cynthia barely had time to breathe, let alone carve out time for this bizarre new experiment called the Lifestyle. Besides, they'd broken their swinging cherry and the afterglow of the evening radiated for several weeks.

Cynthia had a brief panic attack the morning after the couple came to the farm. She began obsessing over the possible ramifications, such as venereal diseases, faulty condoms and estrangement from "vanilla" sex.

"What if we become reliant on sex with other people to keep it interesting between us?" Cynthia asked Jerry. "What if you stop finding me attractive?"

"No matter what we've gone through, no matter how far apart we've ever become, you've never ceased to be the most devastatingly gorgeous woman I've met," Jerry replied, his eyes fixed intently on hers. "There is no woman that could ever outshine you."

The sex that resulted was intensely personal and she cried, but it was cleansing.

As the harvest progressed, it quickly became

apparent that this year would indeed be their breakthrough. The seasons had behaved themselves, no late frosts, no floods, no destructive droughts, no disease.

A second hand tractor appeared, then a slightly used Ford F150. Cynthia began updating her wardrobe with trips to consignment stores. The clothes were technically used, but new to her.

She also began classes during the day, a couple hours while the child was in preschool, just to hurry up her education.

The path had leveled for the young couple, but tribulation was inevitable. The two lovers had one last summit to scale before they could truly see how the remainder of their lives would lay out ahead of them.

Their first glimpse of that final climb came at a much-deserved celebration of a successful year. Babysitting was arranged and a new couple was found through a Lifestyle website. They would meet for drinks at a hip bar in North Oklahoma City called the Electro Lounge. The bizarre "indie" music coming from the jukebox wasn't really up Jerry and Cynthia's alley, but the bar was very urbane and had a great wine selection, so Cynthia made do.

After a few drinks, Cynthia and the woman agreed on a change of venue. The pink-haired beauty, Elena, intimidated Cynthia a little. She was way hipper than what she'd anticipated running into in the Lifestyle. She looked like she spent more on her hair than Cynthia did on her entire outfit. Elena's wardrobe balanced between punk and vintage chic, and the rock star persona seemed an odd fit for her very unrock star husband. The guy, Will, was a little on the short side, had closely cropped red hair and a bit of a pretentious air. He was talkative to the point of exhaustion, but Cynthia decided he was "do-able."

When a dance club was suggested as the next stop, Will was hesitant but Elena asked if he wanted her making out with Jerry in front of his friends.

"No, I suppose you are right," Will sighed and quickly tabbed out.

The dance club was down market, little more than a beer bar with a sizeable dance floor and a clientele that wasn't too scary. Cynthia guessed it was chosen so as to minimize the possibility of running into anyone either of them knew.

The music was all Top 40, which made Will visibly cringe at each new song. Elena reveled in his discomfort by singing along with as many lyrics as she could as loud as she could, and then pulled Cynthia out onto the dance floor. Barry and Will cowered to a pool table.

Cynthia quickly realized that she and Elena were the most attractive women in the bar and men danced closer and closer before finally asking to cut in. Elena quickly nudged Cynthia toward a large, barrel-chested good ole boy, and Elena latched onto a short, cocky Latin guy with a faux hawk. Barry and Will smirked from the sidelines and began discussing particulars.

When the girls returned from the dance floor, Cynthia sat next to Jerry and whispered:

"It's going to be a good night."

Cynthia giggled, a shiver snaked up her back and then she kissed Jerry like a condemned woman seeking salvation.

"Sorry to interrupt," Elena called as she sidled up

next to Cynthia and ran her hand across Cynthia's thigh under the table. "We were thinking about the next stop, maybe somewhere a little more private?"

Jerry couldn't stifle a blush, and a light glaze lifted on his forehead. It made Cynthia giggle.

"Yes," Cynthia said. "But first, I want to take you out to the dance floor one more time."

"Oh, hell yeah," Elena replied, bowing her head and sliding out of the booth. She took Cynthia's hand and they walked back out into the crowd.

"So, where are we going to?" Jerry asked the man.

"Well, are we done drinking?"

Jerry smirked, downed the last of his beer, burped.

"I am."

"Not to pressure you, then, but there are a couple nice hotels around here."

"Sounds good to me."

The women returned to the table, Elena with an amused smile and Cynthia trying to hide anxiety.

"We're thinking about getting a room," the man called.

"Probably pretty good timing," she responded. "There is a really, really drunk girl out there and she was just staring at Cynthia."

Cynthia motioned to Jerry for her purse, anxious to leave. Jerry knew something else was happening.

He stood, leaned in close to whisper, but she just snapped, "I don't care where we go, let's just get out of here."

"Okay," Jerry shrugged, then looking over to the man. "We're following you."

Cynthia was trying to hurry the pace, walking with strides as long as her stilettos would allow, but a name stopped her just before escaping into the night air.

The name was "Carey." The name had been slurred, but it was there. She wanted to continue walking, but instead, she stopped and swiveled toward the voice that had dug back up that horrible word.

"Carey?" the miserably drunk woman repeated. The woman wavered as if she was on a small boat in the ocean. The sickly thin woman wore a pink and black pin-stripped vest and mini skirt with a fedora with a feather tipped to the side on her head. She looked like a meth-ed out stripper at a Halloween party. The woman smiled, showing off two prominent empty slots where teeth should be.

"It's you, right?" the woman asked, holding out a finger with a gaudy costume ring.

"Yeah," Cynthia responded, her face pale as her strength drained.

An equally drunk, much older and fatter man stumbled up next to the woman, put his arm over her shoulder and then cupped the woman's breast.

"Eww, don't be nasty," the woman growled, batting the man away.

"Ya'll wanna party?" the fat man grinned, looking Cynthia up and down.

"Man, show some respect, this here's my little sister."

Tears welled in Cynthia's eyes. She felt small, helpless and shamed. She wanted Jerry to pull her away, hide her, get her away far from this night.

"Pamela?" Cynthia asked.
"Yeah, babygirl, I missed you so much."

—

To their credit, the couple suffered through Pamela's rambling stories, sudden bursts of tears and confessional apologies. Cynthia finally pulled Pamela outside the club as Jerry kept the swingers busy at the bar.

"The bear is coming, Babe," Pamela grumbled as she leaned back against the outside wall of the club and took off the fedora.

"Listen," Cynthia, now Carey, said. "It's all in the past, okay. I'm not worried about some gross man that ruined my childhood. I am only worried about you."

Pamela's broken smile quivered. She raised her thin fingers to Cynthia's cheek. There were red scars on Pamela's wrists, track marks along the inside of her arms.

"You were always so kind," Pamela moaned. "I should have come back, but they took me away."

"You're here now," Cynthia smiled, taking Pamela's hand and cupping in hers. "What can I do to help you?"

"Aww, baby sister," Pamela smiled. "Don't you worry about me, I'm a survivor, always have been."

The fat man emerged through the front door, snapped his fingers together as he walked past Pamela.

"I'm comin' darlin'," Pamela called, then looked back to Cynthia. "It was real good seein' you, you did well for yourself. All grown up."

"Don't go with him. Come back home with us," Cynthia pleaded, tightening her grip on Pamela's hand.

"Aw, honey, you've got friends here, you worry about them."

"Pamela."

"No, baby sis," Pamela replied sternly. "Now, I ain't gonna ruin your night. You have fun and I'll call you in a couple days, okay?"

Cynthia sighed, but didn't let go. The fat man honked his car horn. Pamela eased her hand away from Cynthia, blew her a kiss and hobbled over to the waiting Cadillac.

Cynthia sat on the curb as the car disappeared out of the parking lot. She cried briefly, used a hand mirror to fix her mascara and returned to the club.

The two couples drank heavily as Cynthia insisted repeatedly that she was okay and wanted to "blow off steam."

Despite Jerry's reservations, Cynthia declared that they would rent a hotel room. Once there, Will was too drunk to get an erection, so ultimately the night ended as it was destined, in utter mortification.

Another dry spell ensued as Cynthia awaited the phone call. It came three weeks later.

—

Cynthia wound through downtown Oklahoma City, passing Bricktown until she came to a YMCA a few blocks from the heart of the city. Cynthia had not spoken to Pamela, but instead to the receptionist who had found Pamela passed out in the locker room.

No one remembered Pamela walking into the facility, let alone paying to get in. She'd been found in the morning naked in the showers.

Rather than calling the police, they called the only phone number they could find in Pamela's clothes, which had been spread out across the locker room.

When Cynthia walked in the front door, Pamela was sitting in the lobby with two older men standing on either side of her. Pamela was shivering even though she had a blanket wrapped tightly over her shoulders.

She didn't look up as Cynthia approached and knelt down beside her.

"You're coming home with me," Cynthia whispered. "We're going to get you healthy, okay?"

Pamela didn't respond, so Cynthia straightened to address a stern woman in a business suit and paperwork in her hand.

"The Bear returned, baby sis," Pamela uttered. "Just like I said he would."

"What?" Cynthia asked, kneeling back down.

"Talked to Ma," Pamela muttered, still staring at the ground. "He's back, out of jail. He's comin'. I can feel it."

"No one is going to get you, sis," Cynthia whispered. "Not while you're in my house, you understand?"

Pamela rose her head, looked into Cynthia's eyes and smiled weakly before dropping her head again.

Cynthia kissed Pamela's forehead and stood up.

"We should have called the police," the stern woman snapped.

"I know, thank you," Cynthia mumbled, then signed everything that was put in front of her so she could leave with her sister.

—

Jerry doubled his workload, taking over the work Cynthia normally did so she could stay in the house with her sister. He then traded off duties so Cynthia could go to her classes.

Pamela mostly slept for the first two days. She had a fever, she shook continually and growled in her dreams. Cynthia sent the child to Jerry's parents for a few days until they could figure out what to do about Pamela.

On the third day, Pamela's head was rested in Cynthia's lap as they watched daytime soap operas. Cynthia hadn't watched soap operas since she was a child, since Pamela still lived with the family. Pamela dutifully caught Cynthia up on the various storylines until she began crying. She cried so often that Cynthia learned to just let her finish without saying anything.

Pamela wiped the tears from her eyes.

"I'm sorry, baby sis," Pamela said.

"Don't worry about it, just get well," Cynthia whispered, brushing the hair from Pamela's eyes.

Pamela grasped her hand and kissed it.

"I am just so mad at Ma," Pamela said. "Letting that man back in. And Pa, too. The both of them are no good."

"Dad came back home?" Cynthia asked. "When?"

"He got shot in the leg while runnin' from the cops. He can't walk without a cane. He's pretty worthless now, so Ma just takes care of him. It's been a while since you talked to Ma, huh?"

Cynthia took a deep breath and rubbed tears out of her own eyes.

"It's been a while since I even thought of that entire town," Cynthia finally said.

"Good for you, baby sis."

The two watched the soap opera quietly. Jerry opened the front door and exchanged worried looks with Cynthia before he walked to the kitchen to fix lunch.

"Somethin' has to be done about him," Pamela said, her eyes focused on the television.

"Who, the rich guy having an affair with what's her name's sister?" Cynthia asked innocently, but knowing where this was headed.

"The Bear."

"He can't get you here, sis," Cynthia said, turning Pamela's face to look at her. "Listen to me now, you are safe here. Do you understand?"

Pamela didn't answer.

"Please believe me," Cynthia continued. "They don't know where we live and Jerry and I are sure as hell not going to tell them. We are protected here. We got loud dogs outside, we have a rifle and a shotgun inside. We aren't going to let anything happen to you. Don't worry about back home, you just worry about getting better, okay?"

"Okay."

The next morning, Pamela was gone. So was the shotgun.

Jerry filed a police report and replaced the locks on the doors, just to be safe.

The next call came a month later, just as Cynthia began feeling like herself again. It was the call that finally lured the young, skinny and damaged Carey back home.

FUN FACT: Lifestyle Fashion
What swingers wear to Lifestyle events varies wildly, from business or cocktail attire to lingerie and/or bondage wear. Organizers like themed events and encourage costumes, but it is advisable to err on the side of conservatism until one is familiar with the venue and the people in attendance. Novice swingers are particularly spooked by those flying their freak flag a bit too early in the night.

Superswingers
Part VI

A week and a half passed before the follow up interview. It was held in a hotel bar where a traveling Lifestyle club had rented out an entire wing. The bar was the site of a meet and greet before the participants retired to their private wing and its series of "swinging door" parties.

Barry – "We needed a change of venue, some new scenery."

Mary (timid smile) – "It's the best way to get a fresh start."

Both appeared drunk early on in the night, but switched to coffee at the beginning of the interview. Once the voice recorder appeared, many of the other swingers left the bar. After a few minutes, Mary followed a couple to their hotel room.

Barry – "She needs to blow off steam tonight."

This is not something you really think about dealing with in the Lifestyle, but I guess there is really no escaping it. I'm not so naïve as to think that there is a whole lot of good decision-making going on amidst my peers here, but it's also not like we are criminals or drug users where you'd expect tragedy as part of the job description. You know, let me go check on her."

Mary appeared through the door before Jerry got up from the table. She sat down, stifling laughter.

Mary – "Had a bit of a misfire back there."

Barry – "Oh really, he, uh?"

Mary nodded and giggled.

Mary – "So, where were we? The first time, I think."

Barry met her eyes.

Mary – "I'm fine, Barry. I really am."

Barry – "Okay."

Mary – "So, yeah, our first time."

Barry – "Not exactly our shining hour."

Mary – "No, shit, huh? Well, so we moved and then after about a year, decided to try the Lifestyle again."

Barry – "Only a matter of time, I suppose. As a guy, you hate leaving things off badly. I think it's just the insecurity of being the aggressors during sex, always feeling like you have something to prove, and when sex goes bad, you just really want a mulligan."

Mary – "But now we are three hundred miles away, so we decide to wipe the slate clean and start again. It kind of began with a chance encounter at a party where, after being really drunk, Barry and I found ourselves naked in a side bedroom with a couple."

Barry – "It's not like we were passed out and didn't know how we got there."

Mary – "We knew, but this wasn't exactly that kind of party, you know? I think we only barely knew the people who were throwing the party, and they were Christians, so God knows what would have happened had they walked in on us."

Barry – "I remember how it went, how we got to that place. The girl, I don't want to say her name —"

Mary – "That's probably wise."

Barry – "Well, she'd said her husband was going off to Afghanistan in a few days, so they wanted to make sure they had a proper send-off."

Mary – "Was that why they were having the party in the first place?"

Barry – "No idea. But anyway, Mary said something like 'well, I guess we need to do everything we can to make the night spectacular.' She had those fluttering eyes and everything."

Mary – "In my defense, they had been flirting with us already."

Barry – "You think so? I hadn't noticed."

Mary – "Shut up, they'd totally been grilling our bacon all night long."

Barry – "I suppose so. At any rate, we started talking about trying to strike up a party game like Truth or Dare or Seven Minutes in Heaven, which then somehow led to us looking around for a bedroom with a closet. Mary went in the closet first with the guy and me and the girl were sitting on the couch. We could hear them kissing, then clothes coming off, and then Mary moaning. So, we didn't wait for our turn in the closet and just went for it on the bed."

Mary – "God, I don't even remember, but it wasn't a kid's bed was it?"

Barry shrugged.

Mary – "Let's just say it wasn't, 'cause then I'd feel really awful."

Barry – "It was really fun, though, and fortunately the other couple had extra condoms 'cause I hadn't brought any."

Mary – "Dumbass, I thought you were a Boy Scout."

Barry – "Well, I learned my lesson after that night."

Mary – "Kind of like American Express, never leave home without them."

Barry – "So, after we finished up in the kid's room…"

Mary – "**** you, it wasn't a kids room."

Barry (grinned) – "So wherever it was, after doing the deed, we slipped out of the room separately so as not to arouse suspicions. We met up again in the backyard to talk. The guy asked us to take care of his wife while he was overseas."

Mary – "It was the least we could do. Apparently that's pretty common though, babysitting the husband or wife while the other spouse is deployed."

Barry – "Well, we are a stable couple, and I think some people just understand that infidelity happens during deployment, so better with a couple that won't try to break up your marriage."

Mary – "We started going to dance clubs together, but eventually she took us to our first Lifestyle Club. It was an on-premise house party type club north of Oklahoma City. I don't think it's there anymore."

Barry – "It got exposed when a pissed-off regular called a local radio station and told the DJ about the parties."

Mary – "What an asshole."

Barry – "So, we babysat this gorgeous woman for nearly a year before she got stationed overseas. Mary isn't bisexual, so I sometimes felt like I was getting the better part of the deal, but at the clubs, Mary would hook up with other guys. It was nice, but I was kind of glad when she moved and I was freed up to play with whoever."

Mary – "It was kind of like you guys were dating for a while. I got a little jealous, to be honest. I'd rather us not go down that road again, but I did love her to death. Haven't heard from her in a long time, though."

TRAVELING

Mary – "So, you know what's the biggest pain in the *** in the Lifestyle?"

Barry – "Anal sex?"

Mary – "Do you know what is the second biggest pain in the ***? Going on vacation."

Barry – "That is a pain in the ***."

Mary – "We've done it a couple times, taking trips to other states to meet up with couples, or to go some of the bigger clubs. Taking an airplane is just so unnerving."

Barry – "Yeah, you just never know what to pack."

Mary – "Exactly. What do you do? Bring

everything you want to bring and hope that airport security doesn't have to look through it."

Barry – "Reminds me of that scene from 'Fight Club' where the guy talks about the vibrator being mistaken for a bomb."

Mary – "Right, but if it's in your carry on luggage, then they just open that right in front of God and everyone."

Barry – "Right, but who would take a dong on their carry-on? Then everyone just gets to see it on those x-ray scanners."

Mary – "Oh God, I didn't even think about that."

Barry – "What, you actually did?"

Mary (blushed) – "You remember that time at Will Rogers, on the way to Miami? We were traveling with the ball room dancers?"

Barry nodded his head.

Mary – "He and I had talked about the mile-high thing, and I thought it would be a good idea to, oh, well, then never mind."

Barry – "Wow, I didn't know you guys had planned to do that, but I do remember you disappearing for a while. So what did you have with you?"

Mary – "The Duke."
Barry laughed.
Barry – "Very subtle indeed."
Barry continued laughing.
Mary – "Go to hell."
Barry – "She names her dildos, by the way."
Mary – "Shut up."
Barry – "Well, they already know you've got one named after John Wayne."

Mary – "Shut up!"
Barry (continued laughing) – "Sorry."
Mary – "***hole. Besides, it's not weird to name your dildos. I know plenty of girls that do it."
Barry – "Ok."
Mary – "I do!"
Barry – "I said 'ok.'"
Mary – "I will cut your **** off."

Still laughing, Barry stood to get another cup of coffee from the refreshment table.
Mary – "It's not weird. Guys name their guns, so why can't we name our vibrators, right?"

TOYS

Barry – "Some people are into it and some aren't. Usually it's something that women will play with together, but lots of guys aren't really comfortable with peripherals."
Mary – "The reluctance is usually that first time out of the gate. I think a guy is always a little worried that something is going to get shoved up his butt when he's not paying attention."
Barry – "Yeah, that can be unnerving. In the back of every guy's head is the fear that the other guy in the room is going to turn out to be bisexual and try something weird. But even with girls, you can tell that they have their comfort zone and may not be that interested in big contraptions, sex swings, things like that."
Mary – "Which I'm up for about anything, but if you have control issues, then something like getting

tied up could either be therapeutic or terrifying. You just have to pay attention to the other couple, maybe just start with small vibrators and move up as needed."

Barry – "A massager seems generally acceptable, haven't run into anyone that was unnerved when we whipped it out."

Mary – "It's also not quite so overt or intrusive."

Barry – "Most people aren't going to try to shove something that big into an orifice."

Mary – "Gross."

Barry – "Am I right, though?"

Mary – "So, anyway, girls are a little bit more receptive to new utensils, but you have to make sure you clean them right after you are done. Just letting it sit around is just — unseemly."

Barry – "Yuck."

Mary – "Shut up, I'm still mad at you."

Barry – "Sorry."

Barry leaned in to kiss Mary, but Mary folded her arms. Barry peppered her with kisses until she finally laughed.

Mary – "Still going to cut your **** off."

FAMILIES

Mary – "That is always something that never fails to surprise me. I've been to a club where two siblings where there. They weren't together, they were there with their separate spouses, but were sorta in the same group. Weird."

Barry – "We've even had people want us to bring

over our kids to play with their kids. Maybe if we knew you before we slept together, then I might consider it, but someone we met solely through the Lifestyle? No ****ing way!"

Mary – "But then again, we've never been about that whole communal, love everybody thing. I love my husband, I love my kids. But, I'm just here to **** and chew bubblegum."

Mary raised her hand to Barry. He didn't say anything as he watched a woman at the bar lick salt off another woman's neck, then take a shot of tequila as men cheered. Mary snapped her fingers to draw back his attention.

Barry – "Oh, sorry, what?"

Mary (cleared throat) – "I said, 'I'm just here to **** and chew bubblegum'."

Barry – "And we're all out of bubblegum."

Mary – "Thank you!"

Barry – "You're welcome, gawd."

COMMUNICATION

Barry – "You try to get a feel of what the other people are and are not into, but it's not an exact science. Not everyone is really sure what they want until they've felt it."

Mary – "You just don't spring anything on anyone. Even if you are both into bondage, you still don't bust out the gimp suit on the first date."

Barry – "That's at least four to five dates down the road."

Mary – "Right, and that's really something you

want to discuss before hand. And then, after the fact, we try to chat up the couple for a while before departing, just to get some final thoughts."

Barry – "A few last notes on what we might have missed, or something we should try again."

Mary – "On a scale of 1 –10, 10 being fantastic, 1 being horrific, how would you rate our performance?"

Barry – "Would you recommend our services to your friends and family?"

Mary – "Gross."

Barry smiled and walked to the bar to get a coffee refill.

Mary – "Some couples are really open and honest. They'll tell you straight up they don't like this position or that position. They want you to spank a little or not go down for as long."

Barry – "The ones who don't say anything are usually the ones that will never come back."

Mary – "That's what they said at the restaurant I waitressed at in college."

Barry – "Well, we definitely are in the customer service industry."

Mary – "God, that makes us sound like prostitutes."

Barry – "If only."

WRONG TURNS

Barry – "The biggest surprise for me has been how tight knit the swinger community can become. You really get to know some of these people intimately, which I guess might be inevitable because sex is involved. It's definitely not what I expected, or even really wanted, but then you've slept with this person a couple of times, you start really caring about the ups and downs of their lives. You want them to succeed, and it really moves you when their life hits a snag."

Mary – "You can't save them, though. You try to give them advice, but really, what position are we in to give these people sage wisdom on how to clean up their lives, when we all know what we're really here for? Self-actualization is not really what the Lifestyle is about. You want community and betterment, then you're better off at a church, but we still see people who are clinging to this in really unhealthy ways."

Barry – "Or are in it for the wrong reasons?"

Barry and Mary exchanged glances. Mary sighed and used a napkin to dry her right eye.

Mary – "It's really heartbreaking when you see the damage that this can inflict on those that shouldn't be here. Part of you thinks that if you are there for them, maybe encourage them to slow down and really think about what they are doing, then maybe —."

Barry – "We can't blame ourselves for what happened that night. There's nothing we could have done, and I think her issues went well beyond the Lifestyle. She had a lot of demons, I could tell that from the first time I met her."

Mary – "But we still ****ed them though, didn't we?"

Barry didn't answer, instead took a drink from his mug and leaned back in the chair.

Mary – "I'm sorry, baby, that wasn't fair."

Mary leaned over and they hugged.

Mary (leaned back in her chair, dried her eyes and sighed) – "What could we do? It wasn't really our place."

Barry – "And if you invest yourselves too heavily in the lives of the other people here, then it will get to you. This isn't exactly a place where normal functioning people gather. We're all damaged goods trying to figure out how to get from one day to the next."

Mary – "The best you can do is just try to help them enjoy themselves, for a little while at least. I wasn't with her that night, but it seemed like she did enjoy herself. She seemed happier than I'd ever seen her."

Barry – "They say that's how it usually goes."

Mary – "Poor thing."

FUN FACT: Lifestyle Fashion Addendum
Torn or stained underwear is the quickest way to put an end to an otherwise sure thing. Hygiene-obsessive swingers have even been known to discretely check the condition of prospective playmates' socks during the introduction stage.

The Fishbowl
Part VI

Two and three-quarters days. Sixty-six hours. Three thousand, nine hundred sixty minutes. Two hundred thirty-seven thousand, four hundred sixty seconds.

Michelle felt a little ridiculous calling the intense spell of introspection and change a mid-life crisis since she only had a few days left. "Blossoming" or "awakening" seemed pretentious, but with a need to call it something, she called it "The Arousal." Still pretentious, but also sexy and mysterious.

Perhaps it was just a mid-life crisis. It would be understandable since she had sixty-six hours to balance decades of stagnation with a dynamic burst of creative and emotional growth.

Michelle was roused by a Camera Obscura album playing on her boombox. It had been on repeat most of the night. She didn't remember falling asleep in the armchair surrounded by dozens of painted canvases, paint brushes and empty energy drink bottles. She'd wanted to stay up until her final bow, but also knew that probably wouldn't be feasible if she wanted to keep up her creative momentum.

She could tell it was early by the morning sun peeking up through the bottom of the window.

"Thank God."

Michelle had no time to waste, so she grabbed a canvas and began sketching with a pencil. After a few minutes, a woman emerged on the paper, carrying big bundles of shopping bags. Her legs were trembling as if about to collapse under the weight. Droplets of sweat jumped from her skin.

The voluptuous figure looked like a simple WWII pin-up. She was purposively less emotive and detailed then some of the other single frame paintings around the room, such as the naked woman ripping off the skin on her chest to reveal the Superman logo underneath.

She sketched more. A generic retail store materialized behind the trembling woman with the male clerk craning his head to look out the window. Then rough sketches of people walking by and watching her out of the corner of their eyes and a clock whose hands appeared to be spinning at warp speed.

Just before she laid the canvas down, she drew in a pair of panties that had slipped down to the woman's ankles.

Below the woman, she wrote:

"No time to fret over the little things."

She laughed out loud and sat the canvas down.

She decided late last night not to put the finishing touches on anything yet, just sketch and sketch and sketch. When she decided on which ideas were the best, she would pour her remaining hours on those little details that always took forever. She had so little time left that she had to make the most of every moment.

From time to time, the thought of calling off the countdown emerged. It was only a passing consideration. She was so terrified that if she even entertained the thought too long, she would lose the urgency and the edge that came with it. She couldn't turn back now, because if she did, she'd just end up back where she started.

She was running low on materials, so she found her keys and purse and then opened the door for the first time in half a day. Brad quickly appeared down the hall.

"What the hell is going on?" Brad growled. "What are you doing in there?"

"Art," Michelle shrugged, passing by Brad and then walking down the stairs.

"Well, how much longer is this going to go on?" Brad asked. "I've got work to do and I can't focus with you blaring music all night long."

"Then go over to your office or go see one of your girlfriends," Michelle called as she opened the front door.

"You're not going out like that are you?"

Michelle threw Brad a quizzical smile, then looked down at her paint splattered overalls and bright orange flip flops.

"Why not? I'm wearing a bra."

"You look like ****, Michelle," Brad sighed. "Come upstairs, let's get you a cup of coffee and talk about this."

Michelle shrugged, walked out the front door and closed it behind her. Brad didn't chase after her, but she could see his disapproving face looking through a window as she backed the car out of the driveway. She blew him a kiss.

Michelle had cleared out the nearest art shop, so she had to drive out to a Hobby Lobby. She packed her car with paints, canvases, sketchpads, pencils, markers, easels and whatever else she thought she might possibly need. She had no time for any more shopping, as the hands of the clock seemed to spin faster and faster and faster.

—

She poured the supplies into piles near the door to her art room before going back to the car for another load. As she passed by the bedroom, Brad called to her.

She hesitated, but finally walked into the room where Brad laid on the bed naked. His penis stood straight up like a flagpole without a flag.

"Why don't you take a break and relax with me for a while?" Brad called, patting a spot on the bed next to him.

"Nah," Michelle said with a smirk, then walking back to the stairs to get another load.

"Now hold on," Brad called, climbing off the bed and lumbering down the hall, his flagpole wobbling and whipping around madly.

"Brad, I am busy. You'll just have to take care of yourself."

"Dammit, that's not what I wanted!" Brad growled.

"Oh yeah?" Michelle asked, then motioning to the flagpole.

Brad covered himself.

"It just does that, I thought being naked would make it more intimate."

"Uh huh."

Brad sulked away, disappeared into his bedroom while Michelle finished hoarding supplies and then locked herself inside her art room with a plate full of fruit and a big thermos full of tea.

An hour later, Brad left the house. Michelle guessed he was off to one of his mistresses. Most likely the tall blond model who was trying to convince Brad to fund her way to New York City.

—

Two and one-third days. Fifty-two hours. Three thousand, one hundred twenty minutes. One hundred eighty-seven thousand, two hundred seconds.

Her exhausted eyeballs couldn't focus on the canvas for more than a minute. She laid the pencil down, looked across large stacks of sketches all around her. Small test paintings were tacked to the wall and large puddles of paint scattered around the room.

It was a good day of work. Time to rest.

Brad returned in the afternoon, but didn't bother Michelle. She thought she heard him leave again, but didn't care to find out for sure. Only after digging out her cell phone from under discarded sketches did she realize that her third to last day was nearly gone.

She also saw thirty-two unopened text messages clogging her inbox. Out of curiosity, she began sifting through them. Most were from Brad, asking what was wrong, if she wanted to go to lunch/dinner with him and finally threatening to call her mom if she didn't leave the room.

A few of her lovers also got in on the act. The owner of a national chain of retail stores wanted to take her to an art opening later that night. This was the same man who said he loved her every time they saw each other, even though she never said it back to him.

She despised everything about the man except the way he made her feel beautiful and his ability to quickly find her G spot.

Catherine came in second for most texts and most of them were supportive, but worried. Catherine seemed to think that Brad had hurt her, so Michelle sent her a text back just for reassurance.

"Busy working, no time 2 talk but I assure you I'm fine."

Send.

She deleted the rest and moved to the kitchen to fix her delayed lunch/dinner. She was tempted to grab something fast, maybe a sandwich, but realized she was incapable of working any more that night, so decided to indulge.

After digging through the cupboards, she settled on spaghetti. Lots of carbs, which meant lots of energy for tomorrow.

Her phone buzzed, another text.

When she opened it, a close up picture of Catherine's vagina greeted Michelle. The words, 'Need a break to clear the mind?'

Michelle hated it when Catherine sent pictures of her body parts. It was gross and vulgar.

Might make for an interesting painting though, so Michelle didn't delete it in case she wanted to use it as source material later.

Another buzz.

This one was from a number she didn't recognize.

"Really looking forward to tomorrow night. Want to meet up for dinner beforehand? – Will."

"Dammit," Michelle thought, regretting having to waste time at a club.

She might blow the event off all together, but didn't want to commit to anything yet. She texted:

"Might be too busy for dinner, will let you know. Lots of new work to finish."

Send.

She started the water boiling and her phone buzzed. It was Will again.

"Can I see?"

A smile rose to her face, she blushed slightly, but texted:

"Not now, can't have guests over. Perhaps another time."

When that would be, she did not know. Probably never. She had so little time left.

A quick reply read:

"Then email some pictures. I'm really interested to see where you are going."

—

Two days. Forty-eight hours. Two thousand, eight hundred eighty minutes. One hundred seventy-two thousand, eight hundred seconds.

Michelle finally started eating her spaghetti as she counted down the last seconds of her third to last day. She'd been distracted by setting up a photo studio to take pictures of her work. She only found three near finished works worth sending.

1. The woman with shopping bags and panties around her ankles.

2. A darkly tanned, trollish and humpbacked humanoid with floppy breasts wearing a thong and bikini top. Her nails were long and curled grotesquely as she pointed out of the painting. Under it she'd written: "Sex Appeal."

3. The third was actually a painting she'd attempted a few times before her "Arousal." It was a reference to a film noir movie poster. She'd toyed with the idea of giving it to a girl she knew who owned a little vineyard and needed an image for a wine bottle. She'd never met the girl, but Brad had been emailing back and forth with them for months.

The image wasn't exactly what the girl wanted, but Michelle liked it. She'd painted an idealized image of Will embracing a slightly tweaked image of Michelle as they laid back against a concrete bridge.

The Michelle figure had a word bubble that read:

"But if someone saw us, whatever would they think?"

It made Michelle smile and she thought it would make Will smile too.

She sent them via e-mail, then texted to let him know the images were on their way.

A few minutes later he responded:

"Not what I was expecting. Very impressed. Can I see these in person?"

She bit her lip, ate a few bites of spaghetti and then responded.

"IDK, you'd better be pretty convincing tomorrow night. ;)"

She felt like a silly schoolgirl. It was a nice way to fall back asleep in the armchair.

FUN FACT: Lifestyle Fashion Addendum II
There is simply nothing more charming than an aged and weathered swinger in a schoolgirl outfit or a very obese woman with teeny tiny angel wings. But if you would prefer to people-watch rather than be people-watched, bring a healthy dose of self-scrutiny to your wardrobe choices.

A Charmed Life
Part VI

Jealousy is a fascinating thing, especially now that I find myself on the other side of the scenario.

This is how jealousy usually goes down between Elena and I:

Me: up late at night, staring at the television until I hear the garage door open and her car pull in. I turn off the television and pretend to sleep.

Her: Steals into the bedroom, softly takes off her clothes and slides under the sheets naked and kisses me on the back of the neck. She smells like soap because she showered afterwards, not wanting to come home smelling like another man. It doesn't matter if I already knew that's where she would be.

Me: Still pretend to sleep.

Her: Wrapping her body around me, nibbling at my ear.

Me: Wanting to ignore her, but the jealousy just

turns me on that much more, so we **** like bitter enemies.

But tonight, the scenario flipped and this is how it went down this time:

Me: Opened an email from a bored housewife of a famous politician. Noticed that one of the images attached was a painting of me embracing the housewife. Against better judgment, I mentioned this to Elena. If I'm being honest, I was also a little curious to see what her reaction would be and to show her that other strange, possibly psychotic women desired me.

Her: Muttered "that's nice" and prepared for bed. While lying on her side, she pretended to sleep.

Me: Curled up to her, kissing her neck, saying the sweet things I need to say.

Her: Finally turning to face me, we make love slowly and tenderly. She cried afterwards and I said more sweet things to her.

Me: Realized the end of the Lifestyle is nigh.

It was too much.

I saw a transformation in Elena that night. She'd always known she could have done better than me had she played her cards right earlier in her life.

At the moment she saw the e-mail, she became genuinely threatened and vulnerable in a way I'd never seen.

Later that night, just as I was falling asleep, she whispered, "I need you." For the first time, I could sense she truly meant it.

The thing to do at this point would have been to tell her that I was ready to end the Lifestyle, would never e-mail the politician's wife again, and I was fully committed to this family because I finally felt like it was where I belonged.

I didn't do that, of course. We're just now entering the third act, so I just couldn't let the story end that neatly.

This painter was an enigma, and I couldn't leave it alone. She'd painted me as the romantic lead in whatever bizarre movie she was starring in, and I just had to see where it all ended.

My natural inclination is to resent anyone who wants me, because we both knew she was settling. That didn't seem to be the case with Michelle, and I didn't know why. Unlike every other couple we'd encountered in the Lifestyle, she wasn't putting up with me because her husband liked Elena. It was just all too ****ing fascinating to pack up before the climax, so to speak.

Like a horror movie, I knew this had to get worse; there had to be something dark lurking around the corner waiting to inflict irreparable harm. But, also like a horror movie, it was the ride that kept you young.

—

Charles's number on the caller ID wasn't the first thing I wanted to see in the morning. He'd called me at midnight, but my cell phone had been off.

I didn't bother listening to the voice mail, since he was a notorious rambler. Instead, I just called him.

He greeted me with, "we need to talk. Can you meet me for lunch?"

I sighed and mumbled, "okay."

—

Just spend five minutes in a room with my writing partner and you'll be left with the distinct impression that the man is one hundred eighty pounds of ego encased in a charm-like substance that, like a sugar substitute, had a bitter aftertaste that smacked of artifice.

But he was a decent writing partner because he worked hard, he produced, and was on time. He was very much a follower who believed he was a leader, which worked to my advantage since I just had to throw him a bone from time to time, and he'd do anything I asked.

Like me, he dressed like a man who was dressed by his wife. His suit jacket matched his sweater a little too much, his slacks were a little too well pressed. His eyebrows and nostrils were well kept. His shiny, bald head was moisturized, and he was wearing his "dress" Converse.

So, that's Charles; a charmless man trying to masquerade as a pop star novelist.

We met at a themed restaurant called The Prohibition Room, which served Chicago-style hot dogs and had a really decent beer selection. We always ordered the dogs as the ceremonial meal of our "author meetings."

"So, what's this I hear about you and Trouble[30]?" Charles asked.

I shrugged as I poked a banana pepper back into

---

[30] Names have been changed to protect the innocent.

my mouth after it attempted to squirt off the hot dog in a desperate bid for survival.

The girl in question was a longtime fan who was one of our first readers. I knew for a fact that Charles had tried to kiss her once while drunk at a concert, and Elena and I had successfully sealed the deal two months ago.

Did I do it to spite him? Hell yeah, I did.

Not sure how Charles found out, though. Maybe she told him.

"I'd wanted to discuss this issue with you before now," Charles began, wiping off his fingers and throwing the napkin on is empty plate. He was a fast eater, almost of competitive caliber.

"Okay," I mumbled through a mouth full of hot dog and trimmings.

"Apparently, she told someone that you tried to hit on her."

I shrugged, somewhat relieved that the story culminated with "tried."

"Do I need to remind you that she is a friend of a lot of our friends, many of the people that have bought books in the past and might or might not buy books in the future?"

I shrugged.

"So, I didn't want to write a book about swinging," Charles continued as he held up his empty beer glass to the waitress. She nodded and walked to the bar. "But you convinced me that a book on sex was sure to raise some eyebrows, get some attention directed our way. I say 'yes,' and now that you've finally sent me something to look at, it's all about you and Elena actually being swingers."

I shrugged.

"Dammit, Will, what the hell is this all about?"

I swallowed, took a sip of Dr. Pepper and chuckled.

"I can't believe that you, of all people, are calling me out on infidelity."

Charles grimaced, looked around the restaurant and then leaned over the table.

"That was a while ago, and we were separated," Charles glowered. "It's different."

"Is it?"

"Yes!"

"Okay," I sighed and rolled my eyes. "I like what I've written so far. It's really solid and think I managed to humanize a really taboo subject. It'll get us new readers."

"And tell the world you're a —" Charles leaned over the table to whisper "swinger!"

"Other writers have admitted drug abuse, alcoholism… what's the difference? I'm just being honest."

The waitress approached, set down a beer.

"Thank you, ma'am," Charles said with that coy, smoldering way that really irritates the piss out of me.

"You're welcome, honey."

Their eyes tripped past each other briefly before the waitress walked away.

Charles picked up the beer without looking at me.

"Not the same and you know it," Charles grumbled.

"Okay."

"So, when readers start asking if you're a

swinger," Charles said, then took a sip before continuing. "What do you tell them?"

"I've thought about that quite a bit, and here's what I have." I cleared my throat. "'A swinger will never divulge they are a swinger to anyone they aren't fairly certain they can have sex with. So, no, I'm not a swinger, but if I think we might hook up later? Maybe my answer changes, maybe it doesn't.'"

Charles laughed loud and obnoxiously. The waitress gave us a curious smile. Charles took another drink.

"Okay, Willy Wonka[31], if that's the way you want to go, I'm not going to stop you. But, if this book takes off, we're going to have journalists asking."

"I don't care what they ask, as long as they are asking us something, right?"

Charles smirked, held up his beer and I clinked my glass against the mug.

"Besides, you're the interview guy," I said. "Tell them whatever you want."

"Oh, don't worry about that," Charles chuckled. "It's going to be an interesting book tour."

---

[31] I hate that damn name, FYI.

FUN FACT: Buffet Table.
At many Lifestyle clubs, there will be a buffet table where people can pick from an assortment of candies, cheeses, crackers and other finger food before going back to whatever it is they like to do at a Lifestyle club. Just let that sink in for a few moments.

The Ballad of Jerry and Carey/Cynthia/Veronica Part VII

"I did it, baby sis, I killed The Bear!"

The statement didn't register immediately; Cynthia was too preoccupied with the screaming behind Pamela's voice. The screaming belonged to a woman, and she also heard a man moaning, which were then joined by Pamela's unnerving giggle. It was too much noise all at once.

So Cynthia remained silent, hoping, praying that her older sister was in the midst of a twisted phone prank.

"Did you hear me?" Pamela called into the phone, then talking away from the phone receiver, "Shut up bitch, she can't hear me!"

"You're a demon!" a woman screamed back.

It was Cynthia's mother. After all these years, Cynthia still recognized the ignorant drawl.

"Pamela, what did you do?" Cynthia asked, trying to remain calm.

"I killed The Bear," Pamela boasted, like a proud child. "I told you I would, and I did."

Scuffling could be heard over the phone.

"Sit down or you're next!" Pamela screamed.

"You killed your own father, you whore!"

"You shot dad?" Cynthia asked, almost in a whisper.

Jerry walked into the room with their child skipping behind him, but Cynthia waved them away. Jerry pulled the child back to its bedroom, then returned and studied Cynthia. She turned her back and cupped the phone.

"I shot The Bear," Pamela explained in heavy breaths. "Dad was here; he tried to stop me, so I had to shoot him too. I couldn't let The Bear live. You have a kid now and I can't let it happen again."

"He's dying, Carey!" her mother called. "Call the cops!"

"I said shut up, bitch!" Pamela screamed. "Dad deserved it. He didn't protect us from The Bear. He brought him under our roof and I hope they both rot in hell."

Silence, metal clicking. Cynthia's mind was racing too fast for her to think straight. Should she hang up the phone and call the cops? Should she try to talk Pamela down?

"Baby sis?" Pamela whimpered.

"Yes, I'm still here."

"I'm sorry I left you behind."

"That's okay, let's just figure out what to do now."

"Oh, I got this situation tied down, girl. Don' you worry about that."

"But Pamela—"

"Baby sis?"

"Yes?"

"I love you."

The line went dead. The receiver dropped from Cynthia's pale hand. She stared ahead, unfocused, too stunned to panic, too stunned to act.

Jerry's arms wrapping around her sparked the brain back to life, and she pushed him back and reached for the phone. She punched in 911, but then began crying before she made the call.

"Baby, what's wrong?"

"What the hell am I going to tell them? I don't even know the address to my own mother's house!"

—

Jerry took over, using caller ID to get the number, then putting the rest in the hands of law enforcement. He had no idea what was happening, but just knew there was an emergency.

Cynthia cried in spastic fits for several minutes until life returned to her face. She grabbed a set of keys, kissed Jerry on the cheek and said she'd call later that night.

She was under no delusion she could save anyone. It would take her two hours to get to her mom's house. The one sliver of hope was that there might be a standoff and Cynthia would arrive in time to try to talk her sister into surrendering.

She didn't even know if that's how standoffs

really worked. All she knew was that it was finally time for her to go back home.

After twenty minutes on the road, she realized she still didn't know her mother's address. The woman had moved several times as she jumped from one boyfriend to another.

She wasn't turning around though. She would figure something out along the way. Maybe she should just go straight to the police station. They probably knew more than she did.

"Of course, call the ****ing police," Cynthia sighed, pulling out her cell phone and dialing.

It took a few transfers before Cynthia finally spoke to a sheriff that did indeed know the situation and knew a lot more than he would tell Cynthia.

He did tell her there was no stand-off, no hostage situations, that deputies were on the scene and had secured her mother's house. He told her to head straight to the sheriff station and they would talk there.

"We have everything under control, ma'am," the detective said. "So, if you want to head home and get a change of clothes and then come down, that would be fine."

A change of clothes sounded final, serious. It sounded as if she would be at her hometown for more than an hour. There would be questions, there would be blood, and if Pamela was right, there would be at least two bodies to claim.

———

The lights of the small town rose out of the dark

horizon like fog. She'd driven so far out into rural Oklahoma that there were few houses, few streetlights, only the odd ranch or farm to illuminate the countryside.

But she knew exactly where she was. She could feel the landmarks of her childhood. In another mile, she'd be near the creek where boys had once thrown rocks at her.

Another mile and half past that would be the convenience store she'd walked to on summer afternoons with her first boyfriend. He didn't have a car, so that had been the best date option available. If she drove past the turnoff to the sheriff station, venturing a couple miles back out into the countryside, she would see the dark, dirt road which would take her to the field where the baseball player forced her to give him a blowjob.

Somewhere near the high school was the house where she lost her virginity, and somewhere else out there, by the Baptist church, was the house where she'd first seen The Bear.

She wondered if she'd already driven past the house where deputies were zipping up body bags, collecting hair fibers from carpets and carefully stepping around puddles of blood slowly seeping into the carpet.

The station parking lot was nearly empty; there was only one cruiser left. The rest were out in the countryside, probably all still picking up the pieces. The thought that the deputies were with Pamela was oddly comforting.

"At least she isn't alone."

Sitting behind the receptionist desk was a round,

happy woman. Her smile warmed with sympathy as Cynthia approached.

"Are you Carey?" the woman asked.

Cynthia nodded.

"Okay, you have a seat right over there, and the sheriff will be right out, okay?"

Cynthia nodded.

"Is there anything I can get you? Coffee, water, a soda pop?"

Cynthia shook her head as she sat down and tried to make herself as small as possible. Her hands wouldn't stop trembling.

A door opened and a mountainous black man walked out. He chewed a matchstick as he walked up to the receptionist. They talked quietly, the man looked over at Cynthia and grimaced. He straightened, took the match out of his teeth and tossed it into a trashcan.

"Carey," he called. His voice was as deep as an abyss. He seemed strong, but frustrated. Cynthia could tell he was expecting lies from her. It was her family legacy.

He motioned for her to follow, and the receptionist nodded supportively. At least she had one person on her side.

—

The interview was brief as Cynthia painfully regurgitated the terrifying phone call. The sheriff took in the information passively as he glanced through a file folder. When his eyes did lift from the folder at the reference of "the Bear," his hardened demeanor softened slightly, but only briefly.

When she finished, he sat for a few minutes silently studying her. The long moments were cold, oppressive, and she couldn't stop her hands from trembling. She focused on not crying and not looking up at the man.

Finally, he excused himself to step out of the small interview room so he could get some coffee. She watched the man leave, and drained and empty as she felt, Cynthia was vaguely impressed that her little racist hometown elected a black man to public office.

Minutes passed and Cynthia's mind turned over the events. She began to panic at being held liable for all this, for not informing the police that her sister had threatened The Bear weeks before she killed him.

She decided it was best just to pretend that conversation had never happened. She still had no idea what the sheriff found at her mother's house. They hadn't told her a thing about Pamela, where she was or how she was doing.

There were no answers, just questions, but that didn't surprise her. She had been ready for questions about sex, drugs, family history and a deadbeat dad. All he wanted to know was what Cynthia had heard over the phone line.

But he didn't let her leave the room, so maybe the tough questions were reserved for the last.

The door opened and the sheriff walked in with a short, white deputy in his early thirties.

"Hi, Carey," the deputy said warmly as he approached. "Don't remember me?"

Cynthia shook her head.

"Donnie Adams," he replied, sitting down on the

chair at the other side of the table.

It was the man she'd lost her virginity to. The first boy she'd fallen in love with, who'd cheated on her, lived with a stripper and was as brilliant as he was dangerous.

He was a sheriff's deputy and it made Cynthia chuckle.

"Huh," Donnie shrugged. "I get that a lot."

"He's been a pain in the ass," the sheriff sighed as he held the door open. "But I haven't fired him yet."

"Yet," Donnie echoed.

"Well, you have this?" the sheriff asked, and Donnie nodded.

The sheriff closed the door, leaving Donnie and Cynthia, now Carey, alone. Donnie leaned back in the chair and studied Cynthia with a slim smile.

"Tough day, huh?" Donnie finally said.

Cynthia nodded.

"I know that you had a tough time at home, and I think I remember that this Russell Windstrum had once lived with you."

"Who?" Cynthia asked, but then remembered that was the Bear's real name. She didn't like how the real name made the man seem human.

"Large white male, sixties, tattoos covering his arms, long beard—"

"Yeah, he lived with us," Cynthia interrupted. "I forgot his name."

"Well, he was shot twice with a shotgun, once in the head, once in the groin," Donnie said, watching Cynthia steadily. "Your father, he was also there."

"Are they both dead?"

Donnie paused, still watching Cynthia.

"Yeah, Carey, they're both dead."

"And my sister?"

Donnie glanced back to the door, then turned back to her.

"Carey, your sister set fire to the whole house," Donnie said. "And it went up fast and she was burned alive. We're not sure whether she intended on killing herself or if she'd gotten trapped inside, but she was dead by the time we arrived. I'm very sorry."

"Burned alive." It wasn't just "passed away," "died," or "perished." It was brutal, it was agonizing. It meant a closed casket, it meant no "goodbye." It was the source material for a month's worth of hell and brimstone sermons and the beginning of countless urban legends. Her family was once just a blight on this small town, but it would now be a horror story.

Cynthia grimaced, tears escaped, but she took a deep breath to calm herself. She wiped away the tears and straightened her back. For some reason, it felt important to seem strong, dignified.

"And my mother?"

"She's alive, not a scratch on her. She'd climbed out a window when the fire started."

Cynthia knew instantly how much better she would have felt, in the long run, had her mother died too.

"What do you remember about Windstrum?" Donnie asked. "Did he have any contact with your sister? She'd moved out while you were still a kid, right?"

And there was the question. There was no getting around this moment. The pool of poison that the man had injected into Cynthia's life was what the deputy was searching for, because that would then tie up the investigation neatly. It would make sense of a shooting spree.

Cynthia resisted. It was her secret, the deputy had no right to it. The sheriff had no right to it. The people of the town had no right to it.

But, she thought, would the truth revise the town's image of her sister? Would it reward her for taking an evil man out of this world? Would it punish the memory of her despicable father and scar the remaining days of her weak mother?

"Can you get me a Dr. Pepper?" Cynthia asked.

Donnie didn't answer for a few moments as he stared into her eyes. Finally, he smiled.

"Sure, anything you want."

The deputy knocked on the door, it opened and he disappeared.

Cynthia wanted to cry; she knew the release would make her feel better, but she simply didn't have the emotional resources. She felt empty.

The door opened again and Donnie sat a fizzing plastic cup next to her and then returned to his seat. He was trying to hide that clever smirk that was either infuriating or amusing, depending on what words followed it.

"Where were we?" he asked.

"Windstrum," Cynthia said. "We called him The Bear."

"The Bear? Why?"

"Pamela came up with it," Cynthia answered, clinching her hands to calm the trembles. She took the cup, brought it to her lips and drank it all.

"Bottoms up," Donnie said, that smirk jumping to

his face. He hid it, quickly, then rolled his eyes. "Sorry, not very professional of me."

"Force of habit, I suppose," Cynthia smiled.

"Yup."

Cynthia smiled, lingering on his eyes. She remembered how tender he had been with her. He was an asshole, he was full of himself, but she also trusted him. When he'd cheated on her, it came as no surprise to anyone involved. He just was who he was, and Cynthia was glad that he was the one sitting across the table from her.

"Pamela named him The Bear because he looked like one," Cynthia started. "Especially when we were kids."

"How long did he live with your family?"

"Let's just get to it," Cynthia snapped, taking a deep breath and feeling surprisingly invigorated. "You want to know if Pamela killed him because of drugs or sex. It was sex, he was a pervert, a vicious man and he deserved exactly what he got."

"Why didn't either of you ever go to the authorities?"

"My parents…I don't know why, we just– couldn't," Cynthia answered. "My parents, both of them, are awful people. My sister drove off with me one night to get away from The Bear, but you people just brought me back to this sinkhole of a town."

"Okay," Donnie whispered, pulling out a tissue from a box on the side of the table. He handed it to Cynthia, but she was so numb she hadn't realized she'd finally started crying.

"Did you know that your sister was planning this or even just thinking about it?"

"No," Cynthia answered, perhaps too quickly. Donnie's eyes lingered on her for a few moments, but then dropped away while the smirk returned.

"Can we get you a room at the hotel?" he asked.

"I'm not that easy, deputy," Cynthia laughed.

Donnie chuckled and stood.

"It's late. I wouldn't feel right, you driving all the way back to El Reno at night."

"Don't you worry about me. I'm not a helpless little girl anymore."

Donnie walked to the door and knocked to be let out. He turned back to Cynthia and gave her the clever grin one last time.

"I can see that."

—

Donnie ultimately won out, saying Cynthia was needed for more questioning, thus holding her in town for one more night.

She was worried that she'd placed her trust in Donnie too readily and that after seeing through her lie, he would suggest the sheriff question her further. Then she would be arrested, then she would go to jail, then her baby would have no mommy, then the farm would fall apart and then she would finally become exactly like her mother.

Cynthia thought about having Jerry hire a lawyer, but decided she didn't want to worry him.

She insisted on a room at the motel with no guests on either side. She intended on crying loudly that night and no one in that godforsaken town had the right to hear her.

The emotions that swirled inside her were massive and formless like storm fronts. They approached, they were inevitable, but also indistinguishable. She had a hard time deciphering exactly how she felt.

Sorrow? But for what? A lost father? No. A lost sister? Perhaps?

Sympathy? For her sister, of course. For her mother, no, but there was something there, a pang that she couldn't quite work out. She wasn't sure if it was regret that the woman was so wasted, or maybe fear that her mother's mangled life was the inevitable outcome of her own.

Fear? Yes. The town was a trap, and it had snagged her again. It wanted to destroy her like it had destroyed the rest of her family.

The television flickered deep into the night, well after Cynthia had finally fallen asleep. The Bear waited for Carey in her dreams, but a sense of freedom emerged as she awoke in the morning.

Her dreams were now the last refuge for The Bear. He was the one who was trapped. He could haunt her while she slept, but his shadow would soon fade forever from her waking life. In time, the maggots will have eaten out his cold, evil eyes, gnawed the flesh off his strong, hungry fingers, and burrowed through the man's dark, diseased mind.

The corpses weren't the only evidence found at her mother's house. The Bear had been dealing out of the guestroom, meaning that Cynthia's mother survived a bloodbath just to be sent to jail for the fourth time in her sad life.

Cynthia stuck around just long enough to convince Donnie to let her talk to her mother one last time.

The woman was frail, boney. Her gray roots were chasing the blonde dye out to the tips of her hair. Her eyes seemed like small, glassy marbles.

Her mother managed a smile as Cynthia walked into the interview room. She stood and took a step toward Cynthia, but she was handcuffed to the table.

"Sit down, now," Donnie warned, and her mother complied.

"Hey honey," her mother said, her syllables soft as she showed her exposed gums. The deputies had been unable to find her dentures.

"I need your help, baby. They're trying to pin this on me."

Cynthia sat down silently.

"I need to borrow some money for a lawyer and bail. I can't go back to jail again," her mother pleaded.

Cynthia leaned back, trying to give her mother the same measured stare Donnie had given her. The woman returned the stare with a forced smile.

"You sure did grow up pretty," her mother said. "Are you married? Any grandkids for me to play with?"

"I am married, and I do have a child, but not one you can play with. You will never touch my life again."

Her mother gave a wounded frown, but seeing her daughter's resolve, the frown quickly hardened as she straightened her back.

"You gonna blame me too?" her mother sneered. "That's fine, get on the bandwagon. I only raised you and sent you off to college. Don't mind paying me back for that. Just take advantage of me like everyone else does."

"You ruined Pamela," Cynthia replied flatly. "You ruined me. You knew what that man was doing to us. This is all your fault."

"What do you mean? I don't know what you mean."

Her mother looked away from her, impatient. She tried to fold her arms, forgetting that one hand was handcuffed. "I'm not in the mood."

"You knew the whole time," Cynthia continued. "It was your job as our mother to know when I was suffering and protect me, but you didn't. You could have let Pamela take me away from it all, but you brought me back and sent your other daughter to jail."

"I don't know what you're talking about."

"Yes you do," Cynthia growled. "You didn't give a **** about me, and you sure as hell didn't give a damn about Pamela. It didn't matter who you hurt as long as the drugs kept coming through the door. You tried to ruin my life just like you ruined Pamela, so both of us could be miserable and evil, just like you. But you failed. I'm leaving here. I'm leaving, and I'm taking Pamela with me."

"Huh," her mother chuckled. "She's not gonna be a good travel buddy, what with being dead and all."

Cynthia's face paled.

"I don't know what you're talking about," her mother continued, seeing the exposed nerve. "Maybe something happened, maybe someone touched you."

"Maybe?" Cynthia repeated weakly.

"It's just sex, honey. I don't know why you made such a big deal out of it. We never beat you, we never stole from you. If the worst that ever happened to you was a man got a little handsy, then you're lucky. That's just what men do."

"No, it isn't," Cynthia hissed, her breath lumped in her throat.

"If you think you had it so ***damn hard," her mother hissed, "I can tell you about my childhood. I can tell you about real pain. What I went through—"

"I'm done with you," Cynthia snapped and stood up from the table. She wanted to throw a chair; she wanted to beat the woman's head in, finish the job that her sister had begun. Instead, she turned away and knocked on the door.

Her mother suddenly stood to follow her. The handcuffs scrapped along the bar on the table; she yanked forward like a leashed dog.

"Wait, baby, we ain't done talkin'!"

Cynthia didn't turn around. In her mind, she pleaded for Donnie to open the door and let her out.

"Honey, I'm sorry!" her mother called. "I'm sorry for it all. You're right, I should have protected you. And I will, from now on, but first I need your help. Please, give me another chance!"

The door opened and Cynthia pushed past Donnie and strode through the station toward the font door. Her mother's screaming voice followed her all the way outside, but finally faded as Cynthia reached her car.

Cynthia had planned to leave poor, boney Carey in that room forever, leave her scarred childhood for her mother to live with for the rest of the woman's miserable existence.

But in the end, she took Carey back out with her. Cynthia knew she would be naïve to think her mother would ever feel remorse. She was beyond that now. So, Cynthia took the damaged little girl back to El Reno to nurse her back to health. Carey would live on as a constant reminder of everything she never wanted to happen to her own child.

"I will never be like my mother," Cynthia whispered as her head rested against the steering wheel. "I will never be like my mother. I will never be like my mother. I will never be like my mother."

—

Pamela's ashes were buried near Cynthia's favorite oak tree at the farm. It was tall, strong, and reached its thick branches over Pamela's resting place. Honeysuckle wound around the fence that passed along the grave, and Cynthia seemed to remember that they were Pamela's favorite flowers.

FUN FACT: Alias
Using nicknames or initials is advisable online, but when meeting in the real world, go ahead and give out first names. The last name should be withheld, and the other party really has no need for them anyway. If you are too nervous about a prospective couple to give out your real first names, then perhaps that's a good indication you shouldn't sleep with them.

Superswingers
Part VII

Barry and Mary sipped on cocktails as they glanced around at the stragglers still in the bar. Mary insisted that they wait until they met someone they liked before heading back to the open door parties. She insisted that regardless of how it appeared and what organizers said, there was still a protocol, and an "open door" isn't necessarily an open door to everyone.

Mary – "You get that sometimes with clubs and parties. Some are just so cliquish. It's like an exclusive party that they say is open. They'll take your membership money, but once you're in, unless you know someone within one of the groups, you are just isolated the whole night."

Barry – "And we're some of the most attractive people here, so it's not like we shouldn't have plenty of options."

Mary – "**** 'em if they don't know a good thing

when they see it. Oh well, you can't win every time. We'll hang out a little longer, see if anything develops, but if not…"

Barry – "Do you think the guy with the misfire in the backroom might have poisoned the well?"

Mary – "What, like went around and talked shit about us so now everyone is keeping their distance? Maybe."

Barry – "That happens too, where a rumor spreads about a new couple and then everyone backs off them. You have to pay attention to the grapevine too, because you just don't know what could be out there."

Mary – "Just like a god**** high school cafeteria."

Barry – "So, it's not just being afraid you'll run into someone you know, but also being afraid of pissing off the wrong person."

DRESS CODE

Mary – "It's all what you're comfortable with, really. I don't exactly agree with the wardrobe choices you see made in the clubs, but we aren't as outwardly judgmental."

Barry – "If you have a C-Section scar the size of a machete blade, you probably shouldn't wear low-rise boy shorts, but if you do, no one will say anything to make you feel bad about it."

Mary – "We'll wait until you leave."

Barry – "Right, well, there are limits to our tact."

Mary – "I tend to dress conservatively, or conservatively for the club. Some girls will go walking around with little more than panties on, and that's fine. Clubs will have themes, and some couples will dress up for each theme, like grass skirts, leather, schoolgirl outfits, that sort of thing."

Barry – "I'm not a big costume guy, so I'm not really that into the themes."

Mary – "It's true, he won't even dress up for Halloween."

Barry(shrugs) – "But I do appreciate the effort other people put in. Hell, you'll see costumes that'll rival what you see in some of the high-end strip clubs in Las Vegas. The big difference is, here I have a much better chance of sticking my penis in one of them by the end of the night."

Mary – "Oh, and speaking of strip clubs, don't wear belts with big buckles."

Barry – "Very true. Never do that. You don't want to add another piece of clothing that will limit...access, but also it's bad when girls are giving you a lap dance."

Mary – "There is a lot of grinding going on at these places, so if you have a buckle with an eagle jutting out that's going to jab me in the twat, then don't expect me to be rubbing myself all over you all night."

Barry – "Wasn't there a guy with some kind of crucifix buckle or something that actually cut you on the butt?"

Mary – "Yeah, that was oddly appropriate, I suppose."

RETIREMENT

Mary(glancing at Barry) – "We'll know when its time, I think."

Barry – "We actually talk about this every year on our anniversary, which is kind of weird, but it's an agreement we have."

Mary – "Kind of like an annual review to make sure everyone is still on board. To be honest, there have been times that I've wanted to back away from the Lifestyle for good. It's not an easy thing to do. It's like perpetually dating, which comes with a good deal of rejection and heart break."

Barry – "And I try to be as sensitive as I can, but I'm a guy, so my default setting is to try to spread my seed to as wide a populace as possible."

Mary – "He means that metaphorically. He's fixed."

Barry – "You make me sound like the cat. I still have my nuts."

Mary – "Yeah but they are more just for decoration now, not really practical."

Barry – "Yes, thank you for the clarification."

(Mary smirked, then kissed Barry on the cheek.)

Barry – "Anyway, so I try to be sensitive to her reservations, and when it's time to take a break, we take a break. A lot of times that comes after a couple blows us off or when we get an STD scare."

Mary – "Still clear (knocked on the table). But there will come a time, I think, when we will turn our backs on all this for good. It will be hard, because this is the only social network I've ever really felt comfortable in. There is an all-in-it-together mentality that makes for a really warm environment. There are good times, there are bad times, but the friends we've met here accept us in a way that our vanilla friends never really will. Perhaps some people might think we are just reinforcing each other's bad decisions, but we aren't doing drugs, we're not alcoholics, and I don't see this behavior as inherently destructive to our relationship."

Barry – "It works for us. For some it might not be a good fit."

Mary – "It makes us happy right now at this point in our lives. Maybe it won't tomorrow, and if that's the case, I feel our relationship is strong enough that when this is no longer a good fit for us, we will be able to walk away together."

Barry and Mary smiled at each other, then leaned over and kissed.

FUN FACT: Breaking Up is Hard to Do
Avoidance is the best tactic for breaking up with another couple. A rejection is always personal, even within the Lifestyle, and any break up, no matter how delicate, could distance you from mutual friends. Just fake schedule conflicts, try to avoid going to the same parties or events, and if they don't get the hint, than shift to a scorched Earth policy: sever all contacts and start fresh in a new swinger circle.

The Fishbowl
Part VII

Eight hours, Four hundred eighty minutes, Twenty-eight thousand, eight hundred seconds.

Michelle realized she would have to delay the countdown. There was too much left to do.

In five hours, she would need to drag Brad to The Rumormill to meet Will and his punk princess. That meant in three hours she would need to take a shower, shave her legs, moisturize, set her hair, pick out her outfit, begin on her makeup, make sure Brad was getting ready, curl her hair, find her shoes, look over Brad and make adjustments and then leave.

The sketches went quickly. She had thirty works that she thought were worth finishing. There were five that she loved beyond anything she'd ever accomplished in her life.

Only two were finished. She was being too exact,

but she had to be. This was her final statement to the world. She would have to delay the countdown.

She'd considered backing out tonight, but her hand was cramping and she'd reached her creative wall. Her mind and body needed a break.

She sighed, put down a paintbrush and peeled off her headphones.

"Now you listen to me," an aged and graveled female voice called through the door. "I want this door open now!"

Michelle didn't know how long her mom had been yelling, but smiled at the thought of the former beauty queen and current functioning alcoholic turning progressively darker shades of red as her failure of a daughter had the nerve to ignore her commands. Michelle opened a window and waved the drifting veil of smoke outside.

She'd bought a joint from a girl at the concert the night before. She felt both liberated and ridiculous asking the girl with dark purple hair for something as juvenile as marijuana. Michelle had waited until today to smoke it, and was, sadly, very underwhelmed. She felt more relaxed, but nothing mind-altering. She'd rather be drunk.

She was now able to check it off her list, so it was worth the disappointment and the dry scratchy throat.

Michelle walked to the door and eased it open at first, then realizing she didn't care if her mom smelled the pot, opened the door fully.

Her mother wore the prototypical old woman pantsuit with a bedazzled, black, white, and red swirled top.

She looked up at Michelle with a cold, disapproving stare.

"Can I help you?" Michelle asked formally.

"Brad said you won't come out of your room," her mother grumbled.

"Not true, I've left the room several times. I'm just busy."

"He said he thinks you're depressed."

Michelle glanced down the hall and saw Brad's head peaking around the corner before disappearing like a prairie dog.

"I feel great. We're planning on going out tonight. I just want to finish up what I'm working on before getting ready."

"You're not depressed?"

"No, ma'am."

"You're not a shut-in?"

"No, ma'am."

"Because I didn't raise you to be a shut-in."

"I know, ma'am."

"Okay, then I'm going back home."

The old woman shuffled down the hall, and when she turned the corner to see Brad spying, she shook her head.

"I don't know why my daughter married such an idiot."

And then she was gone.

Michelle would miss her mother.

—

Five and a half hours. Three hundred thirty minutes. Nineteen thousand, eight hundred seconds.

Michelle finally gave up on finishing any more paintings for the night. She would be forced to give herself a reprieve.

Her mind had not sparkled with this level of happiness and optimism in decades. She was thrilled every time she looked across the volume of work, and was deeply in love with this new direction her life had taken.

Did that mean she had days, weeks, months, years left in her life?

She didn't know, but decided that life would tell her when it was her time.

Yet, she still maintained the countdown. If it wasn't to the end of her life, then perhaps something else would change at the zero hour.

Maybe that is when she would tell Brad their relationship was over.

No, that still seemed impossible. She was tethered to the man in a way she didn't fully understand. Perhaps it was habit or residual love that had hardened into obligation.

Regardless of where her path was leading, at this particular stretch, she was happy—whether or not the path would soon lead her off the edge of a cliff.

Her to-do list for the night began with a generous pour of wine and then a long bath. Her gynecologist told her that prolonged baths led to urinary tract infections, but if Michelle did go through with the suicide, then her body wouldn't have time to develop a full-blown UTI. That made the night an opportune time to indulge.

She lit candles, put on a Decembrists album and undressed.

The door edged open and Brad walked in.
"Can I join you?"
Michelle started to say no, but changed her mind. The over-sized tub was big enough to accommodate them both, and this might be the last time she would have Brad alone.
"What the hell?" Michelle smiled.
Brad quickly undressed as Michelle eased into the tub.
"No boom boom until tonight though," Michelle said, watching his erection approach.
"I know," he chuckled as he stepped into the tub.
They both laid back, head to toe. Michelle placed a towel against the lip of the bath and laid her head against it like a pillow. She liked the feel of his leg hair tickling against her. She liked how his subtle movements sent waves toward her. She liked this. If only they could spend the remainder of their marriage in a tub, then they might be happy.
Her eyes shut, she let the warm water soak into her skin without either of them saying a word. After a few minutes, Brad sat up and watched her.
"Yes?" Michelle asked, not opening her eyes.
"I'm sorry I called your mom, I was just worried about you."
"No problem," Michelle answered. "Seems like you got the worst of it anyway."
"Yeah, she's never liked me."
Bard continued to watch her. Michelle didn't mind; she liked to be stared at.
"Are you going to leave me?" Brad asked.
"Sssh. Let's just enjoy this."
Michelle laid her hand on Brad's leg and caressed

it. He placed his palm on her thigh, stroked gently, began wandering northward, but remembering her prohibition until tonight, politely retreated back to her knee.

She knew that her subtle gesture meant, in Brad's mind, "You're being silly. She would never leave you. How could she? It is just one of her phases."

He smiled, laid back against the tub, and there they soaked, silently, for twenty minutes before Michelle was finally ready to face the rest of the night.

—

Three hours. One hundred eighty minutes. Ten thousand, eight hundred seconds.

It was so close now, Michelle had a hard time concentrating on anything else.

Would she go through with it?

She didn't think so. Too much left to paint. They would likely still be at The Rumormill by the zero hour, and she was looking forward to the chance to play with Will and his darling wife again.

The crowd was light as they walked in through the back door. The owners didn't mind if some of their more prominent members snuck in where there would definitely be no photographers, police or any other possible embarrassments.

Michelle saw all the regulars, but no sign of the young couple.

There were Barry and Mary though, talking to a tall bald man with a notepad and a voice recorder lying on the table.

Brad motioned over to the owner, the wife of a

deceased oil man. She'd been swinging since God was a child and had become emotionally attached to the Lifestyle, since it was where her closest friends came from.

    She was always so sweet.

    "What's with the guy with the notepad?" Brad asked the owner.

    "Oh, he's okay," the owner smiled. "He's writing a book about the Lifestyle and came with Mary and Barry. He's not taking names or anything like that."

    Brad nodded and then led Michelle to the other side of the club, just to be safe.

    A few of the lower-end couples were already dancing; two women were making out in the shadowbox. Most everyone else were sitting around tables and drinking to ease the nerves.

    Brad watched the bald man with the notepad skeptically for a half hour, then seemed to forget him and ended up on the dance floor with a homely blonde woman only wearing a teddy. Brad liked to start the night out with a gimmie. He called it his "practice swing."

    Michelle chatted with a Hispanic couple while she kept one eye on the door. The female wasn't sure about the Lifestyle and was clearly just humoring her husband. The man was not so subtly trying to convince Michelle to kiss his wife.

    When Will and Elena finally appeared, Michelle practically jumped from her chair to meet them at the door.

FUN FACT: Alcohol
Most Lifestyle clubs and events are BYOB, so it is recommended to bring a little alcohol to help relax and share with others. What you bring should be fun, perhaps alcohol-infused whip cream or premixed-shots. Just know your limits, because there is nothing more horrifying than a sloppy drunk swinger.

A Charmed Life
Part VII

"Oh Christ, is that really Vanilla Ice?" I grumbled.

We were lingering in the hallway leading to The Rumormill as the music pounded through the building's thin walls.

Elena primped her hair and checked her makeup in a mirror conveniently positioned before the point of no return to the swing club. She smirked and glanced at my reflection.

"Don't try to be superior, Will," she quipped. "'Cause I know for a fact that you still have every word to this song memorized."

She was right, of course, but I refuse to be held to account for any of my misguided choices made during my horrific junior high experience. I simply did not know any better. She'd stumbled upon my unfortunate secret while we were still dating and she'd caught me singing along when Ben Kweller covered it at a concert.

Elena turned from the mirror, placed her hands on my hips and leaned her body against mine.

"Come on now, baby," Elena purred, then began waving her body with the beat. "Go rush the speaker that boom, I'm killing yo' brain like a poisonous mushroom."

"No," I replied flatly.

"Deadly, when I play a dope melody," she continued undeterred, letting her lips brush against mine as she rapped in a whisper. "Anything less than the best is a felony. Love it or leave it, you betta gain way, you betta hit bull's eye, this kid don't play."

She arched her eyebrow. I sighed and mumbled:

"If there was a problem, yo, I'll solve it, check out the hook while my DJ revolves it. Can we go now?"

She turned, grasped my hand and sang the chorus as she led me down the hallway.

"****ing Junior High," I grumbled as I watched Elena's butt wiggle to the music.

Approaching the front door, I heard giggling women and bombastic men. My frown dissipated, replaced by the same nervous grin I get before walking into any swinging situation.

If I can steal a metaphor from my brief and unfortunate high school theater career: Elena and I were enveloped in that eagerness that came when stealing glances behind the curtain at the crowd which filed into the theater and took their seats. We were looking for the faces that we wanted to be there and cringing at the faces that we'd hoped not to see.

Then we vanquished that excitement, because it was now time to get into character.

After paying our way into the swing club, we paused to give ourselves a moment to step into our other skin. I had to find Mr. Asshole. I needed to pull on his clothes, I had to take on his voice, I needed to steal his mannerisms and prop myself up with his inflated ego.

Our grand appearance approached as we awaited our cue while hiding in the shadows. We knew our lines; we knew our blocking. Our costumes were as perfect as they were going to get. Our props were set[32]. There was nothing left to prepare.

It would either be good enough to win the hearts of the audience or we would fall flat on our faces. This being my farewell performance, I needed it to be stellar so I could finish out my abbreviated career in style.

A sense of destiny had taken hold. The evening was out of our control, so all we could do was put on our faces, play our parts, and hope everything else unfolded as scripted.

I realized the doorman was talking to us, or rather, talking to Elena as he put on her wristband. He was tall and imposing—as he should be, since Lifestyle clubs are essentially speakeasies. They are either at someone's house, in far removed locales, disguised within the innards of large hotels, or tucked away in seemingly unused corners of strip malls. For this particular club, located in an industrial complex, there were no exterior markings to distinguish one gunmetal-grey door from any other gunmetal-grey door in the building.

---

[32] Gross.

You were only here if you were in on the secret, and being a part of this hidden world would be something I would definitely miss.

"You are looking great tonight, sugar," the bouncer said to my wife.

"Thanks, honeybear," she replied with a coy smile. "How's the crowd looking?"

"Pretty good already and should get better. We got lots of RSVPs."

"Good news," Elena replied as her eyes passed to me, giving me a wink.

"Aww, ya'll just the cutest couple," a greeter said. The middle-aged woman wearing a silk nightie was one of the old guard. Perhaps she no longer had a sculpted hardbody, and age was showing through the lines in her face, but she was eager, accessible and friendly, which was why her job was to meet newbies and show them around the club.

The most important function of the greeters was to ensure everyone knew what kind of playing field they would be roaming around that night.

And yes, there have been times that women were brought here on dates without being told they were stepping into a swing club. That was part of that sleazy underbelly of the Lifestyle that I definitely would not miss.

The tours were also a handy way to familiarize newbies with all the dark corners of the club that would otherwise be too intimidating to peek into. And what good are dark corners if there is nobody there, right?

There are staples seen at every Lifestyle Club:
1. Stripper Pole(s)

2. Dance Floor
3. A space reserved for those who like to be tied up and spanked.
4. A sex couch.
5. A buffet of snack food and beverages.[33]

    Clubs are dark with copious use of black lights. The low lighting camouflages body flaws like unseemly bulges, scars, or stretch marks.
    The Rumormill had worked out a deal with a nearby hotel for discounted rooms. When guests did retire to their rooms, they were to keep festivities reserved to the floor sectioned out for noisy and sleepless swingers.
    There were dozens of tables spread out across the large room with tablecloths for discretion. A play room was tucked behind curtains in the back, and a human-sized bird cage was constructed near the stripper pole.
    The club had themes for every party, and this one was Hawaiian, so brightly colored leis were sprinkled over the tables. There were many grass skirts shimmying around the club, and coconut-shell bras were worn by several big-breasted women and even one obese man with a cowboy hat.
    The majority of the couples came without costumes, instead opting for whatever they felt most attractive in, or even wearing civilian cloths on the off chance they might run into someone from their

---

[33] Might be unsettling, but once inside a club and stripped down to the bare essentials, one is not exactly in a position for a quick trip to a convenience store.

regular lives. Being inside the club would seem undeniable condemnation, but perhaps they could make a passable case that they had gotten lost looking for the ice machine.

Though swing clubs look very similar to strip clubs, the atmosphere is entirely different. Strip clubs are shark tanks, with the patrons playing the part of hapless fish and the strippers as the single-minded killing machines gliding through the schools of unsuspecting, wide-eyed men to find the meatiest morsel to latch onto.

There is no satisfaction within a strip club, no sense of victory to be had, and certainly no balance between the predator and the prey.

But in a swing club, everyone is there for the exact same reason. It is a social club before anything else. Unlike dance clubs where the music is booming, talking at a Lifestyle event is a must, so the music is kept at a moderate level.

Also unlike a dance club, once the guests are inside, they only leave the club to go to their hotel rooms. When a woman is wearing little more than a thong and body paint, she can't exactly step outside to smoke and shoot the shit with others or jog in her six inch stilettos to the Taco Bell next door.

So, Lifestyle clubs have to stay hidden, have to remain exclusive, and find a way to shelter their customers from the judgmental world outside.

Tables instinctively segregate by socioeconomic status, age, intellect and attractiveness. The older biker crowd gathers in the biggest clusters in the smoking section. This is where the most fun is generally had.

The upper-middle class, middle-aged crowd generally gathers in the non-smoking section near the dance floor. These couples are veterans of the scene and know each other very well, and have slept with most of everyone else in their crowd. The women are, on average, in better shape than the bikers. They have well-maintained tans, subtle tummy tuck scars, and breast implants.

The men are management material with gelled up hair, expensive suits, and midlife-crisis chips on their shoulders. There are also many second wives in this group.

For the most part, the men and women dance throughout the night and are on "dates" with specific couples.

A smaller third group is made up of swingers in their twenties and thirties. They sit in tight huddles, spend most of their time making snide comments about the tragically underdressed. Their standards are so high, they hook up on a much lower rate then the other two groups.

The young swingers sit further back from the dance floor where the people-watching is at its best. They see themselves as the rebellious kids who crouch in the back of the classroom and pass a Dr. Pepper can filled with vodka back and forth while making rude comments about the teacher.

Sprinkled in the very far corners of the club are the newbies. Young and old, attractive or not, the newbies are waiting to be snatched up by one of the cliques. If they are entirely new to the scene, they will almost certainly hook up with someone that night. They'd built the night up so much in their minds that they aren't going home until someone new has ****ed them.

Their standards are low, but if they can hook up with another newbie couple, then they can still do quite well for themselves.

Despite her recent reticence to continue on in the Lifestyle, Elena seemed really excited to come out tonight. She was very handsy, blushed as we pulled up to the motel, and just overall seemed very upbeat. But as I glanced through the crowd and then looked over to my punk goddess, I had the first of many long-awaited epiphanies.

Yes, I know, a little late in the game, but epiphanies come when they are ready. I compared this gorgeous woman who put up with my bull**** for reasons unknown to me to the other women in the room. I was suddenly very ashamed for bringing Elena here.

I'd always felt she was head and shoulders above the other women within the Lifestyle, but she was actually an entirely different breed. This wasn't for her, she had always just been humoring me. This was her price to pay for being married to me. This is how I took advantage of her.

But we were there already, so might as well settle in.

Addiction is a *****.

We'd barely set two feet into the club before I saw Michelle walking our way. She was wearing a black lace top and black boy shorts. She looked incredible, and she was waiting for us, which felt good. Didn't extinguish the shame, mind you, but served as a nice distraction.

Michelle waved at us, but then got cut off by an already drunk and overweight woman who leaned in to plant a kiss. Michelle pulled back and hugged the woman in a stiff-armed way to create distance between the two.

While Michelle was stuck in that unfortunate mess, I took a quick look through the club to see who else was there. My goal for every trip to a club was to kiss at least four women by the end of the night, which is generally easy since it's as acceptable for friendly couples as a handshake.

But it was also something that had seemed incomprehensible for my entire adult life leading up to the Lifestyle.

Around seventy couples were packed in already, a pretty decent showing for one of the clubs' regular events. There were bimonthly parties, which averaged forty couples each, and then four annual blowouts that might get one hundred or more couples. The red-letter days were on Halloween, New Year's Eve, and Valentine's Day, and then a two-day pool party in the summer.

Amongst the sea of candidates was one person whose presence instantly ruined my night. I squeezed Elena's hand and gave her my "Oh shit, let's get out of here" look.

"Where?" she asked, and I nodded toward a table where two of our previous acquaintances sat with a tall, bald-headed man.

"Mary and Barry?" Elena asked. "I like them, they're nice."

"Sitting with them," I whispered.

Elena took a few steps ahead to get a better look.

Her eyes narrowed as her back stiffened.

"That is not ****ing Charles, is it?" she asked.

"It is."

"What the hell is he doing here?" Elena asked, turning her back.

"I don't know, but let's get out of here."

Before I could turn away, Mary stood and waved to me. Unfortunately, I'd already been staring directly at her, so there was no turning away now. As I gazed dumbly ahead, Charles turned toward me and then smiled big and wide.

"F***."

Michelle finally unlatched from the overweight woman and made her way to Elena and I. She hugged Elena first, then me.

"Is everything all right?" Michelle asked.

I pulled her close to whisper in her ear.

"I just saw my business associate here. We need to escape, like right now."

"Oh Jesus, really?" Michelle asked. "Where do you want to go?"

"I don't know, but just not here," Elena said.

"Okay," Michelle nodded. "Let me go find Brad and we'll meet you in the parking lot."

I gave her an inaudible "thank you" and disappeared out the door with Elena in tow. It's not like it made a difference, Charles had already seen me, but I just couldn't be there with him in the room as well.

"Do you think he knew we were going to be here?" Elena asked as we got to my car.

"I don't know," I sighed, unlocking her door and opening it for her. "Do you remember the top secret

project he and I have been working on?"
"Yeah," she replied wearily.
"Well, um, I think he's here doing research," I confessed.
Elena studied me for a few moments.
"You guys are writing a book on the Lifestyle?"
I nodded.
"You are writing a book on swinging?"
"Yes, that is correct."
"Swapping couples."
"The very same."
She tapped her fingers on the car.
"Is that what this whole thing was about? You were doing research?"
"Yes and no," I replied. "Mostly no, I was just horny."
She met my eyes.
"You put us in the book, didn't you?"
My eyes were most definitely shifty.
"Will, please be honest with me."
"Um, well, I kind of needed to because of the way I wrote it."
Elena burst out laughing, but not that delighted laughter, more a maniacal laughter like my mother had when she knew she would be giving me swats once we got home from the mall.
"Jesus Christ, Will, you are such a head case. Did you at least change my name?"
"Yes," I lied.
She laughed. She leaned over and kissed me on the cheek.
"This is good," she smirked as she sat down into the car. "I was worried we were going to run out of

things to talk about in therapy."

She closed the car door and I slowly made my way over to the other side. I opened the driver's side door and she leaned over the consol.

"Out of curiosity, how far along are you?" she asked, looking up at me.

"Almost done, just waiting for an ending."

She patted the driver's seat so I sat down, waiting for a deluge. Instead she put her lips against my ear.

"Well, then, let's get you that ending."

She nibbled my ear lobe and I blushed a fiery red.

She sat back and pulled down the passenger visor so she could look in the mirror.

"Did you say I was pretty in the book?" she asked, not looking away from the mirror.

"Yes, of course I did."

"How pretty?" she insisted.

"Devastatingly pretty. You are my punk goddess, after all."

"Punk goddess," she echoed, blowing a kiss to the mirror. "I like that."

I took a relaxed breath, knowing that this wasn't the end of the matter, but for now, the waters were calm.

"Thank God I came dressed like a normal person tonight," Elena said, flipping up the visor. "Can you imagine if he would have showed up another night when I was dressed like a whore?"

I shivered, wanting to throw up a bit. I glanced in the side mirror to see the club entrance, waiting for Michelle to appear.

I pulled out my phone and began to dial Michelle's number, but then saw her walking alone through the parking lot. She had a skirt and a clingy tank top on. I stood up out of the car and waved.

"Brad is indisposed," she called to me. "Looks like it'll just be me. Can I ride with you?"

Red flags! Many, many red flags!

Her tits did look great though.

"Sure."

Elena was surprised to see Michelle climbing into the backseat of the car, but hid her irritation well. I gave Elena a slight, nervous shrug.

"So, where are we off to?" Michelle asked as she settled into her seat.

I couldn't conceive of ever leaving Elena behind at a Lifestyle event, and I knew she wouldn't ever leave with another couple, so alarm bells were ringing loudly.

Clearly, Brad was somewhere with another woman, which I guess is okay, but us leaving the site with his wife was something entirely different.

"Not sure. Will Brad be joining us later?" Elena asked.

"He met up with some friends in the club and I didn't want to disturb him," Michelle declared. "He'll be fine, though, I assure you."

Elena and I exchanged glances.

"Do you want to come back to my house? Will had mentioned taking a look at what I've been working on lately."

"Did he?" Elena asked Michelle, but while looking at me. "Sounds fun."

This was not how I pictured this night playing

out at all.

—

A brief, silent car ride ended with us parked behind a gas station, Michelle sitting on the hood smoking a joint while Elena and I whispered inside the car.

"What the hell are we going to do?" Elena asked.

"I don't know, I don't think we should ditch her."

"No, we can't do that, but this is weird."

"No arguments, here. I'm sorry, I wouldn't have agreed to give her a ride, but she kind of just surprised me."

"No, no, don't worry about it," Elena sighed, glancing at Michelle's back leaning against the windshield. "Um, she seems like she's in a bad place, and I'm not sure what's up with Brad, but we should take her home. Let's look over her paintings and then get the hell out without making her feel self conscious."

"I'm sorry Honey, I really didn't—"

"It's okay. We're here now, let's just get through the night. This wasn't the ending you wanted, but it'll probably be the best available, given everything."

I nodded, gave her a kiss, and then opened the car door. Elena took my hand and I glanced back at her.

"You owe me something shiny and expensive."

"I figured."

"And you better have called me real f***ing pretty."

"I did."

As I stood out of the car, Michelle craned her head to look back at me. She smiled, scooted over to make room for me, and then patted the hood.

"Hood is still warm, feels good." She smirked, then closed her eyes and settled her head on the glass.

The red bead glowed as she sucked on the joint, and then, a few moments later, a plume of smoke swirled out into the night air.

"What time is it?" Michelle asked, her eyes still closed.

I pulled out my cell phone and checked.

"A few minutes until 10:00 p.m."

"Hmm," Michelle replied, finally opening her eyes to look up at the night sky. "Two hours."

"Two hours until what?"

Michelle smirked.

"I don't know. Something good, hopefully."

—

"So, this is how the other half lives," Elena gasped as our sorely out of place sedan wound through the gated community.

Multi-million-dollar homes packed both sides of the street in a neighborhood that stretched on and on and on. Some already had massive webs of Christmas lights glowing as they wrapped across tree trunks or dangled off roofs. The mailboxes were wrought-iron sculptures; the lawns were lush and green despite the season. Most cars were tucked away for the night in their three- to four-car garages, but a few Lexuses and BMWs lingered in driveways.

Michelle laid across the backseat, and in the

rearview mirror, I could see a glimpse of her panties as her skirt was bunched high on her thigh. She caught me staring and she tugged her skirt down. That seemed a bad omen for my prospects of seeing those panties again.

And yet, despite how the night was shaping up, I still clung to the hope of salvaging some satisfaction.

Am I proud of this? No, but I'm being honest and that counts for something, doesn't it?[34]

We pulled into the driveway of an appropriately gaudy mini-mansion and piled out. I tried to help Michelle out of the car, but she rose without taking my hand. That was a distinctly bad sign.

The heavy front door swung wide open with a creak. Lights inside flickered on automatically. Michelle left us in the living room and disappeared through the dining room. We heard her ascend stairs as we gazed through the very, very white interior. The carpet was pristine, the kind you couldn't normally wear shoes on, so I stepped back onto the walkways, which were marble, therefore more resistant to the unwashed masses.

Everything seemed so clean, it didn't look lived in at all. Rich people homes were always so inhumanely sterile.

"I bet she puts plastic on the bed before she let's you **** her." Elena smirked.

"Nah, I bet you there's a filth room somewhere," I replied in a whisper. "A room where you can be just as disgusting as you want where the walls are painted with the splatters of rich people sin."

---

[34] Nope.

"Hot," Elena laughed, then clasped onto my hand. "You're still buying me something expensive, though."

"Oh, I've already figured out what it is."

"Really, tell me?"

I hadn't actually figured out what I was going to buy her, but I knew she would like the idea that I did.

Elena narrowed her eyes on me.

"It better be ****ing spectacular."

Michelle emerged through the dining room. She was still wearing clothes, sadly. She waved us to follow and then disappeared again.

"How long until we cut bait?" Elena whispered as we walked past a large glass case containing crystal bowls and one that looked suspiciously like a Chihuly, but was probably a knock off.

"She said something about midnight, so let's see what that's all about."

"Okay, if it gets to twelve thirty and this gets weirder or just isn't going anywhere, I reserve the right to pull the plug."

"Yes, ma'am."

As we passed by the kitchen, my eyes trailed over to a window looking out to the backyard. There was a large stack of framed paintings with piles of rolled canvases scattered around it.

"Oh," Michelle said, following my eyes to the backyard. "I'm burning that later tonight. It's all the work that I'm not happy with. I need a fresh start."

Elena nodded and then gave me a wide-eyed smile when Michelle turned away. She mouthed "twelve thirty," and I nodded in agreement.

I watched Michelle's toned calves flex as she ascended the stairs ahead of us.

"Just one more crack at it," I silently prayed.

The second floor seemed a bit more lived in, a few stains on the carpet here and there, perhaps from spilled paint. Michelle led us to a closed door with a sign reading:

"Brad, if you touch this, swear to God I will castrate you!
Mission # 1, listen to Evangelicals. Done!
Mission # 2 Chronic. Done!
Mission # 3 Paint.
Mission # 4 Photojournal.
Mission # 5 See Evangelicals tonight. Done!
Goals, time allowing.
Divebars. Done!
Motorcycle. Done!
Longboard.
Confession. Done!"

Michelle didn't acknowledge the sign as she opened the door and then looked back at us with an eager smile.

"Thank you so much for being willing to look these over," Michelle said as she herded us into the small room filled wall-to-wall with sketches and paintings. "No one else has seen these, I wanted you both to be the first."

"Thank you," Elena said, not very convincingly.

"Are you burning all this too?" I asked.

"No, silly," Michelle whispered as she stepped toward me.

She wrapped her arms around my neck and kissed me. It was abrupt and dreadfully awkward for the first few moments. Our teeth even clinked against each other like we were a junior high couple. Our tongues touched briefly and I settled into the kiss.

Michelle pulled back, and almost like an afterthought, kissed Elena. To Elena's credit, she pretended to be into it. I really did owe her something big.

When their lips parted, Elena flashed a smile before pecking one more kiss on Michelle.

"That was really nice," Michelle gasped, but then pulled away. "I don't want to pressure you; we don't have to have sex. If you just want to look at the art, talk for a while and then head back to the club, that's fine."

"S***!" my body shouted.

"Whatever," my mouth said. "We're following your lead."

Michelle turned and started digging through the canvases. Elena leaned into me to whisper:

"Sorry, honey, but maybe we'll get to watch her burn her shit tonight."

It all seemed very fitting. Mr. Asshole pleaded with me to start angling the situation to get Michelle naked by the time we left.

But I didn't. Instead came the second epiphany of the night. It all suddenly made sense to me. The Lifestyle, the women, the obsession. Everything came into focus in a way so obvious that I felt ashamed it hadn't occurred to me before.

None of it was me. I'd said this before, had meant it to varying degrees, but had indulged this fantasy life and pretended I could keep it from seeping into my real personality. It could just be a mask that I took off when I was finished playing make-believe. I felt I could cordon off Will Weinke from this life, keep him pristine, innocent, and when it was time for me to turn my back on this dangerous lifestyle, I could slip into my old self.

This was not me. Of course it wasn't me. I mean, have you met me? Then surely you know how not me all this was.

But it was what I was doing, and in reality, I'd become nothing more than the sum of my selfish actions.

This moment came with the urgent desire to reclaim myself as I stood there with a crazy woman desperate to show someone her art work, with no interest in me sexually, but hungry for my opinion because, for some reason, she respected it. And Will Weinke would give her that opinion more eagerly than I would have ever f***ed her, because that is what I do.

That is me, that is who I am supposed to be, and that is who I can become again. I should not be in swing clubs, I should not be dating women with liberated world views, and I should not have let my base carnal desires distract me from the only thing I've ever felt comfortable being.

Being Will Weinke.

I looked over to Elena, this woman whose beauty and spirit captivated and mystified me, and saw who I would become, who I was always supposed to become. It was not the brash and bombastic Mr. Asshole; it was not bashful, pensive and self-loathing Will Weinke; it was not the resilient farmer or the balanced and unconventional superswinger. It was something else entirely—something so immediate, intense and irreversible that I was frantic to explain it to Elena, to pull her out of this insane life and away from everything that hurt her and made her feel small. I was ready to apologize, at long last, for being the very person who had made her feel small.

Is this a moment of enlightenment, is this the daybreak that addicts see when it is time to turn their lives around? Did I finally hit bottom?

If I did, I am grateful, because it could have been so much worse.

My fingers laced around Elena's hand. I felt optimistic and proud in a child-like way. I knew it shouldn't have taken me as long as it did, but goddammit, I finally got there.

"Okay," Michelle called as she dug around the room. "I'm a little behind where I wanted to be, but I'm pretty happy with these."

I crouched down and picked up the paintings she'd set aside for me. Elena grabbed the one with Michelle and I in a lovers' embrace. Elena's eyebrows jutted up as she looked over at me.

I was repulsed by the image now and felt guilty, as if I had been the one who'd painted it.

Michelle handed me the shopping girl with the panties around her ankles. I'd seen it in the email, but the colors were crisper than they'd been on my computer screen.

The rest of the paintings were new, though. There was a stark self-portrait with Michelle's eyes bugged and her face contorted in a crazed smile. Underneath was written:

"All work and no play…etc, etc, etc, etc."

Behind the face was the spinning clock, which

appeared in one form or another in each of the works.

I looked up to Michelle's aching eyes. She was pouring her soul out to us and I felt for her, but I'd become so overwhelmed by the moment, I wasn't certain what to say to her.

So instead of something healing and insightful, I asked:

"What happens at midnight?"

"Don't know," Michelle sighed. "I mean, I think I know, but it's a little up in the air."

"Does it involve us?" Elena asked.

"Um, I don't think so," Michelle shrugged. "Maybe."

Elena sent me an "it's time to go" look with raised eyebrows and fixed frown.

I concurred, but had to bow out graciously. Michelle was looking for something to cling to, so I took a moment.

"These are really impressive. I like the stylized, comic book vibe you're going for. It embellishes all these moments, but no so much that they don't seem real. It's kind of surreal, but not absurd."

Michelle nodded her head, still ravenous for my opinion.

"You need to get these out in front of the public. Have you thought about where you are going to have your showing?"

"No," she whispered, tears dripping from her long, fake eyelashes.

I laid down the paintings gently and stood up.

Michelle dove into my arms and was kissing me again, equally as awkwardly as before, just without the teeth clink.

The kiss tasted different to me now. It had become off-putting, but I accepted them all the same.

Michelle took both our hands and led us out of the room and to a bedroom down the hall. She sat down on the bed, and she tugged us down so we are all laying together. There was no more kissing. We just stared at the ceiling fan while I wondered how to get out of the situation.

"I'm sorry if I seem a little scattered and weird, but I'm just so nervous about what I'm doing," Michelle sighed. "I feel like a child again and I think marijuana isn't really helping me relax like I thought it would."

"It hits everyone differently," Elena agreed.

"If I go down this road," Michelle continued. "It'll mean the end of my marriage. Brad won't like where I'm headed. It'll mean the end of my country club friends, it'll mean a new life for me."

"It does sound scary," I said, leaning up on my elbow to look down at Michelle. "But as long as you're still alive and breathing, there is always time to make your life what you want it. You are also in the extremely advantageous position of having some money and no children, so there is nothing holding you back."

"Do you really think my work is good?" she asked me, and only me. Elena might as well have not existed at that moment.

"Yes, I like the path you are on and think you've got some exciting things to look forward to," I said, now sitting up and moving my feet to the edge of the bed.

It was most definitely time to go, and Elena was

rolling off the bed. Michelle was zeroing in on me in a way that made everything feel off and very dangerous.

"Would you help me?" Michelle asked, touching her hand against my arm.

"How?"

"Just," Michelle said, sitting up on the bed, taking my hand into hers, then reaching for Elena's. "I know this all seems weird, but I really just need a few friends to help nudge me in the right direction. I need people to believe in me, to give me more strength."

Elena sighed, walked around the bed and sat next to Michelle. She put her am around Michelle's waist.

"We will both be here for you," Elena said, adding subtle emphasis on "we." "We'd offer you our place to crash at, but we have kids and not a lot of extra room. But if you need emotional support, a person to drink with or to critique your art, then we can absolutely do that."

Michelle smiled and leaned her head on Elena's shoulder.

"Thank you," Michelle whispered, sniffling away tears. "God, I'm a mess. Pot's not good for me."

Elena laughed and nodded.

"Gotta know yourself, honey."

Elena unlatched from Michelle and stood up from the bed.

"I know you guys were probably hoping for something else," Michelle said, standing up and hugging me briefly before pulling away and walking to the bedroom door. "And we still can, if you want."

"Yes! Please!" my body cried.

"That's okay, I think the mood isn't quite there," my mouth countered. "Plus, if you want us as art friends, then it's probably best we don't."

Despite my recent revelation, the last statement physically hurt to say. I felt good afterward, though. I felt like myself. Clearly Michelle didn't need a d*** so much as she needed a new direction in life.

"Wanna watch the bonfire before you go?" Michelle asked, wiping the tears from her eyes while giggling.

"Thought you'd never ask," Elena smirked.

Michelle clapped, then skipped down the hall like a twelve-year-old.

She came to a stop at the sound of a car pulling in front of the house. Headlights shone through the window.

"Dammit," Michelle grumbled to herself, then turned to us. "It's Brad. Bonfire is going to have to wait."

Michelle bowed her head and slowly made her way down the stairs. We followed, and as much as I'd like to have seen dozens of canvases go up in flames, perhaps drift into the air and fly onto the roofs of surrounding houses, starting an inferno leaving hundreds of Oklahoma City's wealthiest citizens essentially homeless, I was eager to get out of this situation before it became even more bizarre.

The front door opened just as we reached the entryway. Brad entered, laughing and hugging a darkly tanned, bleached blonde with ridiculous fake tits. An equally tanned man with bright white teeth followed behind and closed the front door.

Michelle visibly tensed when she saw the couple.

"Oh, hey guys," Brad called as he walked over and shook my hand. "Are you taking off already? Party's just begun."

"We have to get home to relieve the babysitter," Elena said.

"Oh, come on, baby," the blonde purred, running her finger along Elena's arm. "I'll make it worth your while."

The woman switched her gaze over to Michelle and something complicated and nasty passed between them.

"No, they definitely have to go," Michelle said coldly, leading us to the front door.

"Suit yourselves," the blonde said as she led Brad to a couch. The other man followed with a dumb grin on his face.

Michelle ushered us to the front porch and gave us both long, strong hugs.

"Thank you so much," she whispered as she pulled away from me. "I'm sorry this hasn't been the most fun."

"Don't worry about it honey," Elena said, her voice warm and concerned. "We had fun."

Elena took Michelle's hand and pulled her close.

"If you need to come back with us, then come. You can grab some clothes, grab your painting supplies and you can stay at our house tonight. You don't have to go back to that."

Michelle shook her head as a tear dropped from her eye. She then gave a weak chuckled and waved her hands at her eyes to dry the tears.

"It's no big deal," Michelle mumbled, forcing a smile. "It's just sex."

I glanced over at Elena. One of us needed to say something. Neither of did and the moment hung with the three of us frozen on the front porch, music erupting from inside the house.

"What time is it?" Michelle asked, buoyancy suddenly emerging in her voice.

I pulled out my cell phone.

"Eleven forty-five."

Michelle grinned and turned back to the door. Her hand rested on the doorknob.

"Seriously," Elena insisted. "Just crash on our couch tonight."

"Thank you, but I can't impose," Michelle said without looking back at us. "Besides, it's just one more for the road."

She opened the door and was gone.

—

I had a big speech planned in my head, a brilliant plea for Elena's forgiveness, but after turning out the lights, settling into bed and quietly watching a slasher flick on television, I only uttered:

"I'm so sorry, for everything. I promise never to put you through this again."

She replied:

"It's okay, but thank you."

"I don't deserve you."

"Sometimes you do, sometimes you don't, but I believe in you and always will."

"I will be better, from here on out and for the rest of our lives. I know that sounds cheesy and clichéd, but I promise you, it's the truth. When I finish my part of the book, I'll let you read it, and if you're not comfortable with…"

"I trust you, Will," she interrupted. "But you still owe me something expensive."

—

I'd thought the book was done, but then a few days later, I received a package with ten paintings rolled up in a cardboard tube and a flash drive containing hundreds of pictures. They were taken during the final days leading up to Michelle's big moment. Michelle must have sent them right before. I unrolled them, laid them out on my bed and stared at them for hours, terribly burdened that, of all the people in her life, she chose me to trust with her excruciatingly beautiful suicide note.

FUN FACT: Riding the Crimson Tide
Guys should know that if their partner is out of action because of the "monthly gift," then they are both out of action. The upside of the menstrual cycle is that it can serve as the perfect excuse to not sleep with someone without leaving them feeling rejected.

The Ballad of Jerry and Carey/Cynthia/Veronica Part VIII

The season passed with unflinching resiliency. The farm did not care about Cynthia's pain. The crops would not wait for the grief cycle to close. The day she returned home, she was out in the fields, she was playing with her child, she was paying bills.

Jerry tried to ease the workload off of her, but Cynthia refused. She was more likely to cry when she had nothing to do, so Jerry watched her work like a mule for weeks. When there was no work on the land, she would work on the house. There were always dripping faucets, walls that needed another coat of paint, a front porch to rebuild, just to silence one creaky board.

Cynthia worried that long lost associates of her father would call, looking to collect old debts. So far, the phone remained silent.

She worried that her mother would surface

somehow, out on bail and asking for money, asking for a place to live, asking to meet her grandchild.

After a few months, the fear subsided. The farm was now completely isolated from the darkness of her childhood. Carey still lurked in her memories, still dark, unhappy and underfed, but as Cynthia's child grew, so did Carey.

The day that the child insisted on learning to ride a bicycle without training wheels, Cynthia vowed to finally learn how to ride a bike herself. With the bike frames wobbling beneath them, Cynthia and her child tentatively rode side by side down to the road and back all day long, only falling a handful of times.

When Cynthia talked about stranger danger, drugs, and the other evils of the world, Cynthia always felt like she was talking to two children instead of one. She wanted them to know that they would be okay, just as long as they knew how to make good decisions. Above all, she wanted them to know that the farm was safe because they could count on their parents to protect them and be on their side.

Always, no matter what happened.

And after hugging the child goodnight, she would stand by the window and wrap her arms around herself as she watched moonlight splashing across the farmland.

Pamela's grave was set off from the house. The child knew nothing about it, but Cynthia knew she would have to explain the tombstone one day.

Not yet, not now.

As the sun set on the farm, Cynthia would walk out to the grave and sit with her back against the cold stone. She would talk about her day, chat as sisters would, as if their only cares were the length of Cynthia's hair and what she would wear to the farmers' market that weekend.

The tight, white jean shorts, they decided. Cynthia had great legs and they always drew a crowd.

The wedding anniversary came, and the child went off to the grandparents for the weekend. Cynthia hadn't asked for babysitting, hadn't wanted babysitting, but the grandparents insisted. She watched the child leave with an admittedly irrational sense of abandonment.

The grandparents meant well, they just didn't know.

Jerry didn't ask for sex that night, but Cynthia felt obligated since the kid was out of the house.

She burst into tears halfway through.

The rest of the night, Jerry held Cynthia's naked body and silently watched the moon shine through the window.

"I don't want it to be like this," Cynthia finally whispered, hours after Jerry had fallen asleep.

"What?" Jerry snorted as he shook awake.

"Sorry, I didn't want to wake you up, but I wanted to talk."

"No problem," Jerry said, rubbing the sleep from his eyes.

"I don't want it to be like this," Cynthia whispered, tears dripping again. "I want it to be like it was, but—"

"But it's not like it was," Jerry finally finished her

sentence. "That's okay. Things have changed, and we just have to figure out how to change with them. We will, just don't rush it."

"I want to rush it," Cynthia said. "I need that connection, you have no idea how bad I miss that connection. I just don't feel—anything. I feel empty."

Jerry squeezed her tight against him, kissed the top of her head.

"I'm following your lead," Jerry said. "You tell me what you want, I'm there. You want to go to a fancy dinner, I'll set it up. You want to go on vacation, I'll figure out how to get us across the world for a couple weeks. You need to be pampered; I know that."

"You're sweet," Cynthia giggled, then turned to kiss Jerry on the lips. "But you've been pampering me for weeks now. I've noticed, I don't want you to think that I haven't. I've just been doing everything I can to hold it together, and I'm tired."

Jerry began to talk, but a yawn slipped out.

"Oh, I'm sorry. You're tired," Cynthia said, leaning to get up. "I'll go into the living room."

Jerry pulled her back down.

"No, baby, this is the plan. This is you and I. The crops, the house, the fields, everything in our lives centers on what we do here. So, you don't sleep tonight, I don't sleep tonight. I'm not gonna let you fight this thing alone ever again."

Cynthia smiled and leaned into his arms. They had two nights of freedom. One was already almost over, but the next night could still be salvaged. They discussed dinner downtown followed by drinks at a wine bar, then retreat to a dive bar where Cynthia could get desperately drunk and belligerent without

seeming out of place.
They laid back on the bed, their arms and legs tangled. They made love silently, desperately.
They fell asleep immediately after.

—

Cynthia bundled up and took her morning cup of coffee out to see Pamela. With the mist still settling on the dry, dead grass, her sister felt present.
She curled up against the tombstone and cried with deep, quiet sobs. They were the last tears she would shed for her childhood, and as the sun burned the mist away, Pamela felt suddenly absent. Wherever her sister's spirit had gone, she walked hand in hand with poor, little Carey, finally escaping on their last grand adventure.
Cynthia was a frightful mess when Jerry tracked her down, eyes puffy, hair mangled and frizzy, pale and shivering. He was holding a plateful of biscuits and the coffee pot, wearing only boxers and her pink, fuzzy slippers.
The laughter burned the tears away.

—

"So, we're completely committed to going out tonight, right?" Jerry asked.
He was scraping his boots on the front porch as Cynthia read from one of her textbooks.
Jerry's pants were covered with mud. He slipped off his work gloves and kept his distance from Cynthia.

"I think so, yeah," Cynthia replied, not looking up. "Why?"

"Well, if you'd rather, we can skip the fancy dinner, stick around here and you can help me with the septic tank."

"Mmm! As exciting as that sounds, I definitely do not want to be any part of that and would appreciate if you kept your distance until I can spray you down with the garden hose."

"Sexy," Jerry cooed.

"Hmm."

"So, what are we going to do instead?"

Cynthia closed the book and glanced back up at Jerry. He straightened his back and arched his eyebrow.

"You're going to take a shower, first and foremost."

"Roger that."

"After that, we eat, drink and get appropriately stupid and just completely defile each other wherever and whenever is most prudent."

"Want me to make reservations at the Skirvin again?"

Cynthia giggled, stood, and then stalked toward him. She stopped when she could smell him.

"Just go take a shower."

"Roger that." Jerry saluted and walked to the back of the house to strip off his clothes.

—

While Jerry was in the shower, Cynthia pulled up their profile on the swinger website. It had been months since they last logged on, and messages clogged their inbox. She clicked through, looked over pictures, read invitations, read about events scheduled that night.

An email from Barry and Mary caught her eye. They'd asked if they wanted to catch up, "no pressure." The e-mail was a few weeks old, but they had suggested a big party at the Rumormill later that night.

It seemed like fate.

Mary wrote that a novelist was going to be interviewing them for a book about the Lifestyle, but they'd be free afterward.

The shower shut off and Jerry walked into the room with a towel wrapped around his waist. He looked on the screen and his eyebrow arched.

"Just curious," she shrugged.

He glanced back at the screen and she watched his lips move softly as he read. He kissed Cynthia on the head and whispered:

"I want you all to myself tonight."

She warmed and turned to hug him.

"I'm sorry," she whispered.

He edged her away and looked into her eyes.

"It's okay, it really is. But if we are going to do something like that, it has to be when the time is right and when we are doing it for the right reasons."

She nodded her head, a few tears escaping as she smiled.

"I'm sorry. It's been a hard year."

"I know, but we have the rest of our lives, baby. Our roots are strong."

FUN FACT: Long Live the Lifestyle!
True liberation comes when adults possess the freedom to organize the entirety of their life's memories, scars, instincts and delights to form their own singular sexual identity. It is important to remember that sex among consenting adults is a God-given desire, making abstinence the most bizarre sexual perversion of them all.

Superswingers Epilogue

Attendants flocked to the Individual Artists of Oklahoma gallery in downtown Oklahoma City in record numbers that spring. The controversy helped bring the media, the media brought the buzz, and the buzz brought the rubberneckers who loved a good spectacle.

The spectacle came with money as well, so the exhibit was quickly sold off piecemeal. There were lawsuits threatened that could have derailed the exhibit in its infancy, but ultimately the skies cleared and the night was a rousing success.

Few seemed to acknowledge the event for what it really was: a wake. Instead, the crowds hovered in tight groups and discussed the art distantly, analyzing and critiquing rather than empathizing.

Barry – "I think that might have been what she wanted all along, for people to really look at her. As a parting shot for the life of an artist, it's not really a bad way to go out."

Barry and Mary recognized and pointed out several groups of swingers that were, as Mary put it, "in their civilian clothes."

Mary (snickering) – "Just because we have an unusual sexual identity doesn't mean we can't act right in polite society."

Barry – "And when someone you know and care about passes away, you pay your respects just like any close friend. Really, the bond we share with some of these couples is much more intimate than a normal friendship."

Mary – "It is. You connect with these people. Any relationship involving sex is inherently more complex and emotional; you can't avoid it. So, you will look at them differently, you will engage them emotionally in a way you just can't do anywhere else in life."

Barry subtly gestured Mary to keep her voice down as others visibly eavesdropped. Mary shrugged. They walked through the crowd and went out the front door to talk on the sidewalk, away from curious ears.

Barry – "It's really cool that Will put this together, especially in this way. It really legitimizes what Michelle produced those last few days. A lot of us in the Lifestyle were concerned that this would shine a bad light on swinging and lead to a witch hunt across Oklahoma."

Mary – "So far, so good—but it's just a matter of time before somebody starts talking to the media about the clubs, then everyone will go back underground."

Barry – "Let's hope not. Ideally, everyone will see that this is really just all about Michelle and her struggle."

Mary – "I wish I'd known. I saw her at the club, but she was waiting for Will and wasn't interested in talking."

Barry – "The interview creeped her out."

Mary – "The interview creeped a lot of people out. No offense, Charles. We were kind of pariahs for a few weeks after. Oh well."

Barry – "I doubt we could have done anything, even if we did know she was in trouble. I just don't think the Lifestyle was for them. Brad is just so—well, you know."

Mary – "Yeah. The Lifestyle is not for everyone, nor should it be. Swinging doesn't fix your life, it doesn't solve sexual addiction, it doesn't pay your bills. It's just an outlet that some people can enjoy and some people can't."

Barry – "Like golf."

Mary – "Yeah, but it's not boring as ****."

Barry – "And if it takes you five strokes to get in the hole, then you're doing something very, very wrong."

Mary (laughed) – Well played!

Barry – "Thank you.

Mary – "And poor Will and his wife—I'm not sure if he's been outed, so take this out if not—but the two of them just weren't cut out for it either. You can tell when someone is out of their depths in the Lifestyle, and it's just a matter of time. I'm glad they held it together afterward and made a clean break from swinging"

Barry – "Michelle, on the other hand, I think the Lifestyle was the least of her problems. I'm not saying it was good for her or bad for her, I just think she had so many issues to deal with that people pointing at swinging as the reason she took her own life are just being naïve.

"But I guess it would also be naïve to say that the Lifestyle doesn't cause a lot of problems, especially for someone who doesn't know how to moderate their own behavior. That's true of just about anything—if you can't keep it in perspective, then it will take over your life. If you can keep yourself from getting in too deep, then it can be very special."

Mary (giggled) – "'It can be very special'. Fag."

Barry shrugged. A buzz came from his pocket. Barry pulled out a phone and looked at the screen.

Mary – "Is it the farmers?"

Barry nodded.

Mary – "All right, let's get out of here. Everyone here is wearing entirely too many clothes."